QUEEN OF STARS AND WRATH

ARACELI'S BLADE
BOOK THREE

EMBER JOHNSON

CURSEBREAKER BOOKS

Copyright © 2025 by Ember Johnson

All rights reserved.

This novel is entirely a work of fiction. The names, characters and incidents portrayed in it are the work of the author's imagination. Any resemblance to actual persons, living or dead, events or localities is entirely coincidental.

No part of this book may be reproduced in any form or by any electronic or mechanical means, including information storage and retrieval systems, without written permission from the author, except for the use of brief quotations in a book review.

Paperback ISBN: 979-8-9912303-6-0

KDP Paperback ISBN: 979-8-9912303-8-4

eBook ISBN: 979-8-9912303-7-7

No part of this book may be uploaded or used to train AI.

No AI was knowingly used to create the cover or artwork.

Book Cover designed by INK Designs

World Map created by Paige Annabentleah

Character Illustrations created by Valery Maroushchak - @_art_valery

Artwork Backgrounds designed by Ember Johnson

PRAISE FOR PRINCESS OF FLAMES AND FATE

It's spicier, darker and some people deserve to get slapped even harder, as well as most other enjoyable tropes get cranked up and the character growth, I love to see it!

— GOODREADS REVIEWER

This book was like coming home. Idk how else to describe it.

— AMAZON REVIEWER

Ember has a way of pulling you into the story and feeling for EVERY character in it. It's like watching the story play out in front of you.

— GOODREADS REVIEWER

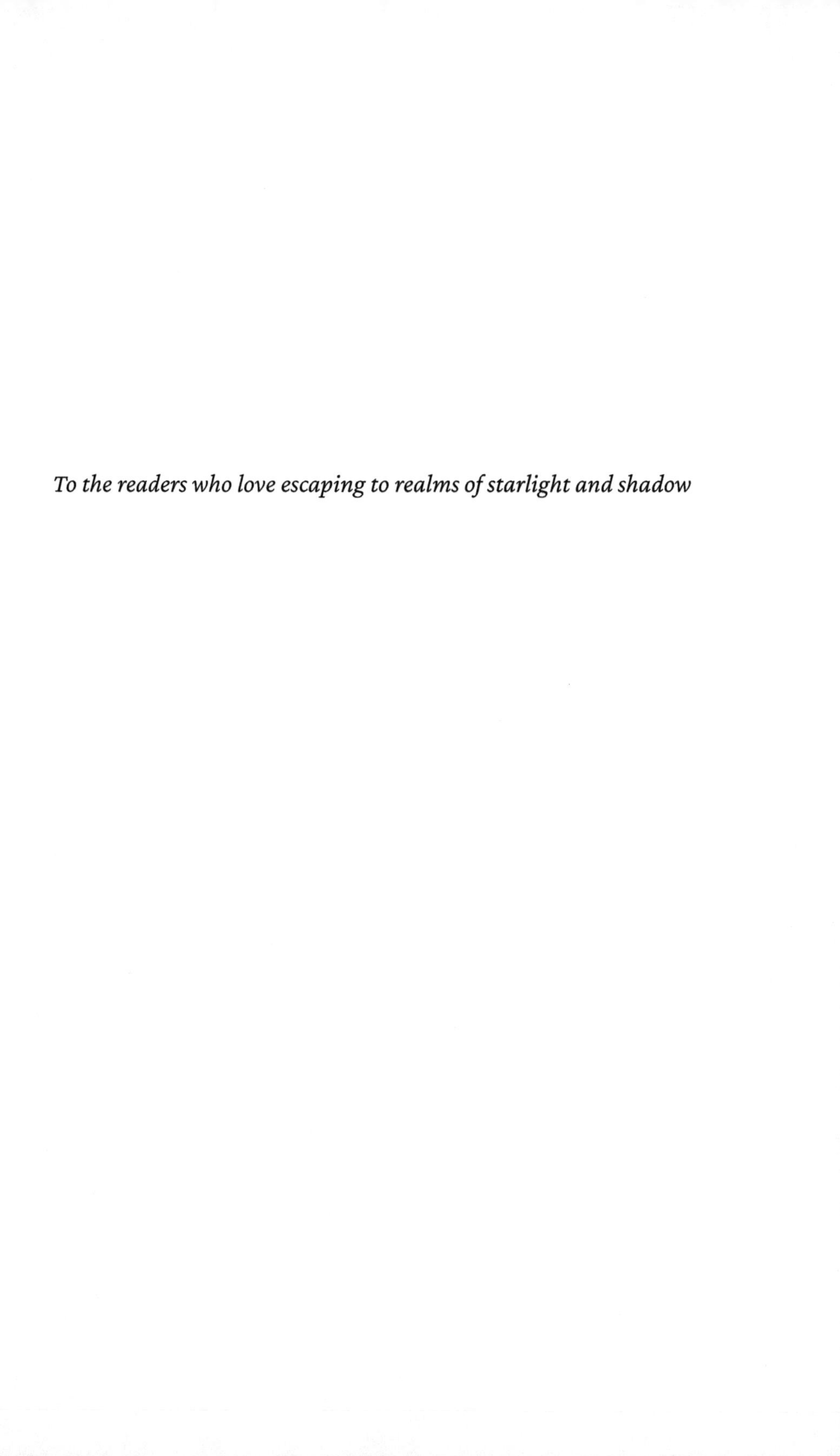

To the readers who love escaping to realms of starlight and shadow

PLAYLIST

Like a Villain - Bad Omens

Like a Prayer (Choir Version) - I'll Take You There Choir

The Water is Fine (Crimson Edition) - Chloe Ament

Iris - MGK & Julia Wolf

Damocles - Sleep Token

Sleeptalk - Dayseeker

Where We Rise - Neoni

Even in Arcadia - Sleep Token

Missing - Seafret

Frozen Pines - Lord Huron

My Blood - Ellie Goulding

Little Bit of Love - Tom Grennan

Ordinary - Our Last Night

Carolina Reaper - Amélie Farren

Eternity - Alex Warren

Figure You Out - VOILA

Things We Lost in the Fire - Bastille

Who's Afraid of Little Old Me - Remember the Monsters

Orpheus - MGK

Creature in the Black Night - Dayseeker

Missile - Dorothy

Tidal Wave - Our Last Night

Colors (Orchestral) - Halsey

Which Witch - Florence + the Machine

End of You - Poppy, Amy Lee, Courtney LaPlante

Up in Flames - Ruelle

How do I say goodbye - Dean Lewis

Iris (Cinematic Version) - Jay Putty & Matt Macleod

CONTENT WARNING

Queen of Stars and Wrath may include the following graphic scenes and difficult topics intended for ages 18+. Please review before proceeding.

Death/murder, suggested rape/sexual assault, attempted murder, deaths of loved ones, abandonment, torture, kidnapping, depression, grief, and other potentially sensitive topics.

ARACELI
THE LOST ISLES
THE WITCH'S COTTAGE
LUMI COVE
ESMERAY
CHERMONA
WILLOWBROOK
OAKSTON
SOUOAK
BRIARWOOD
THE GREAT WOODS
SAINTS LANDING
THE ASSASSIN'S GUILD
BRIDGEDALE
EPHERINIA
SUNNEVA
N

CONTENTS

CHAPTER I

The love of my life's face disappeared into the portal as the other man, the sun prince, who owned my heart carried me from the chaos. Screams echoed against the darkened walls of the chamber as the clang of swords and armor rang out. Sunnevean soldiers were running outside after the king had fled, no doubt acting on the orders of the corrupted man. Only when that door closed, leaving only Oryn, Magnus, and me, did I recognize my own desolate screams.

"Love, I need you to breathe. We'll get him back. But I need you to focus on me so we can get out of here." The edges of my vision swirled, but the warm tenor of the voice that spoke brought me back to reality. Oryn came into view. The first mate I had ever bonded with, the one around whom my anguish had centered around for the last few months. For too long, I felt betrayed by him, believing that he had left me to die in a cold, dark cell. Not only had I believed the words of my captor, I had lost so much precious time with him.

"You might have to carry her out, Your Highness," Magnus, my stoic guard, said. He drew his sword, ready for a fight. Blood trickled down his temple, as if someone had hit him.

But he wasn't just my guard, was he?

I pushed Oryn from where he was crouched before me and rose.

"That won't be necessary. I'm okay." I lied, and I would continue to repeat it until I figured out how I would get Kyler back. Any goals I had would have to wait until the three of us were together again. I had no other choice, especially as the burn from the distance crept its way into me. Oryn's presence stifled it. One benefit of having two bonded men was another connection to help ease that pressure, well, that and the orgasms.

Double the dicks, double the orgasms.

Not the time, Lor, I mentally scolded myself. The only thing that mattered in these moments was finding Kyler.

I knew too well that a single bond stretched beyond its limits was a pain I didn't want to experience again. Despite being so naïve when it came to the mystical connection, I had learned it was less of a "thing" and more like a large part of my very essence. I was drawn to these men, just as they were drawn to me, and I craved their presence even from just rooms away. Kyler was likely experiencing the pain of the separation already, which only gave me more reason to recover him. He was the other half of my heart, he was just as vital to me as the organ itself. The bond connected us in ways we couldn't fathom. I tried reaching out through our mental bond, but all I felt was a wall. I prayed for his safety. I would know if something fatal happened to him, right?

He couldn't be dead. No, even surrounded by the enemy, they wouldn't kill that stubborn man so easily.

I quickly compartmentalized my thoughts, as I always did before and after every mark assigned to me. This became no different. They took my heart, and I was going to rip theirs from their chests.

"Your father-"

"Is a dead man who's probably hiding in his office," Oryn finished as he took my hand and we began rushing down the hall of Sunneva's gilded castle. "We'll figure out where they've gone and rid this world of his filth."

After many twists and turns, we arrived at the locked ornate door. The prince didn't bother with the handle as he kicked the door in. Smashed wood scattered across the floor as a shout from within permeated the air.

"Aurelius, what have you done?" A shrill voice cried out as a scene I didn't expect welcomed us as we entered the room I had not that long ago searched. The king shuffled behind his desk while the queen stood in front of the wooden piece, pleading to him. His hair was in disarray from the struggle with Trinity and her guards. Even his clothes looked a mess compared to the composed ruler that stood in the large portrait behind him. Horror filled her face as she turned to her son. Her very enraged son, whose powerful flames began licking the edges of his hands and arms. "Ory, wait. Whatever happened, we can fix this," she pleaded, a dainty hand reaching towards him.

He ignored his mother as he pressed forward toward his father. As he came around the ornate desk, the king stumbled away towards the back of the room. Magnus and I stepped further into the room, ready if the king made a run for the door. He wouldn't step foot over the threshold without a slit throat.

"Where did she take him?" Oryn demanded.

"Somewhere you'd be a fool to go. Don't worry, he'll be kept alive." The king cackled as he drew his own sword. His other hand held scrolls tight to his chest. "This is your only chance, boy. Join me and restrain that woman of yours, or you'll die by my sword, a traitor to his kingdom. The heir who let his heart turn him into a disgrace."

Unease itched at the back of my neck. The slight bounce on the balls of my feet had my limbs ready for whatever would come next.

A growl rumbled in Oryn's throat. "My loyalty has always belonged to her, and that's where it'll stay."

"Trinity was right about you. She saw your weakness when I failed to." Aurelius shook his head in disbelief. "If you won't get in line to see the world be reborn under our feet, then you can thank your whore for your untimely death."

The king's words were the only warning before crimson flames erupted around his sword and he struck. Another scream filled the surrounding air, and before I could blink, blood splattered onto my golden prince.

Panic had me surging forward. The need to save my mate drove me as I held a dagger at the ready while searching for his wound among the hard planes of his body. My mind wasn't processing the danger of the king's proximity as my movements quickened with each moment, the fear of him bleeding out before me was a vice around my throat. Only when Ryn thrust me behind him, away from his father, did I understand the scene around me.

"Run," a small voice croaked.

His mother lay dead at our feet. Her last act was an act of love to save her oldest son, and her last word hung heavy in the air. Blood soaked through her golden gown as the world seemed to still as her spirit left. A whisper brushed my ears, like a ghost floating by, but I couldn't make out the message.

"Look what you've done," The king sneered. I looked up, expecting to see despair, but the surprise that lit his icy gaze sent a shiver up my spine. "Guards! The prince and his wife have murdered the queen. Seize them!"

I was unsure if shock or absolute horror at what was unraveling held me in place, but the next moment Oryn gripped my hand and we met Magnus at the office door. The wooden barrier was wide open, and the old man was already pushing against the Sunnevean guards that had arrived to arrest us. Luckily, there weren't many yet, but that would change soon.

I tugged against Oryn, looking back at the king, who stood beside his dead wife, sword still protruding from her abdomen.

"We can't let him live," I said.

"We won't be able to fight our way out of this if we give them enough time to surround us," Oryn stated. A golden guard stomped towards us, but I quickly cut him down. "His days are numbered, but we need to regroup. We have to get to Kyler before they change their minds about keeping him safe."

I didn't like the idea of leaving the king breathing. The little information we got was almost useless, but the least we could do was relieve his neck of his head. More guards shouted and chased us as we made our way down to the main floor, the grandiose palace doors within sight. Magnus pushed ahead, barreling through the thick doors. As we leapt into the quiet night, I called on every shadow to cover us.

When we returned, the king's head would decorate one spike on the golden wall.

CHAPTER 2

We kept to the shadows as we ran through the sleepy town of Epherinia, making our way towards the outskirts before more patrols banded together looking for us. We couldn't stop until we were out of Sunneva, which was going to take days on foot.

My lungs burned as I followed Oryn. Magnus stayed right on my heels. It was fortunate, since we were likely to end up back on the king's doorstep if I were to lead. Navigating was never my strong suit.

I prayed to the gods, who had done nothing but enrage me, that Rasher, Lucas, and Luella were alright. And Davian—it felt like chains wrapped around my heart thinking of the boy—poor Davian was left with a murderous father who likely told him his beloved brother killed the their mother. This world was cruel in so many ways, but I feared this was something the young man couldn't handle. It would be a relief if the king placed all the blame on me instead. I could live with Davian hating me, but I couldn't bear the thought of the brothers being at odds.

We found a thicket of trees and stopped for a moment to catch our breath.

"We should head to the guild," I said.

Magnus shook his head. "Your 'uncle' had ties in Bridgedale. A bird has probably already reached the regimen there. They wouldn't waste any time searching the town, including Vanya's place."

"The guild hasn't been searched since I've been there," I challenged.

"Aye, but there hasn't been a royal assassination in that time, either. If Vanya is smart, and from what I remember she was always sharp as a tack, she'll hide what needs to be hidden and let them waste their time searching the place. It's safer to avoid it."

"We'll head north to the Great Woods ," Oryn said. "This is the last stop until we reach them. It's neutral territory. The war is farther east, so there shouldn't be any soldiers lurking about. And it'll give us better cover to stop. We can find a place to hide and figure out how to alert the others—"

"No," I interrupted, "we'll camp out a night, then head to Chermona."

Oryn and Magnus shared an uneasy look. "The Northern Territory? I don't think they'll take too kindly to us, Lor. We're the prince and princess consort of their enemy, and a captain of the Sunnevean palace guard..."

"They will let us in. They've seen me with Kyler, and the queen didn't kick me out immediately last time. We can exchange information about the troop movements to help their side. She's not entirely unreasonable."

The men muttered in acceptance. They either didn't have the energy to fight me on this, or they lacked better ideas.

We continued on, our eyes set towards the thick woods that buffered the two kingdoms. Part of me dreaded seeing Queen Wynaria again, and this time, without her son. Her words from when we met echoed in my head.

Let fate decide what you are and what you are not.

Fate had made its demands, and despite my efforts to resist, I would meet its call.

The harbinger of flame and fate will save us all.

I had no other choice.

CHAPTER 3

It took hours before we could see the Great Woods. So long that the early rays of the sun began peeking over the grassy hills around us.

My legs felt like the rich custard they served at dinner by the time we ducked under the first wall of trees. The cover they provided was a blessing that allowed us to ease our brutal pace. Once Oryn finally deemed we were safe enough, I practically collapsed face first into the ground. The physical and emotional toll of the strained bond and fleeing finally caught up with me. No training could ever prepare me for this.

"Are you alright, Love?" The softness of his words caressed my heart as his firm hands helped pull me up until I was sitting properly.

"I'm fine," I lied, brushing dirt from my tattered dress. "I just need a minute."

Part of me wished we had had time to grab proper clothes. Once we crossed into Esmeray, we'd need to send Magnus to purchase some. Oryn's face was too well known, and my current state would draw too much attention. I was thankful I had armed myself with every blade I owned beneath the deep red dress, but I needed leathers and boots. The intricately embroidered boots abandoned in our wardrobe in Sunneva made my heart ache.

I loved those boots.

Magnus scanned the forest perimeter, his posture rigid as a sentinel. "We rest before continuing, but we can't stay here long."

"Agreed." Oryn's shoulders slumped as his voice carried the weight of our defeat. His eyes, normally bright, had dulled since watching his mother fall and fled the castle without Kyler and Davian. Despite his easy smiles towards me, I knew the world weighed upon him like a crown of stone.

We worked in silence, each of us falling into practiced roles despite never being in this situation before. Magnus gathered wood for a small fire while Oryn cleared a space between three gigantic oaks. I brought enough shadows into our area to conceal us if someone walked by, though our fae hearing would pick up the snap of a twig or the brush of a branch. It'd be enough to alert us before danger struck.

Oryn walked up to the old guard, placing his hand on his shoulder as he finished setting the logs up. Oryn ignited the logs with only a look, and Magnus shuffled off to find something edible.

My eyes tracked Magnus's movements, searching for... what? Some sign that he'd known our connection all along? Some gesture that marked him as my father? The thought sat like a stone in my stomach as I sat by the fire where I could watch more easily.

The signs had all been there.

He had looked at me oddly when we first met, but everything was so natural after I thought it was just the awkwardness of meeting someone new. My grandmother, she always said he was a guard in Bridgedale. That was all my mother had told her. We always thought it meant he died in the line of duty. Magnus was from Bridgedale. The clues had been there, but I had been too focused on Johan and Oryn to notice. If Vanya knew how sloppy I had gotten, how easily distracted, she would kick me out of the guild without another thought. It wouldn't matter how great of a student I had been under her teachings, or my power, or my commitment to the guild's mission. I'd be stripped of my membership and tossed out like moldy fruit.

"We need to figure out where they might have taken him," Oryn said, dropping beside me by the fire.

I nodded. "The other side of that portal was like nothing I've ever seen before. Almost like a stone room, but not as uniform as most of the buildings here."

"I don't think they were in Sunneva, unless they're deep in the desert," Oryn ran his hands through his hair, frustration etched into every line of his face. "There's no telling where they're holding him, but knowing Kyler, he's not made it easy."

"He makes nothing easy." I couldn't help the slight lift of my mouth, thinking about how difficult it would be to subdue him.

Magnus kept his distance, settling on the opposite side of our small camp. His eyes met mine briefly before darting away. Had he always known I was his?

"I can't feel him, it's so numb," I whispered, the admission slipping out before I could stop it. "I miss him."

Oryn's shoulder pressed against mine. "That sounds like what I felt when you were taken." He wrapped a strong arm around me and pulled me closer. "I miss him too, Love."

"We'll get him back," I said, trying to sound more confident than I felt.

"Of course we will. That is, if he doesn't free himself on his own before we get there." Oryn's smile didn't reach his eyes. "You know what Kyler would say if he could see us now?"

"That we're wasting time and should be moving and planning his rescue?"

"Exactly," Oryn laughed softly. "He'd be very annoyed with our moping."

The times Kyler sat beside me patiently, listening to me speak played in my mind.

An absent smile crossed my face. "I don't think he'd be as annoyed as you think. He's dealt with my moping."

"Maybe he's gotten softer as of late," Oryn mused. "Love can do that to you."

Kyler's face was so clear in my mind—his rare smile, the way his eyes softened when he thought no one was looking. The memory of his lips against mine, a stolen moment I'd replayed countless times. How he had claimed me: mind, body, and soul.

"I feel like there's been so much time lost between us. He and I spent the first part of our relationship hating each other..." I trailed off. "I'll get none of that time back. The same happened with you."

Oryn's hand wrapped around mine and gave it a squeeze. "I doubt he hated you as much as he led you to believe. We will have all eternity to make up for what's been lost. You and I are already beginning to make up for it. All that matters is that we're together, the three of us."

Across the fire, Magnus shifted, his expression unreadable as he sat against a nearby boulder.

"You should rest," Oryn said. "We'll need to move again soon."

"I'm not sure I can sleep."

"Try," his voice gentled. "If not for me or yourself, then for him."

I nodded, stretching out on the forest floor, using my arms as a pillow.

I wish I could comfort you the way I'd like to. Oryn's voice caressed the recesses of my head. *But Magnus is watching.*

Another time then, I replied.

I'm going to go find us some food. Don't go anywhere.

You act as if I have a habit of disappearing.

I didn't need to look at his face. The silence on the other end of the bond was loud enough.

Too soon?

It'll never not be too soon, Love.

The sound of his steps carried him away. Whispers caught my attention as I opened my eyes to see Oryn leaning over to tell

Magnus something before leaving our camp. My eyes found Magnus again. He was watching me now, something like sorrow etched into the lines around his eyes.

What had Trinity meant? Could Magnus truly be my father? The man who swore himself to me when I arrived in a court of vipers? Or was this all a twisted game for her? The fact that she's been hidden, scheming all of these years, felt like proof enough she couldn't be trusted. But where her dangerous lies ended and cruel truths began, I wasn't sure.

The questions circled in my head like vultures, but exhaustion pulled harder. My last thought before sleep claimed me was of Kyler —alone, hurt, waiting for us to find him.

I would find him. No matter the cost.

CHAPTER 4

Kyler's face haunted my dreams, his eyes pleading as unseen hands dragged him away. I woke with a start, the dirt beneath me hard and damp.

"You were calling his name," Oryn said softly, crouched beside me with a handful of berries. "Here, eat something."

I took the offering, the tartness shocking my senses awake. "How long was I asleep?"

"A few hours. Not enough, but we need to move."

Magnus was already kicking dirt onto the fire and tossing the little traces that we were there in random directions into the dense foliage. His eyes met mine briefly before looking away, still stoic as ever.

We traveled in silence as the Great Woods thickened around us, ancient trees stretching toward the sky. The familiarity of the woods wrapped around me with a warmth that felt like home. How far was I from where Briarwood *used* to be? I hadn't been back to the site of my long lost home since the night it burned. It became a ghost, just like its inhabitants.

"If we head northeast, we'll be able to get to Suoak in a few days," Magnus said, breaking the silence as we paused at a stream. "It's right on the edge of the woods. It would be better to stop there first."

We spent a moment getting a much needed drink. My throat was thankful for the cool water with every swallow.

"There's nothing there but my father's men," Oryn replied, his head tilted up studying the sun. "Besides, they burned down the part of the forest that touched the town. We wouldn't have the proper cover to scout the area before approaching. No, we need to either go northwest to Willowbrook or press further north to Oakston."

"That'll take days to reach either. And that's if we keep a fast pace," Magnus countered.

"Are you admitting you're out of shape, old man?" Oryn quirked a brow at him, the mirth in his eyes a reminder of the man I had met in a tavern.

Laughter erupted from Magnus, the smile that painted his face the first genuine emotion I've seen from him since we began our journey.

"I'm in plenty good shape, boy. It's not me I'm worried about."

My arms crossed over my chest. "I hope you're not meaning me, Captain."

With a simple shrug of his shoulders, he waved a hand towards me. "No doubt Death's Wraith can handle a bit of travel, but that gown and those dainty slippers cannot. I meant no offense, My Lady."

"Alora," I said. "My name is Alora. No more formalities, especially when..." I didn't finish my thought as my eyes trailed down my attire. He wasn't wrong. My dainty shoes were on the verge of collapse in the mud and dirt, and my dress was entirely impractical for anything but twirling around the ballroom. I unhooked a dagger from the hidden pocket of my corset. Fisting a handful of the skirt of the gown, I began slicing through the fine fabric. The rip echoed among the trees as I tore the bulk of it off until I was left with enough fabric to cover my backside. The ragged edges brushed softly against my upper thighs as the shreds lay on the ground. There wasn't much I could do about the shoes, so I kicked them off. I'd be faster and less of a liability barefoot than if I continued to run in them.

I looked up to find both men gawking at me, though for different reasons. Oryn's eyes narrowed at my now shortened dress. Magnus's mouth pulled into a flat line.

"I guess that solves that," Magnus grunted.

"And creates a slew of other issues," my mate snarled. "You're not traipsing around the forest like that."

Of course, Ryn's possessive side would decide to come out at a time like this.

"I can move quicker like this. The faster we get to Oakston, the faster I can get some proper pants."

He pulled at the strings of his trousers, loosening their hold around his waist. "Take mine."

"Can you both keep your clothes on? We're wasting time here."

"What?" I snapped at Magnus. The sharp tone halted Oryn's stripping. "Don't want to see your daughter's husband give her the literal clothes off his body?"

His eyes widened in surprise at my boldness. The subject that had lurked around us now burst between us like sparks from Oryn's hands. Hurt flashed in his eyes as he let out a sigh and simply gave up.

"Ryn, stop." I quickly tied his pants back in place. "I appreciate the sentiment, but I think you've forgotten something."

"Lor, I can't bear the thought of anyone seeing—"

His words fell silent as my power swirled around me. Shadows crawled up my legs to mimic pants, wrapping around my exposed skin in a protective embrace. It wasn't the same barrier as clothing, but at least it would keep me covered.

Oryn's mouth pulled into a tight line as he studied the shadows that now caressed my skin. "I guess that's fine."

"It is more than fine." I patted his chest as I stepped around him towards Magnus. "Now let's go."

The terrain grew steeper, roots and rocks making each step treacherous. I missed the thick soles of boots beneath my feet.

My thoughts kept drifting to Kyler—was he cold? Hurt? Did he think we'd abandoned him?

"He knows we're coming for him," Oryn whispered, catching my hand as I stumbled. His fingers squeezed mine before letting go.

THREE DAYS of hard travel later, we crossed into Esmeray under the cover of darkness. The earthy pine was a welcoming scent, as was the distant curve of its great mountains.

"Oakston is a day's walk," Magnus said, pointing north, where the tree line thinned. "If we don't stop, we should reach it by midday tomorrow."

"And then Chermona is another two days," I added, recalling my travels with Kyler and Rasher.

Oryn nodded. "We'll need supplies and proper clothing." He aimed a pointed look my way. "We can't walk into Wynaria's court looking like we've been dragged through the forest."

"Even though we have," I muttered, picking leaves from my hair. "I'm ready for a warm bath and a soft bed."

"Not a fan of camping?" Oryn mused.

"It's not my favorite."

"She practically lived in the library," Magnus added. He seemed to brush off the earlier spat with ease. Our travel party had quickly gone back to silent steps until now. "If there were a way to bring a library of books here, maybe the lady might enjoy it."

They shared a laugh despite how I rolled my eyes.

"Maybe I'm not a fan of insects. I'm surprised the golden prince has taken to roughing it so well."

"Ah, your prince spent most of his days with his men around the realm," Magnus said. "Even as a boy, he was always sneaking off for days. You could hardly keep the boy inside."

"I've always loved sleeping under the stars, and exploring unknown places." Oryn's voice drifted off dreamily. "Always seeking the next adventure, until my father put a stop to it. Then you came along." His eyes met mine. "I knew I wouldn't take another step on unknown land unless you were there with me. I never thought I would ever leave you until my father threatened me the morning after our wedding. The choice of leaving you there has haunted me every day since."

"You didn't know what was going to happen. You were just as much a victim, Ryn."

Magnus cleared his throat. "It's my fault for not watching my charge as I should have."

"Neither of you are at fault," I said. "Gods, it's my own fault for letting my guard down." They both looked like they were about to protest, but I held up my hand. "All that matters is we stop it from happening again."

Ryn nodded as Magnus quietly agreed.

We continued on our trek in silence until I finally asked the question that had been plaguing me.

"What did your father threaten you with?" I asked Oryn. "That morning, you said you had refused, but he made a threat that clearly got to you since you left."

Magnus continued to walk ahead of us as Oryn's steps slowed to match my own.

"He threatened to chain you to a bed for... breeding. Then, once an heir was born, he'd have you sent to the gallows," he said. "He always said having a heart was only for weak fools, and he could see mine walking at my side." The Esmeranian countryside sprawled before us, a beautiful backdrop to a somber conversation. "I knew right then it was a mistake to keep you under his thumb. I had planned to run once I returned. Appease him, then slip out in the dead of night."

"But I wasn't there."

"You were not. And I could only hope he hadn't gotten to you. His story about your kidnapping was convincing enough. I should have realized it was nothing more than another one of his lies."

We could circle this painful truth for days without changing anything. Previously, I believed he had been behind everything, but I knew better. It didn't stop the guilt that settled into me now that I knew the thing his father held over his head was me. Part of me wished I had told him who I was earlier. Maybe that threat wouldn't have held so much power. Would we have fled right then in a flurry of swords and arrows, battling our way out of his father's clutches?

"I would have followed you anywhere, Ryn."

"You would have regretted that choice after the first night of sleeping outside."

"Well," I nudged his shoulder, "maybe I can learn to love it as much as the man I love does. Relationships require effort on both sides, right?"

"Right."

The soft smile that graced his face eased the weight that had settled between us. We'd be okay as long as we had each other, and if there was anything I knew, my mates would never be without me again.

Death be damned.

CHAPTER 5

Magnus' estimation was accurate as Oakston rose before us around midday the next day. The air had a chill to it that brought Kyler to mind. Even the underlying scent of rain in the air brought the prince's face to the forefront of my mind. Each passing day was a battle within me—terror that we were taking too long to reach him, that Trinity had already inflicted irreparable damage. The other side of me tried to remain calm, to trust Kyler to take care of himself until we could arrive. He's kept himself alive this long, surely he can hold out a bit longer.

But what if he couldn't?

I shook my head to clear the idea. No, he has to. He would never give up, not the man who ran into battle to save a town despite the odds stacked against him. He loved this land—and perhaps me—far too deeply to surrender before his final breath.

The patchwork of stone buildings and thatched roofs of the town nestled between rolling hills. Unlike the capital cities with their imposing walls and grand architecture, this humble trading town had appeared charming the first time I had visited. Now, it felt gloomy, haunted by memories of a happier time, even if Kyler and I were at each other's throats once the spell of our shared dance broke. I would take that over the hollow feeling of his absence any day.

"Keep yourselves hidden," Magnus instructed as we approached the town's edge. "I'll find us some proper clothing. Find somewhere quiet to wait."

I nodded. "We'll need supplies, too."

Oryn passed the guard a stack of coins.

"And supplies," Magnus gave a curt nod. "I won't be long." With that, he slipped into the flow of people entering the town, his broad shoulders soon disappearing among the crowd.

Oryn and I skirted the busier streets, finding a quiet spot between a tailor's shop and what looked like a bakery. The narrow alley offered decent cover while still allowing us to observe the main thoroughfare. The scent of fresh bread and honey wafted through the air, causing my stomach to growl, reminding me of how little we've had to eat. I took better care of myself while I was a drifter, but I also wasn't rushing across the land to beat the dark cloud that hung over us.

"What do you think our chances are of passing through unnoticed?" I asked, leaning against the rough stone wall.

"Depends on how quickly the news has traveled." Oryn's eyes scanned the street, ever vigilant. "Small towns like this are usually the last to hear royal gossip, but the first to spread it once they do. We also don't know how vocal my father has been about placing the blame on me. If he's keeping it just to the palace, we'd have a little more time. But if he's plastering it on every wall and town," he scratched at his chin in thought, "we're probably already days behind."

We fell silent and turned, hiding our faces as a group of merchants passed by, their conversation drifting toward us.

"—saying Death's Wraith herself was seen heading east—"

"—nonsense, I heard she was in the west, at that port—"

"—killed his own mother, they say—"

My blood ran cold. I glanced at Oryn, whose jaw had tightened.

"I think we've solved that mystery," I whispered. "Hopefully, Magnus acquires cloaks. Nothing good will come from someone recognizing you."

"Maybe you should tie my wrists and parade me around like a bounty," Oryn murmured.

A low chuckle escaped me. "Something tells me you'd enjoy it too much. That dazzling smile would be a dead giveaway that I was not leading you to some unfortunate fate."

"Maybe we should practice later. When we're not running for our lives." His eyes sparkled with mischief.

I met the deep blue of his eyes. "If we have a private moment, maybe."

My mate beamed at me, his natural beauty the worst distraction there ever was. I looked away to maintain focus and prevent us from being seen.

Another group passed by, their voices low but clear enough.

"—Prince Oryn stabbed her—"

"—betrayed his own kingdom, his own kin—"

"—bounty on their heads would feed a village—"

The minutes crawled by, each snippet of conversation more concerning than the last. By the time Magnus returned, arms laden with bundles, my nerves were frayed.

"We need to move quickly," he said, thrusting clothing into our arms. "The town's already buzzing with rumors. Your father must've sent a raven to every territory."

I ducked behind a stack of barrels, the damp area dark enough for me to call on my power for extra coverage. My trembling hands fumbled with the ties of my dress as I changed, yanking the simple tunic over my head and pulling on the pants. It wasn't my usual style, but more practical than the ballgown I had left discarded on the ground.

Coming back to our spot, Magnus handed me a woolen cloak and a pair of socks and shoes. Both he and Oryn had already changed into similarly plain outfits like my own. It would keep us from garnering too much attention. Oryn knelt down before me, gently taking my foot in his hands to slide on the socks and secure my shoes.

"Better," Magnus approved. "But we should—"

The shuffle of feet caught our attention as two drunken men wandered closer to us, snickering to each other.

"Oi, any of the lot of ya have any coin?" The plump one to the left asked.

"Just spent our last one." Oryn stepped in front of me, blocking me from their view. "We don't have any left to spare, unfortunately."

"You hear that, Horace?" The willowy man on the right asked his friend, waving around an empty bottle. "They ain't got no more coin."

"Can't let ya through without paying the toll." Horace said. His dark eyes looked from Oryn to Magnus, then settled onto me. "We take payment in... other forms."

Snickers tumbled out of the slim one.

"Your payment is me allowing you to walk away with your life right now," Oryn's voice dropped to a dangerous tone.

"There's three of us and only two of you," Magnus pointed out. "Why don't you be on your way and we'll be on ours?"

"No, no, no, no, no," the smaller of the two whined. "Horace, make them pay the toll."

"Don't worry, Arnold." Horace said, a dagger brandishing from his hand at the ready. "We just have to take care of these two. She'll be too weak to fight us off."

A feral growl tore from Oryn's throat as he launched himself at Horace. The two men struggled on the ground. The other, Arnold, looked ready to pounce on Magus and me.

I would show them a weak woman. The bond connected the rage Oryn and I shared; there was no longer a separation between what he felt and what I felt. We were one in the same, our emotions merged. I called to my shadows, pulling them to me until I was nothing but a creature of pure darkness.

"D-D-D-Death's W-W-Wraith!" The putrid smell of piss filled the alley as Arnold's eyes grew twice their size. Frantically, he stumbled away, past his friend, who Oryn had pinned to the ground, his face already a bloody pulp. My husband reared back his fist and delivered one final blow, knocking the drunk man out.

Releasing my hold on my power, I pulled Oryn off of the man, inspecting his bloody knuckles.

"Are you okay?" I asked.

"I should be asking you that." His finger hooked under my chin, tilting it up until I met his eyes. He placed a gentle kiss on my lips before pulling back and assessing me for injury.

"That idiot didn't even try us," I said. "Too scared of your sweet little companion." I batted my eyelashes while taking on a sweeter tone.

Magnus choked behind me. "Nothing sweet about what he just saw. That man will likely never harass a lady again."

"Good—"

Hushed voices began trickling towards us from the street.

"Is that her?"

"Did you see what she did? It has to be her."

I cursed, realizing too late that my little show exposed us.

"It's them!" someone cried. "Death's Wraith, and that must be the traitor prince!"

The crowd that had peacefully gone about its business transformed in an instant. Faces contorted with fear and anger, hands reaching for weapons.

"Run," Magnus growled, shoving us toward the town's edge.

We bolted, dodging between buildings and leaping over carts. Behind us, the mob grew, their shouts echoing off stone walls.

"Catch him!"

"Kill him!"

"We should let his own soldiers have their way with his traitorous ass."

A rock sailed past my head, missing by inches. Another struck Oryn's shoulder, making him stumble.

"This way!" I grabbed his hand, pulling him down a narrow passage between two buildings.

We burst through to the other side, finding ourselves at the town's edge. Without hesitation, we plunged into the cover of the forest beyond, the angry voices from Oakston fading behind us as we fled deeper into the evergreen wilderness.

CHAPTER 6

The forest swallowed us whole, branches whipping at our faces as we ran. My lungs burned, each breath coming in sharp, painful gasps. Behind us, the sounds of pursuit gradually faded, replaced by the natural chorus of the woods.

"I think we lost them," Magnus panted, finally slowing to a brisk walk.

Oryn nodded, one hand pressed against his side. "For now. Let's keep moving, we don't want to risk them catching up before we reach Chermona."

We pushed onward through the day, avoiding roads and settlements, speaking little to conserve energy. The sun tracked across the sky, casting long shadows through the trees as afternoon melted into evening.

"Chermona lies just beyond that ridge." Magnus pointed as we crested a hill the following day. The journey had been punishing— we couldn't risk stopping for food, the three of us too exhausted to sleep. With every step, we looked over our shoulders.

The capital city spread before us, nestled in a valley surrounded by ancient trees. Unlike Sunnevean towns, Chermona seemed to grow from the earth itself—buildings of living wood and stone. The city curved around the southern palace grounds, with sprawling trees dotting the northern side. Unlike Epherinia, it was beautiful, without banners and insignias glittering with gold. It's just as stunning as the last time I saw it.

"It's breathtaking," Oryn murmured, genuine awe in his voice despite his exhaustion.

"And heavily guarded," I added, noting the men positioned along the tree line. "Stay close to me."

As we approached, guards emerged like ghosts from the forest, arrows nocked and aimed at our hearts.

"I am Alora Satori," I called out, raising my hands. "I seek an audience with Queen Wynaria."

One warrior stepped forward, his silver eyes narrowing. "What about them?" He nodded his head towards Oryn and Magnus.

"Under my protection and not to be harmed."

A tense moment passed before the warrior nodded. "The queen will want to see this for herself."

They escorted us through the city, drawing curious stares from its inhabitants. Children peeked from windows. Elders with silvery hair paused in their work to watch us pass. I felt Oryn's wonder through our bond, his gaze darting everywhere at once.

There are more humans here than I thought.

They value humans and half-breeds just as much as they do the fae, I answered back. *Something Sunneva could learn from.*

It'll be hard to change the habits of the nobles, but it'll be necessary. It's time our kingdom steps into unity.

I accidentally hummed in agreement out loud, earning me a look from the leading guard. The quirk of his eyebrow was full of suspicion and confusion.

The palace rose before us, a towering structure of stone and crystals that caught the late afternoon light and scattered it in rainbow patterns. Under different circumstances, I might have allowed Oryn a moment to appreciate it. Instead, we were hustled inside and straight to the throne room.

Ruby hair cascaded around Queen Wynaria's face as she sat on her throne. The woman was just as regal as she was intimidating. Dark eyes, black as a starless night, stood out against snow-white skin as she fixed an icy glare on us as we entered.

"Well, well," she drawled, leaning forward. "Death's Wraith returns to us, and with interesting company." She paused a moment, looking toward the door and then back at me. In an instant of realization, her words grew sharper than steel. "Where is my son, little bird?" She demanded.

I bowed my head, respect battling with exhaustion. "Queen Wynaria, I'm afraid he's been taken."

"Taken? By who?" She asked. "Don't tell me you left him in that dreadful palace and brought *this* prince in his place."

A pang of guilt struck my chest. Her words didn't surprise me, but the thought of ever purposely leaving Kyler behind was like tearing out my own heart. Especially when I was ready to swap places with him if ever the opportunity arose.

"King Aurelius has garnered favor with someone who toys with the natural balance of things." Because no matter how I explained it, there was nothing natural about stony soldiers. The queen's gaze only narrowed more in disapproval. "We're seeking refuge and protection while we gather intel and forces to rescue him."

The sovereign leaned back in her seat, fingers thrumming against the armrest.

"Mate of my blood, you'll have your wish, but you will return my son to his home. His *true* home. No more of this nonsense of playing savior in the south as some knight in that," she sneered, "*gold* plating."

"Thank you." Dropping into another bow, I didn't want to consider how Kyler would take my swearing to bring him home. It was a problem for another day.

"Though," she continued, "I find it odd you'd even request such a thing. Our traditions guarantee your safety upon this soil, at least with our people. Do you not think of us as honorable, little bird?"

My brow quirked at that. "Being chased out of Oakston was not the most welcoming experience."

"Ah, but were they chasing you? Regardless, I'll send ravens to our territories alerting them that our princess has come home. You won't have any issues while you're here."

"I'm sorry," I said, "what do you mean 'your princess'?"

"Exactly as I said. Did you get dropped on your head in that pretty little cage? You are my son's mate. We honor the laws of our gods and recognize fate's bond as absolute. Mate, wife, it's all the same. Despite his absence, my son is still the prince by title. Therefore, you are not only royal in the southern lands, you are royal by right here."

A cold familiarity swam around me as I tried to steady myself. Once again, in this very room, Queen Wynaria proved to have more cards than she showed. It was concerning, to say the least, imagining what she hid behind her sly looks and sharp wit.

The ethereal queen stood, her arms raised out, a predatory smile crossed her lips.

"Welcome home, Princess Alora." The words spoken with power echoed against the cavernous walls. Every guard stationed around the room dropped to one knee. The clang of metal rang as they slammed their fists against their chests. Their voices were powerful with conviction as their chant became the only song in the room.

"We serve you with honor."

Wynaria relaxed in her seat and looked me up and down. "You've been busy since we last spoke. One moment you're rejecting the plan the gods have laid at your feet, and the next you're assassinating the

Queen of Sunneva and showing up here with their prince. I must say, your ambition has grown."

"I did not kill Queen Lianna," I said coldly.

"Oh, that's right," Wynaria's gaze slid to Oryn, who stood tall despite the hostile stares directed his way, "her son did. The very son who's an enemy of our people and now his own that you have brought to our doorstep. Bold move, even for you."

"It's much more complicated than—"

"Oh, I'm sure it is." Wynaria cut me off as she rose, gliding down the steps of her dais with predatory grace. She circled Oryn, studying him like prey she wasn't quite ready to devour. "The son of the man who would see all Esmeranians exterminated, standing in my throne room. Tell me, Prince of Sunneva, what should prevent me from executing you on the spot?"

Magnus shifted closer to us, hand resting on his sword hilt though it would do little good. We were outnumbered, both here and in the halls outside the grand doors.

"Your Majesty," I interjected, "King Aurelius murdered his own wife. Oryn is not the enemy—he's been Kyler's biggest ally in ending the bloodshed."

Wynaria's perfect eyebrow arched. "Is that so? I want to hear it from the golden prince himself."

"It's the truth," Oryn stated, meeting her gaze without flinching.

"Truth," Wynaria laughed, the sound like ice crackling over a frozen lake. "That's a rare commodity these days, isn't it, assassin?" The queen gave me a pointed look despite responding to Oryn. "Everyone's always hiding something." She brought a dainty hand up, brushing her long locks from her shoulder. "Luckily for you, I'm all too familiar with your father's lies, and his missive that's been spreading around reeks of them."

She snapped her fingers, and a man materialized at her feet, a fresh scroll in his hands. She snatched the item from him and handed it to Oryn, who took it without hesitation. His silence was deafening as he studied its contents before rolling it back up and placing it in the old man's hands.

"What is it?" I asked.

A look of resignation and grim acceptance took over my husband's face. "Exactly what we expected. He's claimed that I murdered my mother and went on the run. You and Magnus are listed as accomplices. A bounty of a hundred thousand gold coins rests on each of our heads."

"It'll be hard for anyone to ignore a price like that," Magnus added grimly. "The reaction in Oakston makes more sense now. Other than hating those from Sunneva in general."

"Yes, your father drives a very tempting offer." Wynaria remarked. "But that wasn't all, was it?"

My eyes met Oryn's as he sighed in defeat.

"What else, Ryn?" The worst came to the front of my mind. No, it couldn't be Kyler; he would be safe. They'd keep him safe to get to me, right?

"It seems, in the wake of my mother's funeral," Oryn said, "my father has secured an engagement, to 'strengthen the realm'."

"An engagement?" I looked to Wynaria, expecting her to admit to agreeing to marry such a putrid man. If only to slit his throat once the moon was high. But she met my eyes with a slight shake of her head, the disgust at the mere thought was evident in the curl of her lip.

"It's Trinity, Alora." His lowered tone did not soften the blow. "He plans to place your mother on the Sunnevean throne."

CHAPTER 7

"Trinity?" My voice came out as a strangled whisper. The room tilted around me, and I had nothing to grip for support. "That's not possible."

"I'm afraid it is," Oryn's face had gone pale as death. "My father has always been ambitious, but this…"

"Fuck," Magnus spat, his hand tightening on his sword hilt. "That's not just an alliance. That's…"

"The end of everything," I finished for him. The realization crashed over me like a tidal wave. Trinity—the same woman who had tortured countless innocents as well as her own daughter. A woman who was just as greedy as the king in her quest for power— would soon sit on the throne of Sunneva.

Wynaria's eyes narrowed. "Who is this Trinity?"

"She's the one who has Kyler," I said, my voice trembling with fury that burned like ice in my veins. "She has abilities unlike anything I've ever seen, a hunger for power like the king. I think she may have less of a conscience than he does."

"She's been consorting with the king this whole time," Oryn added, running a hand through his golden hair. "And she's been researching the magic of the gods. Nothing good will come from this. If she gains a crown…"

"She'll have legal justification to wage war on an unprecedented scale," Magnus concluded grimly. "She wouldn't need to kidnap Alora and do gods' knows what with her. A simple order would have the entire kingdom dragging her back."

The queen's expression hardened. "She's been playing with magic? Godly magic?" She tapped a long, spindly finger to her chin in thought, the speed increasing with every breath that passed. "And with your father's armies at her disposal—"

"It won't be just Esmeray that falls," I cut in. "There's no telling what her true motivations are, but the entire realm would surely suffer."

A heavy silence fell over the throne room. The guards exchanged nervous glances, and even Wynaria seemed momentarily at a loss.

"How much time do we have?" She finally asked.

Oryn shook his head. "The announcement was made three days ago. The wedding is set for the new moon—less than a fortnight away."

"Then we need to act quickly." I paced the polished floor, my mind racing. "We need to find Kyler. Without him, she'll lose her leverage on me. I'm the one she wants. I'm surprised she hasn't already demanded me in exchange for him."

"And how do you propose we find him?" Wynaria asked, her tone softening slightly. "Do you know where she's taken him?"

I shook my head. "We got next to nothing from Aurelius, and I've tried reaching out to Kyler." The queen quirked a confused brow my way. "We have a mind bond," I explained. "But I haven't been able to hear him, any emotion he has is muffled. I know he's alive, but I cannot feel what's happening."

The queen studied me for a long moment. Could she sense the trust I had just awarded her for freely giving such information? As her gaze turned toward the tall windows, where the distant mountains were visible through the glass, her expression changed. It became contemplative, almost uncertain.

"There is... one possibility," she said slowly. "Though I've never resorted to it before."

"What is it?" I asked, desperate hope clawing through the darkness in my chest.

"The witch of fate," Wynaria said, her voice barely above a whisper. "Elisana. She may be able to help us find him."

Oh, no. Not *her* again.

The silence that followed was so deafening that all I could hear was my own heartbeat pounding in my ears. Even recalling my brush with the bizarre woman and her nonsensical rambling made a shiver crawl up my spine.

Who is this witch? And why does she have my wife trembling? Oryn asked through our bond.

She's a haunting experience.

"And this witch is your ally?" Magnus questioned carefully.

"In a sense," the queen confirmed. "She's never wished harm on Esmeray, or myself, but is still very dangerous. No one enters the mountain who she does not wish to. She sees things others cannot— threads of destiny woven through time. Her prophecies are rarely straightforward. But to call her down from the mountain, there'll be a price to pay."

"I don't care," I said firmly. "If she can help us find Kyler, I'll pay whatever price she asks."

Wynaria's lips pressed into a thin line. "You say that now, Death's Wraith, but the witch's price is never what you expect. She doesn't deal in gold or favors—she deals in fate itself. She may decide not to answer our plea for aid."

"We're out of options," Oryn said, stepping forward. "And soon out of time."

The queen nodded slowly. "Then I will do something no ruler in Esmeray has done in over a thousand years. I will call Elisanna down from her mountain." She turned to a guard. "Prepare her a chamber. And bring me the silver bell."

As the guard hurried away, Wynaria fixed me with a piercing stare. "I hope you understand what you're asking for, Alora. Once the witch of fate is summoned, there's no turning back from the path she reveals."

I met her gaze steadily. "Some paths were chosen for us long before we knew we were walking them."

CHAPTER 8

Wynaria rose from her throne, the silver fabric of her gown catching the light. "I must prepare for the summoning. It's not a simple matter to call Elisanna down." She paused, studying me with those unfathomable dark eyes. "But I believe you'll want to see who arrived at court yesterday."

She gestured toward a side door, and my heart faltered as two familiar figures strode into the throne room.

"Our beautiful goddess has returned!" Lucas shouted, sprinting across the floor towards me.

"Lucas?" His name was the only word I managed to say before being swept into his arms. We spun around for a moment before he placed me back down. A shadow covered us as I looked up at the owner's kind face and smiled. "Rasher, this seems oddly familiar."

"Somewhat," a grin spread across his face. "Only this time, my limbs aren't aching from sleeping in that blasted chair beside your bed."

We shared a laugh while Lucas and Oryn looked lost. I could hardly believe my eyes seeing our friends once again. It wasn't long since we had seen them, but it felt like an eternity after confronting the king during the ball.

Lucas wrapped an arm around my shoulder. "Where's the tall one?"

My mood darkened instantly. What little joy the reunion had brought vanished like smoke.

Magnus cleared his throat somewhere beside me, but it was Oryn who spoke.

"Kyler was taken, but we're going to find him." His blue eyes met mine. "We will get him back."

Rasher's face fell. Lucas's face went neutral for a moment before he smiled once again. Though instead of his beaming, joyous smile, it was one of reassurance.

"Yeah, we'll get him back, sweet girl. We've faced gods, what's one little recovery mission?" He squeezed me once more before letting me go.

Wynaria cleared her throat. "Rasher will help you all get settled." She fixed Rasher with a stern look. "Make sure everyone knows Prince Oryn is a guest of the crown and is to be unharmed while on Esmeranian soil."

"Yes, Your Majesty," Rasher replied with a small bow.

As the queen swept from the room, Lucas pulled me into another hug. "Gods, I've missed you."

"I've missed you too." I pulled back suddenly, remembering. "What about Raven? Is he—"

"Safe and sound despite the hell he put me through," Lucas said. "That demon threw me off at least twenty times on our way here. Tried to take one of my fingers, too."

Relief flooded through me. My loyal steed had made it safely out of Sunneva.

"Lucas," Oryn stepped forward, a warm smile breaking across his handsome face. "It's good to see you."

"Your Highness," Lucas dipped in a flourishing bow before abandoning all pretense and embracing Oryn too.

"Just Oryn will do," he replied, clapping Lucas on the back.

Magnus stood awkwardly to the side until Rasher approached him, extending a hand. Magnus took the offering. The two men exchanged warm welcomes without a word.

While the others exchanged pleasantries, Rasher moved to stand beside me, his presence steady as stone.

"How are you holding up?" he asked quietly.

I swallowed hard. "I'm functioning."

"That's all any of us can do right now." His voice dropped lower. "He's strong, Alora. If anyone can survive being in enemy territory, it's him."

"I know," I whispered, the words burning in my throat. "But that doesn't make it any easier."

Rasher nodded, understanding in his brown eyes. "We'll find him. And in the meantime, we should resume your training."

I hesitantly agreed, not once thinking about the training we attempted when I first came here. Without Kyler there to douse my wild flames, I found it hard to imagine it would go well.

After a moment, he straightened his shoulders. "Come on, let's get you settled. You look like you haven't slept in days."

"That's because we haven't," Magnus muttered.

Rasher led us through the winding corridors of the castle, pointing out important locations as we went. He was a much better guide than his prince. He showed Magnus to a comfortable chamber near Lucas's room.

"Sorry, I promised a certain someone that I would let them know when I came back." Confused, I watched Rasher knock on the door on the other side of Lucas's room, and when it opened, I gasped.

"Luella?"

My lady's maid stood in the doorway, her eyes widening before filling with tears. "My Lady!"

She rushed forward, propriety forgotten as she embraced me. "Thank the gods you're safe."

"How—" I started, looking between her and Rasher in confusion.

"We found her wandering Bridgedale as we were leaving," Rasher explained. "Glad we did, too. There's no telling what could've happened to her if she had made the journey on her own."

For the first time in days, I felt something close to hope blooming in my chest. I wasn't alone in this fight. Not anymore.

Luella wiped her tears, then straightened her dress as if suddenly remembering her position. "I've been so worried about you, my lady. I tried to find you, but there was so much chaos. But I remembered the promise I made to you."

"Luella, please, no more formalities. Please call me Lor. I'm so relieved you're safe." There was no telling what Miss Gregoria would do to Luella if she ever found out how close we had become. With the king ready to use me as he pleased, surely he'd let his staff manager do whatever she wished to the poor maid.

"I've been given a lovely room here," she continued, her words tumbling out faster now. "The Esmeranian servants have been most kind, though they do things quite differently here. Did you know they use pine oil instead of lavender for the linens? And their morning tea is served with honey crystals rather than—"

"Luella," I cut in gently, a smile tugging at my lips despite everything. "We can discuss all of this tomorrow. Perhaps you could also show me around the parts of the castle you've discovered?"

Her face brightened. "Oh, yes! There's a most beautiful garden with the strangest flowers I've ever seen. And the library—" She caught herself. "But tomorrow, as you say. You look exhausted, Lor."

"I am," I admitted. "It's been... difficult."

Her eyes softened with understanding. "Tomorrow then. I'll come find you after breakfast."

We parted ways, and Rasher continued leading Oryn and me through the dark stone corridors. The deeper we ventured into the castle, the more I recognized our surroundings. We were heading toward the wing I had originally woken up in.

"This way," Rasher said, turning down another hallway. He opened the second door on our left.

The room came into view, but it wasn't the room I had used prior. Stepping into the grand space, I took a deep breath. It smelled of fresh rain on the tall pine trees that covered the northern territory. This *wasn't* my room. By scent alone it was clear these were the prince's quarters. Even though he's been gone, his room seemed to capture his very essence. Dark marbled floors with thin rivers of silver woven throughout, dark curtains that reminded me of a clear night sky adorned the windows. The furniture a rich woodsy color, but without any luxurious touches like glittering gems. Everything had that quality you'd find in any regal residence, but was just as unassuming as its owner could be.

"I don't understand," I said, looking up at Rasher in confusion. "I thought we would be staying in the same room as before."

Rasher shook his head. He stepped aside to let Oryn through and then leaned against the heavy door. "He'd kill me if I put you anywhere else."

His belongings appeared as if he'd only left the room moments ago: a book splayed open on the desk, a jacket tossed over a chair, and boots lined up neatly by the wardrobe. I wandered to the desk. My fingers trailed over the back of a chair where he must have sat countless times.

"I don't know if I can—" My voice cracked.

"You can," Rasher said firmly. "And you will. He'd want you here. Hell, he even had the wardrobe stocked with clothes for you the day after you two made up. This is your room as much as his."

Oryn stood silently between us, his blue eyes taking in everything. "It's as meticulous as his room in Sunneva," he mused.

A lump formed in my throat. "I shouldn't be here without him."

"This is exactly where you *should* be," Rasher countered. "The room you stayed in before is just through that door." He looked towards Oryn. "I can't say I understand a bond with multiple mates, but if you need a separate room, you can use that. The bathing room is fully stocked, and I'll go talk to the cook about dinner once I find the tailor. His shirts may fit you, but his pants would be puddles around your feet."

Oryn laughed. "He's only got a few inches on me. How about I join you?" He turned to me. "Love, why don't you take a bath, get cleaned up, and I'll be back with some food soon?"

I nodded; I didn't trust my voice any longer. I was sure that the next time I spoke, it would cause a flow of tears.

Rasher bowed slightly. "I'll leave you to settle in. Training begins at dawn, Alora." His eyes held a warning. "I don't think I have to warn you not to be late."

With a mischievous grin with his warning, he left with Oryn in tow. I stood frozen in the center of the room, afraid to touch anything else, afraid to disturb what Kyler had left behind. That was until I caught a whiff of myself. Not able to bear the thought of losing his scent surrounding me with my own stink, I made my way into the bathroom.

CHAPTER 9

I turned the brass faucet, watching as steaming water gushed into the massive marble tub. The bathroom itself was easily double the size of my entire childhood bedroom——a reminder of the vastly different world I came from compared to both of my princes.

My fingers trailed through the rising water, testing its temperature.

Perfect.

I added a splash of oil I found on a nearby shelf, inhaling deeply as the familiar scent of rain filled the steam-clouded room. It smelled like him.

"Gods, I miss you," I whispered to the empty room, wishing Kyler would materialize from thin air. The room stayed empty aside from myself.

I peeled off my filthy clothes, letting them drop in a heap on the floor. Days of travel left them beyond salvaging. I sank into the hot water with a hiss, my muscles first screaming in protest before surrendering to the blissful heat.

You're going to find him, Maël's voice drifted through my mind, so shockingly clear I almost looked around the bathroom for him.

"I know," I answered aloud, leaning my head against the edge of the tub. "But what state will he be in when I do?"

The silence that followed wasn't reassuring. I closed my eyes, letting the water rise to my chin.

He's stronger than you give him credit for, Maël finally replied. *And so are you.*

I wished I could believe that. The memory of Trinity's cruel smile flashed behind my eyelids. What was she doing to him? The thought of her touching him, hurting him, made my stomach clench painfully. Our muted bond was a dull ache that made every bone in my body feel hollow with despair.

"She'll pay for this," I promised myself. "Whatever she's done, whatever she's planning—I'll make her regret ever opening a portal into that room. She'll wish she never crossed me, or my mates." The water rippled around me as my hands clenched into fists beneath the surface. Heat built inside me, not from the bath, but from somewhere deeper. An internal flame stirred, responding to my rage.

I jerked upright, water sloshing over the sides of the tub.

No.

Not now.

Breathe, Lor, Maël's voice said soothingly. *It's only you here. You're safe.*

But that was the problem. I wasn't safe—not from myself. The fire inside me felt different now, hungrier, erratic. Ever since that night I spent with both my mates, I'd felt it pushing against my control, eager to break free.

I stared down at my hands beneath the water's surface. They looked like mine, pale and pruning slightly from the heat. But I knew what they were capable of. I was all too familiar with my power's thirst for destruction.

"What if I can't control it?" I whispered out loud. "What if I hurt someone I care about?"

You won't.

"You don't know that."

But I know you.

I sank lower into the water. The queen had summoned the witch to help us find Kyler. But even if we located him, what then? Trinity would be there. Her soldiers of stone would be there. Even the king may be there. And I would need every weapon at my disposal to get Kyler back and out of there safely.

Including my fire.

I lifted one hand from the water, watching droplets slide down my wrist. A flame burst to life in my palm before I shoved my hand under the water to extinguish it.

"I need to master this," I said quietly. "Ignoring it has only led to it growing more unpredictable."

You need to stop fearing it, Maël said. *Fear will only make it harder to control.*

He was right. I'd been running from this part of myself for as long as I could remember, terrified of what it meant, what it could do. It wasn't like my shadows that answered my every call, knowing exactly where I wanted them to go and what to do. The flames didn't care about order, only feeding themselves and burning everything in its path. Frustration gnawed at me. But Kyler needed me—all of me, including the parts I feared the most.

I closed my eyes again, feeling the fire inside me, acknowledging its existence instead of shying away. Its warm essence caressed me like a forgotten lover.

"For a moment, I thought I might have gained some semblance of my sanity back. I hadn't spoken to you in a long time," I mused.

You haven't needed me as much. Besides, the only time you've been truly crazy is when you thought you could take me in the training ring.

"I held my own just fine, thank you," I laughed. "There would never be a day where I don't need you." The overwhelming sadness that has cloaked me since the night my world burned to ash washed over me. A handful of my final memories of his face replaying in my head, his eyes lit with joy and that stupidly charming smile beamed at me as I let myself drift deep into the scene. "Why couldn't you have survived that night?" The whisper pierced the quiet of the otherwise tranquil room.

If I had, you wouldn't be here. You would have married me and never have met your true mates.

"You were my mate too, even without a bond. I chose you first."

And I you, little hunter.

CHAPTER 10

A splash of water hit the floor as I shifted. The sound of movement from the main room caught my attention. I stilled, listening. Footsteps. Too heavy for a woman, so it couldn't be a servant. And it sounded too purposeful to be an intruder.

"Lor?" Oryn's voice called out, followed by a gentle knock on the bathroom door.

"In here," I answered, sinking deeper into the water to wash away any tear marks left on my face. The door creaked open just enough for Oryn to peek his head in, his eyes finding mine immediately.

"I brought food," he said, his gaze deliberately fixed on my face despite the temptation I knew he felt to look elsewhere. "Rasher convinced the cook to make a small feast, so I hope you're hungry."

"Starving, actually." I hadn't realized how empty my stomach felt until he mentioned food.

Oryn's eyes darkened as they finally slipped down to where the water lapped at my collarbone. "I'd offer to join you, but I don't think either of us would eat if I did. And it'd be a shame to let it grow cold."

Heat that had nothing to do with the bathwater rushed through me. "Probably not."

He cleared his throat. "Are you almost finished, Love?"

"Just about." I made no move to rise, suddenly shy despite everything we'd shared.

Oryn seemed to understand. He disappeared for a moment, returning with a large towel. "Come on. Let me take care of you."

I stood, water cascading down my body. Oryn's sharp intake of breath was the only indication that he was affected as he wrapped the plush towel around me, his touch lingering at my shoulders.

"You're making this very difficult," he murmured, his voice rough.

"Making what difficult?"

"Keeping my hands to myself." He helped me step out of the tub, his fingers gentle as they tucked the towel more securely around me. "You need to eat first. Rest."

"And after?" I couldn't help asking, a small smile playing at my lips.

His answering grin was wolfish. "Afterward, I'll show you exactly what I've been thinking about since I walked in here."

I let him guide me to the bedroom, where he'd laid out a veritable feast on the small table by the window. Fresh bread, cheese, sliced fruit, and what looked like seared chicken filled the plates.

"Sit," he commanded, pulling out a chair for me. I obeyed, clutching the towel to my chest. Oryn took the seat opposite, but instead of reaching for his own food, he tore off a piece of bread and held it to my lips.

"I can feed myself," I protested, though my heart fluttered at the gesture.

"I know." His eyes were serious despite his easy smile. "Let me do this for you, Lor."

Something in his tone made me relent. I opened my mouth, accepting the morsel from his fingers. The bread was still warm, crusty on the outside and soft within. I closed my eyes, savoring the simple pleasure.

When I opened them again, Oryn was watching me with such tenderness it made my chest ache.

"What?" I asked, suddenly self-conscious.

"Nothing." He offered me a slice of cheese next. "Just... happy to see you eat."

I took it, chewing softly. "You should eat, too."

"I will." But he continued feeding me, piece by piece, ensuring I had my fill before taking anything for himself.

As my initial hunger subsided, the weight of everything settled back onto my shoulders. I accepted a slice of apple from Oryn's fingers, but my appetite had begun to wane.

"We're going to find him," Oryn said quietly, reading my thoughts. "Whatever it takes."

"And what if we're too late?" The fear that had been building since Kyler's disappearance finally spilled out. "What if Trinity has already—"

"Don't." Oryn's voice was sharp. "Don't go there, Lor. He's alive. We would know if he weren't. He would do whatever it took to make it back to you, he would survive anything."

I nodded, though the reassurance felt hollow. "The bond is so faint when it's closed off like this. He should never have pushed me out of the way."

"If it wasn't him, it was going to be me. Despite everything, the bond is still there." Oryn reached across the table, his fingers finding mine. "And as long as it's there, we have hope."

"I can't lose him," I whispered. "Not after everything. Not when we've barely had any time together."

"You won't lose him." Oryn's grip tightened. "*We* won't lose him."

I looked up, meeting his gaze. The golden flakes in his deep blue eyes seemed to glow in the dim light of the room. "I can't lose you, either."

Something flickered across his face—pain, perhaps, or resignation. "You have me, Lor. Always."

I nodded, soaking in the comfort of his words. "Do you ever feel like the worst has not yet passed? Like there's another attack just around the corner waiting?"

Instead of answering, Oryn stood, circling the table to kneel before me. His hands framed my face, thumbs brushing away tears I hadn't realized I'd shed.

"Even if there is, I know we're strong enough together to take it. That sea serpent was no match, though I could've done without you going right into its mouth."

I leaned into his touch, seeking the comfort only he could provide. "I'm worried, Oryn."

"So am I." The admission cost him. I could see it in the tightening of his shoulders. "But I'm more afraid of losing you than anything else."

His honesty broke something inside me. I slid from the chair into his arms, the towel loosening as I pressed against him. Oryn caught me, his arms encircling my waist as our foreheads touched.

"I need you," I breathed against his lips. "Tonight, I just need to forget everything else."

His response was to capture my mouth with his, a kiss that started gentle but quickly blazed into something desperate and consuming. I clung to him as he lifted me, carrying me to the bed without breaking the kiss.

The towel fell away as he laid me down, his eyes darkening as they roamed over my bare skin. "Gods, you're beautiful."

I reached for him, tugging at his shirt. "Too many clothes."

He smiled, a flash of the playful man I'd fallen for. "Impatient as ever."

"Always, when it comes to you."

Oryn stripped quickly, each piece of clothing discarded left me burning with anticipation. When he finally joined me on the bed, the feel of his bare skin against mine sent electricity coursing through my veins.

"I've missed you," he murmured, trailing kisses down my neck. "Missed this."

"Then show me," I challenged, arching against him.

His answering growl vibrated through me as he claimed my mouth again, his hands exploring with familiar reverence. Each touch was a balm to my fractured soul, each kiss a promise that somehow, we would find our way through this darkness.

I lost myself in him—in the feel of his hands mapping my body, in the taste of his skin beneath my lips, in the weight of him pressing me into the mattress. For these precious moments, there was no war, no Trinity, no uncertain future. There was only us, finding solace in each other's arms.

"Stay with me," I whispered as we moved together, my fingers digging into his shoulders.

"Always, Love," he vowed, his eyes locked with mine. "In this life and whatever comes after. My wife, my soul."

We found our release together, clinging to each other as waves of pleasure washed over us. In the aftermath, as our breathing slowed and our heartbeats gradually returned to normal, Oryn gathered me against his chest, his fingers tracing idle patterns on my back.

"You should eat more," he said eventually, though he made no move to leave the bed.

I nestled closer, unwilling to break the fragile peace we'd found. "Later."

He pressed a kiss onto my forehead. "Later," he agreed.

We lay in silence for a while. The only sounds were our synchronized breathing and the occasional hoot of an owl hunting in the night. The darkness from beyond the window seeped into the bedroom, broken only by the glow of a fire.

"Tell me something good," I requested softly. "Something to hold onto when things get dark again."

Oryn was quiet for so long, I thought he might have fallen asleep.

Then, his voice rumbled in my ear. "When I was a child, before my father took an interest in my upbringing, my mother used to tell me that souls who are meant to find each other always will—no matter how many lifetimes it takes."

I lifted my head to look at him. "Do you believe that?"

His smile was sad but genuine. "How else could I explain how you came into our lives? Kyler and I were drawn to you like moths to a flame."

I laid my head back on his chest, listening to the steady beat of his heart. "Then we'll find him again. And we'll bring him home."

"We will," Oryn promised, his arms tightening around me. "Together."

CHAPTER II

I jolted awake before the sun had fully risen, my body tense with anticipation. Beside me, Oryn slept peacefully, his features softened in slumber. I traced the line of his jaw with my fingertip, allowing myself one moment of tenderness before slipping from the warmth of his arms.

Rasher would expect me soon. Today was the day I'd confront the fire that burned inside me.

I dressed quietly, pulling on the leather pants and fitted tunic that had been hanging in the wardrobe for me. The fabric was supple yet sturdy—practical clothing for combat training. I plaited my hair into a tight braid that hung down my back, keeping it out of my face.

Oryn stirred as I laced my boots. "Where are you going so early?" His voice was rough with sleep.

"Training with Rasher. He expects me there at dawn."

He propped himself up on one elbow, eyes still heavy-lidded. "There's still plenty of time before dawn, come back to bed."

I leaned over and pressed a kiss to his forehead. "Go back to sleep. I'm taking a little extra time for a walk."

Understanding flickered across his face, knowing there were

plenty of reasons for me to want to be alone with my thoughts. "I'll see you down there soon."

"Alright." I answered with a forced smile.

I slipped from our chambers into the silent hallway. The castle was stirring, servants moving silently as they prepared for the day. I'd asked for directions to the training grounds from the first guard that I passed, trying to memorize the path he described before his duties took him in the other direction.

Left at the grand staircase, through the eastern corridor, down the servant's stairs, across the inner courtyard, and through the armory.

Simple enough.

Says the girl who could barely find her way home after gallivanting in the woods all day.

I don't need your sass, Maël, I shot back in my head.

Thirty minutes later, I was hopelessly lost.

I'd taken what I *thought* was the eastern corridor, only to end up in the kitchens. From there, I'd attempted to find my way back, only to discover an entirely new wing of the castle I hadn't seen before.

"Gods-damned castles and their unnecessary size," I muttered to myself, turning down yet another cold, gleaming hallway decorated in silver and black.

Castles tend to be large, otherwise, they would be no different from a country cottage.

"For once, I just want to get somewhere without losing my mind," I muttered to myself.

The only thing you've lost is your sense of direction. But you never really had that, did you?

Fighting the urge to take the bait my imaginary Maël dangled in my face, I continued on with my head held high. The grounds couldn't be too far.

Two guards stood at attention at the end of the corridor I'd been walking down. They straightened as I approached, their expressions carefully neutral.

"Excuse me," I said, forcing a polite smile. "I'm looking for the training grounds."

The taller guard pointed down a side passage. "Through there, my lady. Follow it to the end, then take the stairs down."

"Thank you." I moved to pass them, but paused when I caught fragments of their whispered conversation.

"—witch could arrive any day—"

"—heard she sees your death—"

"—I've never had the balls to even set foot on her mountain. She—"

"—Queen must be desperate to call her—"

The fear in their voices was palpable, making the hair on my arms stand on end. Fate's witch was no ordinary woman. As helpful as her visions were, her delivery was a haunting song of nonsense and riddles. Their fear was justified. The witch might appear as just an old woman, but the dread she inspired was bone-deep.

The woman inspired dread with every syllable. I just hoped that whatever she shared wouldn't be unsolvable.

I hurried down the passage, eager to reach the training grounds and focus on the task at hand.

Following the guard's directions, I finally emerged into a large, open courtyard. The space held the same sections it had before: the table laden with weapons, an archery range, and enough room for sparring.

It wasn't surprising to find Lucas and Oryn circling each other in the center, swords in hand. Despite leaving long before him, my husband had beaten me here. The twisting routes of the castle took more time than I had anticipated. Both men were already sweating, their movements quick and precise. Lucas feinted left before striking from the right, a move Oryn anticipated and blocked easily. The smiles on their faces with every swish of a sword both warmed my heart and concerned me. If they became too close of friends, we would all be doomed to constant mayhem.

"You're practically calling out your attacks before you strike," Oryn criticized, though there was no heat in his words.

Lucas grinned. "And you're still favoring your right side."

On the far side of the yard, Rasher stood with his arms crossed, watching me with narrowed eyes. As I approached, he made a show of looking up at the sun, now fully risen.

"Decided to join us after all, Lor?" His voice carried across the yard, causing both Oryn and Lucas to pause their sparring.

I lifted my chin. "I got lost on the way."

"Of course you did." The man's mouth twitched, almost smiling. "I was beginning to think you had changed your mind about training."

"I'm here, aren't I?"

Lucas bounded over, his face flushed with exertion. "Lor! About time. Rasher's been working me like a dog, not that I mind." He winked at the large man. "Let's show them what it's like to fight the best damn assassins that ever were."

The tone of his voice was light, but humor and excitement didn't hide his true motivation. They must have been putting Lucas through the ringer for him to be determined to beat them at their own game. But now, his best ally had arrived: his partner in crime, in many, many crimes.

"You seemed eager to fight me," Oryn said, joining us more sedately. His eyes swept over me, checking for signs of something out of sorts. Finding none, he relaxed slightly. "I'm curious what it'd be like for my wife to dominate me, in the ring that is."

The heated look that accompanied his innocent comment made my cheeks warm. "I'd be happy to show you what it's like, but I'm not sure you're ready for that."

Rasher cleared his throat loudly. "If you two are finished making eyes at each other, we have work to do." He gestured for me to follow him to an empty section of the yard, away from the others.

The space was bare except for a series of stone targets arranged in a semicircle. The ground had been cleared of vegetation, leaving only packed earth. Fire precautions, I realized with a twist of apprehension. We didn't have the luxury of having Kyler here to put it out if it got out of control like last time.

And I was certain it would leap beyond my control.

"Have you attempted to call your fire since the last time?" Rasher asked without preamble.

I shrugged. "A few times."

"And?"

"And it felt like it was a moment away from consuming everything." I answered.

"Why do you think that is?"

The question was simple, but the answer wasn't. I stared at my hands, remembering the times the flames had danced across my skin. "Because I lack control. Because the power is stronger than I am."

Rasher nodded as if he'd expected this answer. "Fear is your enemy here, Alora. Not the fire."

"Easy for you to say," I muttered. "Your power doesn't have the potential to burn down an entire city."

"No," he agreed. "But I've seen what you're capable of. Strength is not what you're lacking."

From the corner of my eye, I saw Oryn and Lucas had moved closer, watching our exchange with matching expressions of curiosity and concern.

"What do you want me to do?" I asked, resignation coloring my tone.

Rasher pointed to the center of the cleared area. "Stand there. Close your eyes. Feel the fire inside you."

I moved to the spot he indicated, my heart hammering against my ribs. The morning air felt suddenly too thin, too cold.

"Now what?"

"Now you stop fighting it." Rasher's voice was firm but not unkind. "The fire is part of you, Alora. Not something to be feared."

I closed my eyes, trying to focus on the spark I always felt lurking beneath my skin. It was there, waiting—a lone ember ready to flare to life.

"I can't," I admitted, eyes still closed. "When it comes, it just... consumes everything."

"That's because you're resisting it," Rasher said. "You're treating it like an enemy to be subdued rather than a part of yourself to be embraced."

I opened my eyes to find him standing directly in front of me, his expression serious.

"Think of it like your blades," he continued. "When you first learned to fight, did you have perfect control?"

"No, but—"

"Did you cut yourself? Others?"

I frowned. "Yes, but that's different."

"Is it?" Rasher raised an eyebrow. "All power requires practice, discipline. Your fire is no different."

He stepped back, gesturing to the targets. "Start small. Light one of them on fire."

My stomach knotted. "And if it grows out of control?"

"Then we'll deal with it," Oryn's voice came from behind me, steady and reassuring.

I turned to find him watching me with absolute faith shining in his eyes. Beside him, Lucas nodded encouragingly.

"You've got this, Lor," Lucas said. "Just try not to singe my eyebrows. I'm rather attached to them."

Despite my nerves, I found myself smiling at his attempt to lighten the mood.

Turning back to the targets, I took a deep breath and held out my hand. The spark inside me stirred, responding to my intention.

"Don't force it," Rasher instructed. "Invite it."

I closed my eyes again, focusing not on pushing the fire out, but on allowing it to flow through me naturally. I thought of the heat that always lingered beneath my skin, the warmth that flared when I was angry or afraid.

Or when I needed to protect those I loved.

The image of Kyler's face flashed behind my eyelids—his sharp eyes paired with that gentle smile of his. Then came Trinity's mocking laughter, the thought of her holding Kyler captive while I stood helpless.

No, she won't hold him for long. Not while I still breathed.

Heat rushed down my arm, pooling in my palm. I opened my eyes to find a small flame dancing above my hand, its light reflecting in Rasher's approving gaze.

"Good," he said. "Now direct it toward the target."

I focused on the stone marker directly ahead, visualizing the flame striking at its center. With a flick of my wrist, I sent the fire flying—

Only to watch it veer wildly to the right and grow four times its size, igniting several of the target dummies.

"Shit!" I gasped as one by one the dummies burst into flames.

Lucas let out a startled laugh. "Well, at least you hit something. Not what you were aiming for, but something."

"This isn't funny, Lucas." Panic clawed at my throat as I tried to stay calm and douse the flames. The white tendrils wouldn't bend to my will, instead growing higher and higher, their heat increasing rapidly.

"Focus, Alora," Rasher instructed. "You can do this."

His muffled voice sounded a million miles away despite his closeness. The sight before me transported me back to that blood-soaked night when flames devoured everything I'd ever known and everyone I'd ever loved. My vision tunneled as I tried to focus long enough to gain even an ounce of control of my power.

I couldn't let this continue. Kyler's freedom—his life—depended on my success.

But still, the fire didn't heed my call. With everything in me, I tried to force it down, to extinguish itself. A flicker occurred here and there, but the flames wouldn't extinguish.

I was losing this battle.

A warm hand wrapped around my arm. The tug of my mate bond pulsed through me as I looked up to find Oryn at my side. His cerulean eyes focused on the wildfire. With a sweep of his hand, golden flames mixed with mine until it was hard to tell where one ended and the other began. The fire began to subside, dying down until all that was left were glowing embers on the ground.

I slumped against him, relieved the danger was gone, but disappointment started to take hold.

I failed today, and I was going to fail Kyler.

"It was a good attempt, Lor," Rasher said, his voice soft, and his eyes looked upon me with kindness. "You kept it contained. It's a start."

"I almost burnt the entire place down!" I exclaimed. "All three of you could've been hurt—"

"But we weren't," Oryn cut in, grabbing both of my hands and forcing me to look up at him. "We are fine. The grounds are fine. It'll be better next time."

"There won't *be* a next time." I muttered.

Rasher and Oryn shared a brief, quiet look before meeting my eyes once again.

"Alora, it's only the first day. These things take time."

"We don't have time," I argued. "Kyler is out there right now suffering gods knows what tortures while we play with fire."

"And we will consult with this witch to try to locate him," Oryn said. "In the meantime, how about I work with you? If there's one thing I know, it's fire. Let me help you with this."

"It's a lost cause. We should just go look for him. At least we would be doing something productive."

"Wandering around aimlessly is not productive. Patience, Love. I know it's difficult."

My arms crossed in front of my chest as I brought my eyes towards the ground. The thought of these warriors wasting precious hours on my hopeless case made my stomach turn. It was a lost cause. At the very least, if we needed to resort to this power, I could try to get everyone to flee, and I could let it loose and hope they would extinguish the flames before it could do any more damage beyond what I would intend.

"Fine," I said.

I would give my life to free him. Whether they agreed with me or not, at least it was an option, a plan when all others failed.

Slow clapping sounded from behind me. I turned to find a woman in leathers. One side of her head was shaved, and it looked like a blind man had hacked off her black hair on the other side. She was nothing short of intimidating as she took confident steps towards us.

"If this is the one who's supposed to save us, then we're all doomed," the newcomer said.

CHAPTER 12

I stiffened at the woman's remark, my eyes narrowing as I took in her battle-worn appearance and the casual way she dismissed me. Her deep umber eyes shone against golden-brown skin.

"And you are?" I asked, my voice sharp.

The woman's lips curved into something that wasn't quite a smile. "Candra." Her gaze slid to Rasher, and her expression softened marginally. "Good to see you back, old friend. Been too long."

Rasher nodded, his posture relaxing slightly. "Candra."

She crossed the training grounds with the confident swagger of someone who knew every rock and bit of dirt personally. The twin axes strapped to her back gleamed in the morning light as she turned to face Rasher, well-used but meticulously maintained.

"Last I saw you," she said to Rasher, "you were being dragged to the Sunnevean dungeons after you shoved me through a window." She tapped her fingers against her thigh before lowering her voice. I leaned in to listen. "You didn't have to do that. You didn't need to be there alone."

"I wasn't as lonely as I would have preferred to be," Rasher's eyes met mine briefly before looking back to Candra. "But it made no sense for us both to be there. I was prepared to make that sacrifice, and you had a long life ahead of you still to live."

"That was my choice to make," Candra snapped. "Even so, I'm grateful."

"You were part of the team that attempted to assassinate the king?" I asked, putting together the pieces.

Candra's eyes cut to me, calculating. "That's right. Failed mission, obviously. Though from what I hear, you've had better luck getting close to royalty." Her gaze roved over me again, this time with open skepticism. "Hard to believe you're the infamous Death's Wraith after that display. I expected something... more."

The dismissal in her tone made my blood simmer. I'd faced this before—people underestimating me based on appearance alone. Usually, I let my blades do the talking.

Lucas stepped forward, positioning himself between us. "I wouldn't judge too quickly. I've seen Alora take down men three times her size without breaking a sweat. *She* is the deadliest person I have ever met."

"Is she now?" Candra raised an eyebrow, unimpressed. "Because what I just witnessed was a novice at best. Not exactly the legend I've been hearing about."

"You don't know what you're talking about," Lucas said, his usual playfulness gone.

Candra ignored him, her attention shifting beyond us. Her entire demeanor changed in an instant—her body tensed, hand reaching for one of her axes as her eyes locked on Oryn.

"What the fuck is he doing here?" She growled, taking a step forward.

Oryn met her gaze evenly, not reaching for a weapon, but I could feel the tension radiating from him. Would he let her make contact just to prove he wasn't a threat? Part of me knew he would, but I wasn't as noble as he was. My muscles tensed, ready to spring into action to protect him. She could try, but she'd lose her hand before that axe ever touched his skin.

"Stand down, Candra," Rasher commanded, his voice cutting through the sudden tension.

"Stand down?" She looked at him as if he'd lost his mind. "That's the son of the very man we've been trying to kill for ages. Our enemy. And you're telling me to stand down?"

"By order of Queen Wynaria herself," Rasher said firmly. "Oryn is Princess Alora's honored guest and is not to be harmed on Esmeranian soil."

Candra's laugh was harsh and bitter. "Princess? Since when? Last I checked, Prince Kyler hadn't claimed a mate." Her eyes narrowed as she looked between Oryn and me. "There's no way he'd choose someone like you. Not when he could have—"

"You?" I guessed. My chin lifted, taking the woman in with fresh eyes after seeing her reaction to Rasher's words.

"At least I can wield effectively." Tendrils of water emerged out of the ground and swirled around her. "At least I wouldn't bring our enemy home. Was one prince not enough for you?"

"Careful," Oryn warned, his voice deceptively calm.

"Or what?" Candra challenged. "You'll kill me like you've killed so many of my people?"

The accusation hung in the air between them. I could see the pain flash across Oryn's face before he masked it.

"We're here to help," I said, stepping forward. "Kyler needs us, and—"

"Don't speak his name like you *know* him," Candra cut me off. "Prince Kyler is our future king. I refuse to acknowledge you as our princess until he decrees it himself."

"Kyler is my mate," I said, the words coming out stronger than I expected.

"So you claim." Candra's eyes were cold. "Yet here you stand with another male. *Mate* must be a confusing word for you."

Rasher moved between us, his massive frame blocking Candra's path. "That's enough. Kyler is missing, and we need to focus on finding him. Alora is his mate, Candra, whether you believe it or not. The gods have blessed the three of them with a fate none of us could understand. But just so we're clear, Kyler would demand respect for them, and he's already validated his bond."

"The three of them?" She shook her head. "Gods, it's worse than I thought. Our prince entangled with a hopeless girl, but also sharing her with the enemy." She spat on the ground. "Kyler deserves better than this."

"You don't know what you're talking about," I said, my hands curling into fists as I fought to keep my fire contained. "Kyler deserves to be rescued, but instead, you're wasting our time with your jealousy."

"Jealousy? You think I envy the bitch that led him to his death?" Candra's accusation hit like a physical blow.

"That's not what happened," Oryn said, his voice tight with anger.

Candra ignored him, her focus on me now. "You think you can just walk in here, play pretty princess, and we'll all bow down? You can't even control your power. I saw that pathetic display. What good are you to Esmeray?"

"That's enough."

The shift in me was so sudden I wouldn't have been surprised if it had been audible. The once sunny sky was now plunged into darkness. My shadows engulfed the five of us as my patience ran dry. Flames licked at my boots, our only source of light, as I sent inky tendrils to wrap around Candra. Her eyes grew wide as my shadows lifted her just above the ground. All I could see was red, bloodlust pulsing through me, a silent chant for me to show this woman exactly who I was.

"I didn't ask to be your princess," I said, my voice hollow and cold. "I never asked to be anyone's princess. I will find Kyler, who is my *mate*, just as Oryn is. Who are you to deny what the gods have deemed to be? I didn't demand to be Death's Wraith, but I'll gladly show you exactly how I've earned that nickname."

"What is happening with her eyes?" Lucas said quietly from Oryn's other side. The look of panic on Candra's face, paired with my mate's and friend's expressions of horror, snapped me out of the trance that had its claws deep in me. The moment broke as I dropped her back to the ground and the blackness around us dissipated until the sun shone above us once again.

Rasher tried to help Candra up, but she only stumbled, shaking with fury as she created distance between us.

"Told you not to mess with Lor." Lucas snickered, his humor a thin mask over the fear I heard only a moment ago.

The woman finally steeled herself, brushed the dirt off her pants and lifted her chin high.

"You're a loose cannon, and you're only going to get us all killed."

"Enough!" Rasher's voice boomed in the air surrounding us. "Candra, you're out of line. They are welcome here, and that's the end of it."

For a moment, I thought she might defy him again. Then she sighed, shaking her head as if in disbelief that he defended me.

"Fine. I'll respect the queen's wishes." Her eyes met mine, burning with hatred. "But when Esmeray falls because we welcomed vipers into our nest, remember this moment. Remember that you couldn't make the simplest spark, let alone protect our kingdom."

She turned to leave, but paused, looking back over her shoulder. "Our prince is out there somewhere, and I intend to return him. I won't let you ruin our chances."

With that, she stalked away, leaving a heavy silence in her wake.

I stood frozen, her words cutting through me like glass. The worst part was that she'd voiced my own fears—I wasn't enough, that I was failing Kyler with every moment I spent failing. Was she better suited to rescue him?

"Don't listen to her," Lucas whispered as he stood beside me.

"She doesn't know what she's talking about. Besides, I'm pretty sure you made her piss herself."

But the seed of doubt had been planted, taking root alongside my existing fears.

"What did you mean about my eyes?"

Lucas avoided my gaze, suddenly finding the ground fascinating as he fidgeted uncomfortably. "They turned white while you were using your power. It was a little creepy."

Great.

Not only did I have the fate of the world on my shoulders, but now I needed to worry about my eyes and what that meant.

"What if we're not fast enough?" I asked the question that had been haunting me since we'd arrived. "What if Kyler doesn't have that kind of time?"

Rasher's expression was grim. "Then we work with what we have. The witch should arrive soon. Perhaps she'll have the answers we don't."

I nodded, trying to hold onto that hope. But Candra's words had cut deep, feeding the fear that had been growing inside me since Kyler had thrown himself into that portal in my place.

If I couldn't even wield what the gods had given me, how could I possibly save him? And what if Candra was meant to save him instead?

The training dummy's charred remains smoldered, a stark reminder of my failure.

"I think we're done for the day," Rasher said. "How about we find your friend?"

The large man led the way back into the castle, Oryn gently pulling me along. When our eyes met, he graced me with a gentle smile. But his eyes shone with the fear we all felt.

What if we were too late?

CHAPTER 13

We walked back through the corridors of the castle, my feet dragging with each step. The weight of Candra's words hung over me like a storm cloud, threatening to burst at any moment.

"Don't beat yourself up," Lucas said, falling into step beside me. "First day jitters and all that."

I shot him a withering look. "Jitters don't typically result in nearly killing someone." My voice cracked with bitterness.

"To be fair," Oryn interjected from my other side, "she was asking for it."

"That's not helping." My voice came out sharper than intended. "I need control, not excuses."

Rasher turned to look at us from several steps ahead, where he led our small procession. His broad shoulders tensed as his eyes met mine. "Control comes with practice and trust. You've barely scratched the surface of what you can do, but you need to trust yourself to do it."

"And what if I scratch too deep?" The question slipped out before

I could stop it, revealing the fear that had been gnawing at me since the incident in the training yard. "What if I lose myself completely?"

"Then we'll pull you back," Oryn said simply, his fingers finding mine and squeezing gently.

We rounded a corner, the corridor opening into a more ornate section of the castle. Rasher stopped before a door inlaid with delicate silver filigree. His hard knocks echoed down the hallway.

The door opened to reveal my former handmaiden. No longer a servant of the Sunnevean palace, Luella was free to be herself. My friend's eyes brightened when she saw us. "You're finished with training already?"

"Let's just say it was cut short," Lucas replied with a smirk.

Luella's gaze settled on me, her expression shifting to concern.

"It's fine," I said. "I needed a break, anyway."

She stepped out, closing the door behind her. "How about we lose ourselves in a good romance?" She linked her arm with mine and giggled.

"That's why we're here," Rasher said. "We're headed to the library to search for anything that could help us find Kyler." He spoke with a stern finality, clearly not in the mood for frivolity.

Luella nodded as we followed him to our destination. "I'm sure we can sneak away and find something good," she whispered to me.

Lucas came to my other side and leaned in towards us. "Count me in," he whispered, eliciting giggles from both Luella and me.

As we passed another door, it slowly creaked open to reveal Magnus. His solemn face greeted us as he cleared his throat.

"Sorry," his voice was gravelly, "must've overslept."

"Traveling like we were will do that to you," I said. "Do you wanna join us in the library?"

He must have seen my words for what they were, a peace offering. It was like dipping one toe into the waters neither of us knew how to navigate. He nodded and followed us quietly.

Soon, the library doors loomed ahead, massive oak panels carved with scenes from Esmeray's history. Rasher pushed them open, revealing a cavernous space filled with towering shelves that disappeared into the shadows above.

"Gods," I whispered, momentarily forgetting my troubles as I took in the sheer magnitude of knowledge contained within these walls.

"Where do we even start?" Lucas asked, voicing what we were all thinking.

Luella stepped forward confidently. "We need to find the oldest texts."

"Follow me," Rasher said. He led us through a maze of shelves to a secluded corner where the books looked older than I'd ever seen. The shelves groaned under volumes bound in cracked leather, their pages yellowed to amber, alongside ancient scrolls that threatened to disintegrate at the slightest touch. Dust motes danced in the shafts of sunlight streaming through high windows.

"These are the oldest tomes we have," Rasher explained, gesturing towards the worn shelves. "If there were any books about the lost gods in this library, it would be one of these. There are some older maps I want to study, maybe there's something we're missing in locating Kyler."

"It's nice to see someone respect history," Oryn added quietly as he selected a book from the shelf. Clouds of dust drifted around us.

I glanced at him. "Does Sunneva not value the gods?"

My husband let out a derisive snort. "My father believes himself to be a god most days."

"He had all records prior to his rule burned long ago." Magnus chimed in. "He called it a *rebirth*, but now..." His voice trailed off.

"Now, I wonder if he was destroying evidence of his corruption," Oryn finished.

Luella's face reflected how I felt, sad for the stories forever lost and worried that what we needed lay in the ash that would've been left.

"There were still stories about the forgotten gods," Oryn added. "He could burn the paper they were written on, but there was nothing he could do about the stories told around a fire. Children's tales mostly, even the ones about finding one's mate." He sighed. "Nearly forgotten tales about long forgotten gods."

Luella pulled a massive tome from a shelf. She placed it on a nearby table, opening it carefully.

"Whether they abandoned us, or they were deliberately hidden, we'll find them," confidence reinforced every word she spoke. She opened a section at random, devouring the pages with her eyes as she began her search.

Oryn nodded in agreement. He sat beside my friend as he began to look through the book he had selected. Quickly, Rasher, Lucas, and I each grabbed a book off the shelves and brought them to the table. Magnus brought an entire armful to the table, saving us several trips back and forth to the shelves. Silence blanketed around us, only broken by the turning of pages and occasional murmurs as someone found something that seemed promising.

I ran my finger along a passage describing Chaos—the primordial force from which all magic stemmed. According to the text, it wasn't inherently destructive, but rather the raw potential of creation itself, unfiltered and unpredictable. It was this unpredictability that gifted fae their abilities. A gift bestowed upon his worshippers that had grown into something more than he intended.

"Listen to this," I said, reading aloud. "Chaos, so moved by the outcries of those who bowed before him despite their impending doom, blessed the people of this land with what they needed to survive the famine. Seedlings to grow food, water to quench their dire thirst, and fire to keep them from freezing in the night. He gave them ears that could pick up an animal from miles away in order to hunt. These gifts manifested, into the fae and their elemental affinities. The great god brought order through purpose. He wielded his powers with intent, to shape the path Fate called for, rather than destroy life itself."

"Intent," Oryn repeated thoughtfully. "Not control."

"He doesn't sound half bad," Lucas mused.

Oryn, Magnus, and I exchanged a look. If Trinity's actions were in his name, it was hard to believe him to be some benevolent being.

"There's more here about the gods," Luella said, turning her book for us to see. "Five in total, embodying different aspects of existence."

The illustration showed five figures arranged in a semicircle: Life, Death, Chaos, Power, and Fate. At the center was an orb that glowed with threads that connected it to each god.

"Look at this," I murmured, tracing the central point. "Was this what held it all together?"

"Whatever it is, it must be keeping things balanced," Rasher added grimly, pointing to the next passage on the page. "Without it, everything fell into discord."

"At some point," Luella continued as she read the next page, "people began to notice a rift in the gods. Soon, very few could hear their words, their voices dimmed. Some of the last things the other gods mentioned was that Chaos had ruined them all." Her eyes searched the worn pages. "That's the last entry. Everything else looks like regular logs when the monarchies began to take control over territories."

Lucas groaned, stretching his arms above his head. "This is fascinating and all, but my brain is starting to hurt." He stood suddenly. "I need food if I'm going to keep reading about ancient cosmic betrayals."

"I'll help you," Rasher offered, rising as well. "The kitchen is a maze for newcomers."

"You don't need to make any excuses to bask in my company, big guy," Lucas said with a playful wink.

The two departed, leaving Oryn, Luella, Magnus, and me alone among the dusty tomes.

We sat in silence for a while until Oryn leaned forward. "Have you noticed anything... odd between those two?"

I blinked, momentarily pulled from my thoughts about the gods. "Between Lucas and Rasher?"

"Have they not always been this close? I thought they were good friends." Luella said.

"They were total strangers not too long ago," I said, recalling my time with both of them. Their mannerisms, the things they said, turned in my head. "They got closer after we faced the serpent."

"You mean, when you decided to be its lunch?" Oryn quipped.

"I did not decide to be its next meal," my false sense of sternness only caused my mate to smirk. "I thought it had more to do with Lucas' seasickness."

"They acted the same when we met them at the bookshop," Magnus added. "Like the four of us had... interrupted something."

Luella let out a small giggle, quickly covering her mouth with her hand. "Lucas has been pretty flirtatious."

I rolled my eyes. "Lucas has always been a charmer. When we met..." Oryn's eyes darkened, halting my words as my train of thought vanished. "Anyway, that's just his personality."

"I think it may be more than that," Luella mused. "He hasn't flirted with me once since we met. And I think I'm quite the catch."

I stared at her for a moment before understanding dawned. "Wait, you think they're—"

"Shhh," Oryn hissed suddenly. "The lovebirds are coming back."

The nickname was enough to send Luella into a fit of giggles. She slapped her hand over her mouth to smother the noise, desperately trying to compose herself before our friends joined us once again.

We fell silent as Lucas and Rasher returned, arms laden with bread, cheese, and fruit. They set their bounty on the table, careful to avoid the ancient texts.

"The cook wasn't happy about us raiding her pantry," Lucas said, breaking off a piece of bread. "But Rasher here has quite the silver tongue."

Rasher's dark ears appeared to redden slightly. "I simply explained our situation."

I caught Luella's eye, and we both quickly looked away before we could burst into laughter.

"Did you find anything useful while we were gone?" Rasher asked, clearly trying to change the subject.

I nodded, pulling my book closer. "Maybe. There's something here about the gods only speaking to those who appeared at their altars."

"Like that temple," Rasher said.

"Exactly," I answered. "Death spoke to us because we came to his altar. Perhaps if we found Chaos' altar, we could speak to him."

"You think he'd grant us an audience?" Magnus asked.

I shrugged. "Clearly, Trinity needs me for some part of her plan. Her plan revolves around Chaos. Why wouldn't he appear?"

"It sounds like a trap," Oryn said.

"That's all well and good," Lucas said around a mouthful of cheese, "but how does this help us find Kyler?"

The question sobered us all. I turned back to the book, scanning the pages for anything that might point us toward my missing mate.

"The old gods lived in their own realm," Oryn noted, pointing to a passage in his book. "A place between worlds where they could exist without overwhelming mortal beings."

"Like the portal Trinity opened," I said, the memory of the swirling darkness flashing in my mind. "The void that took Kyler."

Rasher nodded slowly. "If Trinity could access another realm..."

"Then Kyler might be in one of them," I finished, the pieces starting to fall into place. "And if she can harness the power..."

"You might be able to, too," Luella whispered, her eyes wide. "If Chaos' gifts affected generation after generation," she furiously flipped through the pages in another book she had discarded moments ago. "And you mentioned Death spoke to you. You're touched by Death, so your direct connection and your powers could create a bridge." She slammed the book down, pointing to an illustration of a god seated upon a throne, a similar swirling essence behind them.

Hope bloomed in my chest, fragile but persistent. We were still missing crucial pieces of the puzzle, but for the first time since arriving in Esmeray, I felt like we were moving in the right direction.

I reached for Oryn's hand under the table, finding comfort in his steady presence as we continued our search for answers among the forgotten histories of gods long lost to time.

Our ancestors knew what it meant to be touched by a god, and I needed to understand how to use my power to bring a god to his knees.

CHAPTER 14

Hours passed as we combed through the ancient texts, my eyes burning from strain. The stack of books I'd already searched grew taller, each one yielding only fragments of information. Frustration clawed at me, but I pushed it aside. Kyler was out there somewhere, and I wouldn't rest until I found him.

"Listen to this," Luella said, her finger tracing a line of text. "When Death walks among the living, Chaos trembles."

"What does that even mean?" I sighed, rubbing my temples.

"Maybe it means you scare Trinity," Lucas offered, leaning back in his chair.

"She didn't seem scared to me."

The library door burst open with a bang, startling us all. A young man stood in the doorway, chest heaving as though he'd run the entire length of the castle.

"She's here," he gasped, eyes wide with a mixture of fear and awe. "The witch has arrived!"

My heart stuttered. Elisanna had heeded our call for help, that was one less thing to worry about.

"The Queen demands your presence in the main hall immediately," the boy said, already backing toward the door. "All of you."

We exchanged glances, a silent conversation passing between us. This was what we'd been waiting for—our chance to find Kyler.

"Well," Magnus said, closing his book with a thud. "Let's not keep the witch waiting."

We hurried through the winding corridors, Rasher leading the way. My mind raced with questions and worry. I knew what to expect from the old hag, but how would everyone else fare? Lucas couldn't control his mouth any more than he could control the weather, so what would the madwoman do if he offended her with one of his jokes?

Could Elisanna hold the key to finding Kyler, even if he was held beyond our realm? Could I trust her with his fate?

A thought dawned on me from the last time we had met.

"Have you ever met her?" I asked Rasher as we descended a grand staircase.

He shook his head. "Few have. She rarely leaves her mountain. But I heard enough stories to make me wary of ever finding myself on her bad side."

"Is that why you stayed behind?"

"The horses needed tending," Rasher said. "But yes, even without needing to keep the camp ready for your return, I wouldn't have gone with you. It was meant for you and Kyler to walk alone. It was not my path."

"I've heard stories since we've been here," Lucas whispered, his usual bravado subdued. "They say she can see your death, that it'll drive you mad with fear until that day comes to pass."

"It wouldn't surprise me," I admitted.

The main hall loomed ahead, its massive doors thrown open. Guards stood at attention, their faces unusually pale. As we approached, I caught snippets of whispered conversations.

"...spoke to no one, maybe she saw a ghost before her..."

"...knew my name without being told..."

"...laughed at nothing and then smacked Gregory for no good reason. The poor lad was just sitting there, minding his own business..."

My steps faltered, the heaviness of her presence crept back into me. It was the feeling of wrongness and confusion as she mumbled about everything and nothing all at once. Oryn's hand pressed against the small of my back, steadying me.

Together, he murmured through our bond.

Together, I repeated.

We entered the hall to find an unusual scene. The long dining table had been set for a feast. The candles flickered in ornate holders. Queen Wynaria sat to the right, her posture rigid, ruby hair gleaming in the light. Tension tightened her face.

And beside her, at the head of the table, sat Elisanna. Her silvery hair was braided down her back, adorned with small wildflowers. Her aged face still hinted with a touch of youthfulness, but her eyes... those milky orbs stared straight into my soul as a crooked grin crept across her face.

"Ah, Death's pretty pet! Come, come," she called, her voice melodic and slightly manic. She waved her hand to the empty seat across from Wynaria. "And you've brought the golden one. How delightful!"

I froze, unsure how to respond. Her tone was light but Wynaria's strained face set my nerves on edge.

"Don't just stand there gawking," Queen Wynaria commanded, though her voice held a tremor. "Sit. Eat. The witch has much to say."

Elisanna giggled, reaching for her wine glass without looking. "Oh yes, much to say indeed. The little whispers have kept me up at night, you see. Your name has interrupted my sleep night after night since you left my humble home, Alora Satori. Or is it Artan? Or Evander? How does one choose a name when they cannot choose one mate?"

The way she said my name sent chills down my spine, and the way she prattled off both of my mate's surnames...

"Satori," Oryn answered for me. "No sense in soiling such a beautiful woman with a vile man's name."

He led us to our seats, the closest to Elisanna. As we took our seats around the table, I couldn't shake the feeling that our lives were about to change irrevocably.

"Aye," she said. "Smart man for one so burned by the sun. Maybe not all is lost in the golden flames."

"I hope not." Oryn kept his composure, the unease I could feel through the bond hidden behind his stoic face. Meanwhile, Lucas and Luella watched our interaction with wide eyes, and Rasher was doing everything but looking at the witch.

As uncomfortable as the other dinners in Sunneva were, they were pleasant compared to this one. *This* was a dinner from hell.

Elisanna picked around her food before dropping her fork down onto the porcelain plate.

"Now," the witch said, tilting her head as though listening to something none of us could hear, "shall we discuss how to retrieve your stolen star?"

"We don't need a star," Wynaria hissed as she rolled her eyes. "We need to find my son."

"Yes, yes, the prince with two lives, two names. Lost to you, lost to himself. Beyond the seas, below the lands. Not here, nor there." Elisanna's voice became lower with each word. A prickle stirred at the back of my neck. "Blood betrayals will keep you apart. Drowning under the weight you carry. Flame to heart. Ice and stone. Will you go where one cannot go?"

"Go where?" I asked, unable to hold my tongue as I burned each word into my memory.

That misty gaze locked onto me. "You will doom us all if you cannot see. The bonds of blood are a noose around your neck, heart of ice that cannot trust. Don't believe what you see, follow that which you're blind to. Follow the path. Always changing, a river of tears. Bonds will break to forge the blade. How far can you bend? Will you break?" Elisanna met the eyes of everyone seated at the table as she threw her head back with an unbidden cackle.

"I don't understand." The words had barely left my mouth before her head snapped back to me.

"Don't be so coy. You've seen what you need, the well of power. Too afraid to wield that which has been bestowed upon you. I see everything, yet you see nothing. Why, I see nothing but death for you, my dear. If you can't see what you already know, your path will be shrouded with death. Could be the death of your friends, your mates, or the one that belongs to you. One foot in the grave, they say."

"What do I already know? Can you see where they're keeping Kyler? Is he alive?" The last question was a desperate plea from my lips. I knew to expect nonsense from the old woman, but I had hoped she'd tell us *something,* anything.

Knobby fingers wrapped around her glass and lifted the wine as a toast.

"A sacrifice to appease the gods, may we all live to tell the tale. Death's pretty dead pet. Death's pretty dead pet."

CHAPTER 15

E lisanna's milky eyes suddenly focused on something beyond the wall.

The chill that had been creeping up my spine now enveloped my entire body. The witch's words hung in the air, poisoning the atmosphere. No one dared to speak, not even Wynaria, whose knuckles had turned white around her goblet.

"His soul calls to yours," Elisanna suddenly announced, pushing back from the table with surprising strength. "May you journey to faraway places, where metal burns flesh and souls are currency. That is the only plane where a god finds mortality, harbinger of flame."

"Where?" I demanded, rising to my feet. "Please, where is he?"

But Elisanna was already gliding toward the door, her bare feet making no sound on the stone floor. "The doorway is closing. Fate waits for no one, not even its witch." She paused at the threshold, her head tilting as if listening to distant music. "Be wary of the bonds, Death's Wraith. Be swift, for your path will end in blood and fire. You and yours will be consumed by flame."

And with that, she was gone, leaving nothing but the echo of her cryptic warning and the scent of something wild.

"Useless!" Wynaria slammed her fist on the table, sending goblets wobbling. "Absolutely useless! Why did I even bother summoning that madwoman?" Her voice cracked on the last word, betraying the desperation beneath her rage.

"Your Majesty," Rasher began carefully. "Maybe there's something in her riddles—"

"Fuck her riddles," Wynaria's eyes flashed dangerously. "My son is out there somewhere, and all she gives us are nonsensical ramblings!"

I sank back into my chair, the weight of Elisanna's words pressing down on me. *Death's pretty dead pet.* The idea of death never scared me, not until I found Oryn and Kyler. Now, I had people to stick around for. The lack of a straight answer made my blood boil, but I would spend all night trying to untangle her words and make them make sense.

"Where metal burns flesh," Oryn murmured beside me, his mind clearly working through the puzzle.

Lucas pushed his plate away, untouched. "I've lost my appetite after that show. What the fuck was that?"

A sentiment shared by all of us. The food that had looked so appetizing moments ago now seemed as appealing as ash.

"That," I said, "was Fate toying with us."

"We should reconvene in the morning," Wynaria finally said, her voice hollow. "Perhaps with clear heads, we can make sense of it." She rose, her shoulders slumped with the burden of a mother missing her son. "You're all dismissed."

As we filed out of the dining hall, my mind raced with possibilities. Was there an entire realm of metal that could burn the skin off a body? Logically, anything hot enough could do that, but how would one survive long enough to search for another? The pieces refused to fit together in any meaningful way.

"I'm going to Kyler's chambers," Oryn whispered to me. "How about I draw you a bath?"

I nodded, ready to follow him, when a hand touched my elbow. I turned to find Magnus, his expression uncharacteristically vulnerable.

"Alora," he said. "Might I have a moment of your time?"

Something in his tone made me pause. I glanced at Oryn, who nodded slightly.

"Go," he said. "I'll be waiting."

I turned back to Magnus. "Of course."

He led me through a series of corridors, neither of us speaking. The silence between us felt different from our usual comfortable quiet—it was thick with words unspoken and secrets newly unearthed.

We emerged into a garden bathed in moonlight. The air was cool and fragrant with night-blooming flowers. Their sweet scent drifted on the light breeze that ruffled the trees. Magnus walked to a stone bench beneath a flowering tree and gestured for me to join him.

"I've been meaning to speak with you," he began, his hands clasped tightly in his lap. "About many things."

"Is this about how I deceived you when we met?" I asked, my mind still preoccupied with the witch's warnings.

Magnus shook his head. "No, though I wish you *had* told me instead of prowling around the palace alone at night."

"And then what? You were loyal to Sunneva, so I assumed you would've arrested me."

"Possibly," he mused, "or maybe I would have seen what the kingdom needed in you." He sighed as he looked ahead. "No, this is about us."

Something in his tone made my heart skip a beat. I turned to face him fully, suddenly reminded of the moments we had spent avoiding this very conversation since leaving the southern kingdom.

"I never knew I had sired a child, Alora," he began. "I met your mother one summer, entirely captured by her spell. I had loved her, and I thought she felt the same. That was until I woke up one morning to her absence. I didn't think—"

"You didn't think she'd run off to have your child and leave her with her grandmother while you lived your life none the wiser," I finished.

He winced as he finally met my gaze. "I would have married her if I had known. If she didn't want me, I would have at least done what I could to bring you home. Raising you would have been the honor of my life, and I'm sincerely sorry that you grew up without a father to protect you. I hope..." he swallowed and I watched the little ball in his throat bob. "I'd like to make things right, to be what I should have been all along."

My throat tightened as I stared at Magnus—my father—his weathered face vulnerable in the moonlight. A face I'd studied these past days, searching for pieces of myself. The sharp jawline, and the way his brow furrowed when concentrating. Even the way he spoke, all little fragments of identity I'd never known were mine to claim.

"I don't blame you," I said finally. "How could you have known? No one but my mother was privy to the information."

Magnus's shoulders relaxed slightly, though the tension never fully left his face. "Still, I should have—"

"What? Tracked down a woman who clearly didn't want to be found? Somehow sensed you had a daughter out there?" I shook my head. "We can't rewrite the past. Trust me, I've tried."

A breeze rustled through the garden, carrying the sweet scent of night flowers. In the distance, an owl called out, its mournful cry echoing my own conflicted heart.

"Tell me about your childhood." His usually curt tone had been replaced with gentleness, and it betrayed him, showcasing how lost he felt in this situation.

"My mother abandoned me just as she had you." My eyes shuttered closed for a moment, thinking about how easily Trinity had thrown us both away: a man she pretended to love and the child that love resulted in. "My grandmother raised me in a quiet village. Not much happened there, but we were happy." My childhood flashed before my eyes, Maël and I running through the dirt paths, helping my grandmother in the garden, picking up a bow for the first time. A tear threatened to escape my watering eyes.

Those were the days, Maël's voice echoed in my mind. *Though nothing will ever beat watching you pummel Thomas until you broke his nose.*

I'd give anything to go back to that time, I replied.

So would I.

"What made you become an assassin? Kids from good homes don't usually take such a path." Magnus asked.

He made no mention of the tears that began to stream freely down my face as memories of that night flooded me. The screams of everyone I knew and loved echoed around me like a blood-drenched symphony. The sound of steel rang in the air. I tasted ash and smoke filled my lungs as I desperately searched for the one person I needed most in this world. Bright flames engulfed everything, leaving me empty and alone.

I steeled myself, fighting to keep my words from shaking. "Everyone I loved was taken from me, so I vowed to take everything from the men responsible."

He said nothing for a while, either contemplating how to handle a murderous daughter or uncomfortable with such an admittance. I couldn't tell as I kept from meeting his eyes as silent tears continued down my face.

"But I knew love," I added. "I had friends, was trained by one of the best men I knew, and I was to be married to my best friend before he too was taken from me. Before everything became dark, I had a full life being a part of a community and losing myself in books."

"I'm very sorry, Alora," Magnus said.

I plucked a fallen petal from the bench between us, rolling it between my fingers. "What was she like? My mother?"

Magnus's eyes grew distant. "She was like wildfire—beautiful, untamed. I was young and captivated." He smiled sadly. "You have the same fire, though you wield it differently."

The irony wasn't lost on me. The thing I feared most.

"How?" I asked.

Magnus's brows drew closer, as if he was considering his next words carefully. "She drew people in, not caring if they got burned being too close." He turned to face me. "You burn brightly from a distance, like you know what would happen if someone got too close."

I couldn't help the dark chuckle that escaped. "Nothing good will ever come from being with me. If you value your life, you should leave and go live a quiet life. The path Fate has given me will end in blood and fire. You heard the witch."

He gave a slight nod. "I heard her, but I've fought many battles, and I would not dare be anywhere else but by your side in this one. And I know I'm not the only one who feels that way."

No, he wasn't. Every day I wished the ones I grew to care about would leave, to save themselves from entangling their fates with mine.

You were never meant to be alone, Lor. Maël said.

Brushing off the emotions both men stirred in me, I flicked the petal to the ground. "I don't know what to call you." I changed the subject. "Magnus seems wrong now, but 'father' feels..."

"Too soon," he finished for me. "I understand. I haven't earned that title yet."

The honesty in his voice caught me off guard. I'd spent so long building walls around myself that I'd since given up any hope of having a traditional family.

"When this is over—when we find Kyler and deal with Trinity—perhaps we could..." I trailed off, unsure how to finish.

"Spend time figuring it out?" Magnus offered. "I'd like that. You have grandparents in Bridgedale that would be delighted to meet you one day." The older man flashed a smile. "I haven't met a person my mother wouldn't embrace warmly upon their first meeting, so be prepared for that."

Waves of warmth and regret crashed against each other as I considered what it could mean to accept more family into my life. A comfortable silence settled between us. For the first time since discovering our connection, I didn't feel the need to fill it with words or escape it altogether.

"The witch's riddles," Magnus said eventually. "What do you make of them?"

I sighed. "Something about metal burning flesh. A place where gods find mortality." I shook my head. "It sounds like nowhere I've ever heard of, and I wouldn't know where to start with trying to reach them."

"The only metal I know to burn flesh is iron," Magnus frowned, his eyes suddenly distant. "But it only burns fae. Humans can wield it without injury."

Iron... a thought, a memory veiled in shadow came to mind, but I couldn't quite see it.

"Maybe we can find evidence of a realm of iron," Magnus continued, rising from the bench. "Tomorrow. For tonight, you should rest."

As we walked back toward the castle, I felt something shift between us—not a complete healing of what had been broken, but the first tentative bridge across the divide.

"Magnus," I said as we reached the corridor that would lead to Kyler's chambers where Oryn waited. "Thank you for everything."

He bowed his head slightly, emotion flickering across his face. "The honor is mine, Alora."

CHAPTER 16

When I turned to open the door, I paused. Inside was Oryn, waiting for me, my sanctuary of comfort and warmth. But also inside was a reminder of who wasn't there.

I pushed the door open quietly. The gentle amber glow of a solitary lantern consumed the room. Oryn sat propped against the headboard of Kyler's massive bed, a book open in his lap. His eyes lifted to meet mine the moment I entered.

"There you are," he said, closing the book. "I was beginning to wonder if you'd gotten lost again."

"Very funny." I closed the door behind me, leaning against it. "The castle's layout is unnecessarily complicated."

Oryn's lips quirked up. "So it's the castle's fault, not your terrible sense of direction?"

"Exactly." I pushed away from the door and moved towards him, peeling away my outer layers with each step toward the bed.

"Would you like me to draw you a bath, Love?"

"Not right now, I just want to lie next to you."

The room smelled faintly of Kyler—that crisp winter scent that always clung to him. It made my heart ache. His absence was a wound carved between Oryn and me that no amount of time could fill. A dull pain that never left.

"How was your talk with Magnus?" Oryn asked, lifting the covers so I could slip in beside him.

I nestled into the pillows, turning to face him. "Surprisingly... not terrible."

"High praise indeed." His fingers found mine beneath the covers.

"We talked about my mother," I said, shifting to my back to stare at the canopy above us. "And about family. He has parents—my grandparents—in Bridgedale."

"How does that make you feel? Knowing you have family out there?"

I considered the question. "Strange, as though I've wandered into a story that was never meant to be mine." I turned to look at him. "For so long it was just me. My grandmother was the only family I ever knew. The idea of having more blood relatives out there feels... like a dream I never dared to have."

Oryn's thumb traced circles on my palm. "Family isn't always blood."

"No," I agreed, thinking of Lucas, Luella, even Rasher. "But it's odd to think there are people who share my blood, who might have my eyes or my laugh."

"Are you going to meet them? After all this is over?"

"Maybe." I sighed. "If we survive all of this."

Oryn pulled me closer, his warmth wrapping around me like a shield against the darkness. "We will. Then you can decide what kind of relationship you want with your father and his family."

I nodded against his chest, letting the steady rise and fall of his breathing lull me. "I miss him," I whispered.

"I know." Oryn pressed a kiss to the top of my head. "So do I."

MORNING CAME TOO QUICKLY. The weight of Oryn's arm around my waist, the warmth of his breath against my neck—these comforts made the prospect of leaving bed nearly impossible.

"Rise and shine, lovebirds." Lucas's voice filtered through the wooden door. "Rasher says if you're late again, he's adding an extra hour to training."

I groaned, burying my face in the pillow. "Tell him I'm sick."

"Heard that," Lucas called back. "And he says nice try."

Oryn chuckled against my shoulder. "We should go before he comes in and drags us out."

"Fine." I threw back the covers with more force than necessary. "But I'm not going to be happy about it."

"You're never happy in the morning." Oryn stretched, muscles rippling beneath his skin. "That's half the problem."

I shot him a look as I pulled on my leathers. "The only problem I need to be focused on is trying to control something that doesn't want to be controlled."

"Maybe that's the issue." He stood, grabbing his own clothes.

I paused, my dark boot half-laced. "What do you mean?"

"Just a thought." He shrugged. "We can talk about it at training."

The training grounds were already busy when we arrived. Candra was there, throwing her twin axes at a target with deadly precision. Her eyes tracked us as we entered, narrowing with obvious disdain.

"Look who finally decided to grace us with their presence," she called out, loud enough for everyone to hear. "The traitor princess and her pet."

Oryn tensed beside me, but I placed a hand on his arm. "Ignore her."

Rasher strode toward us, arms crossed over his broad chest. "You're late."

"By three minutes," I countered.

"Late is late." He gestured to the open area away from the others. "You're working on your fire today. We need to see progress."

I swallowed, looking around at the crowded training grounds. "Here? With everyone watching?"

"Yes, here." Rasher's tone left no room for argument. "If you can't handle an audience, how will you handle a battlefield?"

Across the yard, I spotted Magnus and Lucas beginning to spar, their swords flashing in the morning light. At least they were too busy to watch my inevitable failure.

Oryn guided me to the designated area, his hand warm at the small of my back. "We'll take it slow," he murmured.

I nodded, trying to ignore the knot of anxiety tightening in my chest. The memory of our last training session—of the fire raging beyond my control, of Oryn's panicked face—was still too fresh.

"Focus on your breathing first," Oryn instructed, standing opposite me. "Center yourself."

I closed my eyes, drawing deep breaths. The sounds of the training yard faded—metal against metal, grunts of exertion, Candra's derisive laughter—until all I could hear was my own heartbeat and Oryn's steady breathing.

"Now, call to it. From deep within you, find it and pull it out until it's a small flame."

I extended my palm, picturing a tiny flicker of fire within me. I pictured my power like a well, and I pulled slowly at the rope that held the bucket. The familiar heat built beneath my skin, traveling up my arm and pooling in my hand. A small flame danced to life, no bigger than a candle's.

"Good," Oryn said softly. "Now, try to shape it. Make it taller."

I concentrated, willing the flame to stretch upward. It responded, growing into a slender column about a foot high.

"Perfect, Love. Now wider."

The flame spread outward, forming a disk that hovered above my palm. Sweat beaded on my forehead from the effort of maintaining its shape.

"You're doing well," Oryn encouraged. "Now, try moving it. Send it to my hand."

It was one thing to make it taller and wider. But moving it seemed like an impossible task. I barely controlled it within my grasp, but what would happen when I tried to move it?

"You can do this," Oryn said, holding out his hand. "I trust you."

Those words—*I trust you*—sent a sharp pang through my chest. After everything, after my treatment of him, after the chasm that had opened between us... he still trusted me, even when he knew I was likely to fail.

Suddenly, I wasn't sure I deserved that trust. I was never the mate he deserved. I doubted our bond and had turned my back on him for a time. The old scrolls I'd studied showed high regard for connections like ours, as if no one would have dared to do what I had done, to deny it. Your mate was the other piece of your soul. They completed you as much as you did them, a profound love that one could not survive losing.

And for a time, I had lost it.

The flame wobbled, expanding erratically. I tried to rein it in, but my concentration was fracturing.

"Alora," Oryn's voice sharpened. "Focus."

"I'm trying," I gritted out, panic rising as the fire grew. It was happening again—the loss of control, the surge of power that I couldn't contain.

"You're fighting it too hard," Oryn said, stepping closer despite the danger. "Don't try to force it."

"It's taking over!" The flame was now a roaring ball of fire, pulsing with my heartbeat.

"And there she goes again," Candra's voice cut through my concentration. "Watch your eyebrows, lest they get singed."

The fire flared higher, feeding on my anger.

"Back away," I warned Oryn, my voice tight. "I can't—I can't hold it."

But instead of retreating, he stepped even closer, his hands coming up to frame my face. "Look at me, Alora. Not at the fire, not at Candra. Just me."

I met his eyes, those deep blue pools that had once looked at me with such coldness, now filled with nothing but warmth and confidence.

"Maybe we're going about this all wrong," he said quietly. "We're trying to contain it, but maybe it's meant to flow. Fire isn't static— it's not a thing. It moves, it's life. Let's stop trying to cage it, and start *directing* its path instead. Its fate is in *your* hands."

"I don't understand."

"Think of a river. You can't stop the water, but you can build banks to guide where it flows." His thumbs stroked my cheeks. "Don't fight against the current. Work with it."

I took a shaky breath, trying to see the fire as he described—not as an enemy to be subdued, but as an ally to be guided. The flame still burned between us, dangerous and volatile.

"Close your eyes," Oryn instructed. "Feel the fire. Not with your hand, but with your mind. Feel its edges, its heart, its hunger."

I did as he said, reaching out with senses I didn't know I possessed. And there it was—the fire had a pulse, a rhythm all its own. It wasn't fighting me. It was waiting for direction.

"Now, imagine a path from your hand to mine. Not confined, but a channel."

I visualized it—a bridge of energy connecting us. And with a gentle mental nudge, I sent the fire along that path.

The heat left my palm, and I heard Oryn's sharp intake of breath. My eyes flew open to see the flame hovering above his outstretched hand, smaller but still burning brightly.

"You did it," he whispered, awe in his voice.

I stared in disbelief. "I did it."

"How touching," Candra drawled from behind us. She was

leaning on one of her axes, watching with undisguised contempt. "She managed to pass a tiny flame without burning down the training yard. Shall we throw a feast?"

Rasher, who had been observing silently, turned to her with a scowl. "Enough, Candra. Back to your own training."

"Why bother?" She gestured toward us. "If this is our great hope, we might as well surrender now."

"I said *enough*." Rasher's voice carried a warning that even Candra couldn't ignore.

She shrugged, spinning her axe. "Fine. But when we're all dead because you put your faith in the wrong people, don't say I didn't warn you."

As she stalked away, Oryn turned back to me, the flame still dancing above his palm. "Ignore her. This is progress, Alora. Real progress."

I nodded, still stunned by what I'd accomplished. "It feels... different. My shadows hardly need a thought, and they act how I command. With fire, it was more like working with it, not bossing it around."

"Exactly." He smiled, a genuine, proud smile that made my heart flutter. "That's exactly it. Now, let's try something more complex. Can you split the flame? Make it into two separate fires?"

I bit my lip, considering. "I can try."

And so we continued, with Oryn guiding me through exercises that felt more like dancing than fighting. The fire responded to my direction with increasing ease, splitting and merging, growing and shrinking at my command.

Across the yard, Magnus and Lucas had paused their sparring to watch, their expressions a mixture of amazement and pride. Even Rasher couldn't hide the fact that he had long since given up on training and watched the dance of fire and flame Oryn walked me through.

Only Candra remained determinedly unimpressed, her axes

thudding into targets with vicious force, each impact seeming to say: not enough, never enough.

A glimmer of hope had entered my soul. Not only did my fire feel more familiar, but I could wield it—no longer a burden to bear, but a weapon to master.

And with Oryn beside me, his faith unwavering despite everything that had come between us, I believed maybe we stood a chance after all.

CHAPTER 17

I spent all day becoming one with the flame under Oryn's guidance. The sun gradually drifted until it sank beyond the horizon. We took a rare break for food and water, but all I could focus on was pushing my skills further and further. Stars were beginning to sparkle when Rasher finally forced us from the grounds.

"You're not doing yourself any favors by overdoing it," he said and the stern look he gave was enough to halt me in my tracks. Magnus and Lucas had picked up discarded weapons from their sparring, and soon the training field was properly set up for the next day.

Everyone was exhausted, at least that's what Lucas claimed as he dragged Rasher away with him, claiming he needed his help with something. Magnus and Luella joined us for a quiet supper before we all retired for the night, though Wynaria never joined us.

I let out a bone-deep sigh as I collapsed onto Kyler's bed, every muscle in my body protesting the day's exertions. Oryn closed the door behind us, his movements more fluid than mine despite having trained just as hard. He stopped at the wardrobe to pull a nightdress out for me and brought it to the bed.

"I might never move again," I groaned, face half-buried in Kyler's pillow. His scent had faded, but if I breathed deeply enough, I could still catch traces of fresh rain.

Oryn chuckled, the sound warm and rich in the quiet room. "You pushed yourself too hard today."

"Says the man who insisted I try to create a tornado of fire."

I let him lift the tunic from my body and pull my trousers from my legs. He slipped the light dress onto my frame before tossing the worn clothes to the side. I laid back down, more comfortable without the constraints of real clothes. Though I'm sure my comfort wasn't his only motivator for helping me change, the new garment left little to the imagination and was surely a sight for him.

"That was impressive, by the way." The mattress dipped as he sat beside me, his hand finding my lower back and pressing gently into the sore muscles there. "I think you about gave Magnus a heart attack when you chased him and Lucas with it."

I rolled over to face him, a laugh bubbling in my throat. "Magnus wasn't the target. Unfortunately, he was too close to Lucas."

His bright eyes softened as they met mine. "I'm sure he'll find it in his heart to forgive you."

"Maybe." I mused. I stared up at the canopy above us, doubt creeping in despite my exhaustion. "What if I can't figure out how to channel this into a portal? What if—"

"Stop." Oryn's finger pressed against my lips. "No more what-ifs tonight. You need rest."

I caught his hand, holding it against my cheek. "How are you so certain about everything all the time?"

Something vulnerable flashed across his face before he masked it. "I'm not. I just don't see the point in dwelling on uncertainties when there's work to be done. A soldier shouldn't go into battle thinking about the loss that has yet to come. And I believe there is no sense in assuming we'll fail when we have every opportunity to succeed."

"The ever-practical warrior," I teased, but there was truth in it.

"Someone has to be." He stretched out beside me, propping himself up on one elbow. "Usually it's Kyler, but…"

"But he's not here." I finished.

"Yeah," he sighed. Silence grew between us. He leaned down, pressing his forehead to mine. "We're going to find him, Alora. We're going to bring Kyler home, and he can take over being the brooding realist of our group, and I can go back to being my charming self."

His joke was subtle enough to draw out a smile from me. The difference between the two men often seemed stark, but they were near twins at their core.

"Tell me something about him," I said suddenly, "and you. Something I don't know."

Oryn pulled back slightly, surprise flickering across his features. "What?"

"Tell me something I don't know because I want to know everything about you both."

He was quiet for a moment, thoughtful. "He's terrified of spiders."

I blinked. "What?"

"The fearless Kyler freezes like a startled deer at the sight of even the tiniest spider." A genuine smile spread across Oryn's face. "I once watched him leap onto a table during a meeting because one scurried across the floor."

Laughter erupted from my chest, unexpected and unburdened. "You're lying."

"I swear on my sword." He placed a hand over his heart, eyes dancing with mischief. "Ask him yourself when we find him. Or better yet, get Lucas to bring a little friend."

"Why don't you bring the creature?" I questioned.

His warm chuckle filled the room. "Because I value my life, and he would expect it from me. Something tells me Lucas wouldn't have a problem terrorizing the man."

We shared another laugh at the thought of my friend risking his life to scare Kyler. He wasn't wrong, this was the kind of thing Lucas lived for. Other than fucking anything with a pulse.

"What about you?" I asked him.

"Me?" Oryn shifted. "I'm not afraid of anything."

"Everyone is afraid of something," I teased.

His face sobered as he considered his own fear. I had thought he would have admitted to a fear as tame as spiders, but suddenly the air felt heavier.

"I've always feared that I would one day become the monster my father wishes I would be," his voice was quiet with the admittance. "Until I met you. Then my biggest fear became the thought of you being taken from me."

Struggling to swallow my guilt, I placed a gentle hand on his arm. "You could never be a monster, I know that now. And, I'm so sorry that your fear about me came true."

"It's not your fault, Love." Oryn cupped my hand with his own, stroking his thumb against mine. "But enough about me. Did you know Kyler sings when he thinks no one can hear him? Has a decent voice, actually."

I smiled at the thought. "I've never heard him sing."

"You will." His fingers combed through my hair, gentle and soothing. "And," he chuckled, "he used to make the new recruits steal sweets for him from the kitchen before feasts. Said, 'he needed to see their worth.' We had to let some go after the cook nearly beat them to death."

Each small revelation was a gift, filling in the gaps of the men I loved. "Tell me more."

Oryn continued, his voice growing softer as he shared memories —Kyler teaching himself to skip stones across a lake, his terrible habit of leaving books open and face-down, and the way Kyler always paused to help anyone who asked, regardless of their status. My favorite was a story where a young girl had showered my mates in floral crowns that had Kyler sneezing for a week.

My eyelids grew heavier with each story, Oryn's steady heartbeat beneath my ear a comforting rhythm.

"He's going to be so proud of you," Oryn murmured, his lips brushing my temple. "When he sees how far you've come with your fire."

"If I don't burn down the castle first," I mumbled drowsily.

His chest rumbled with quiet laughter. "There is that risk."

I wanted to ask more, to hear more stories, but exhaustion pulled at me insistently. "Thank you," I whispered.

"For what?"

"For loving him. For loving me. For not giving up on either of us."

His arms tightened around me. "Never."

Sleep came over me like a gentle tide, pulling me under before I could say anything more.

My dream began as it often did—with darkness and silence. Then, slowly, shapes formed around me. I was in a forest clearing, moonlight filtering through the canopy above. The air was cool against my skin, and somewhere in the distance, water rushed over rocks.

I was alone, but the hairs at the back of my neck rose. I was being watched.

"Hello?" I called, turning in a slow circle.

In this dreamscape, I had no weapons and I was clothed only in an airy lilac nightdress that was sheerer than I would have preferred. It was what Oryn had dressed me in before we fell asleep. As the breeze blew against me, my nipples grew taut and noticeable through the thin fabric. The trees rustled, and from the shadows stepped Kyler.

My breath caught.

He looked exactly as I remembered—tall and imposing, dark hair falling across his forehead, and those penetrating eyes fixed on me.

"Kyler," I whispered, taking a step toward him.

"Princess," he held out his hand. I reached for it, our fingers almost touching—

"What about me, Love?" Oryn's voice came from behind me.

I turned to find him standing at the edge of the clearing, moonlight illuminating his features.

I looked between them—Kyler silent and watchful, and Oryn, approaching with feral intent in his eyes. My heart hammered in my chest as warmth flooded me.

"What is this?" I asked, though some part of me already knew.

"Whatever you want it to be, Princess," Kyler said. His low voice sent shivers cascading down my spine.

They were both close now, one on either side of me. I could feel the heat radiating from their bodies, smell their distinct scents mingling in the night air.

"I wish this were real," My voice came out wistful. I relished in the reprieve this dream was giving me. I turned. to Kyler. "We miss you so much, it's hell without you."

Kyler's hand cupped my cheek and I leaned into the familiar comfort. "I'm here now."

Oryn's hand slid to my waist, pulling me back against his chest. His lips found the sensitive spot just below my ear. "Would be a shame to waste such a perfect moment. Taking our mate hasn't been nearly as enjoyable without seeing her caught between us."

I turned in Oryn's arms to face him, my lips finding his in a hungry kiss. His hands tangled in my hair, holding me close as if afraid I might disappear. When we broke apart, I felt Kyler step closer, his chest pressing against my back.

"My turn," he murmured, gently turning my face toward him.

His kiss was different from Oryn's—more controlled, but with an underlying intensity that made my knees weak. I reached out, threading my fingers through his dark hair, holding onto him to prevent losing him once more. Two desperate lovers separated for too long. Even if this was a dream, this moment would keep me going until the day it would be real once again.

Oryn's hand wandered down my sides, finding the hem of my nightdress and slowly drawing it upward. Kyler's hands joined his, their fingers occasionally brushing against each other as they worked together to undress me.

The night air kissed my bare skin as the fabric was lifted over my head. I should have felt exposed, vulnerable, but instead I felt powerful—desired by these two men who meant everything to me.

"Beautiful," Kyler breathed, his eyes traveling over me.

Oryn hummed in agreement, his hands continuing their exploration of my body. "Perfect."

They undressed themselves next, their movements unhurried yet purposeful. I watched, mesmerized by the play of moonlight on their skin.

We sank down onto a bed of soft moss that hadn't been there before. This dream must materialize anything we needed, I thought distantly, just as it brought Kyler to me. All coherent thoughts fled as four hands and two mouths began mapping my body.

Kyler's lips traced a path down my neck while Oryn's mouth claimed mine again. Their hands worked in tandem, stroking and teasing until I was arching against them, desperate for more.

"Please," I gasped when Oryn released my lips.

"What do you need, Love?" He asked, his voice rough with desire.

"Everything," I answered. "Both of you."

Kyler's chuckle vibrated against my skin. "So greedy."

"Can you blame me?" I turned to look at him, reaching up to trace the sharp line of his jaw.

"Never," he said, capturing my hand and pressing a kiss to my palm.

What followed was nothing short of a dance of desire and desperation—Kyler's cool touch contrasting with Oryn's natural heat, their movements perfectly synchronized as if they'd done this a thousand times before. I lost myself in them, in the pleasure they wrought from my body, in the whispered words of devotion and desire.

When release finally came, it crashed over me like a tidal wave. I couldn't help but scream their names as I reached the peak. They followed soon after, a chorus of growls and my name echoed through the forest.

We lay tangled together afterward, their bodies cradling mine from both sides. Kyler's fingers traced lazy patterns on my hip while Oryn pressed soft kisses to my shoulder.

"I could stay like this forever," I murmured.

"Our days will soon be like this," Oryn promised. "Once we find him."

"When I escape," Kyler corrected, his eyes meeting mine with an intensity that made my breath catch. "Promise me you won't step foot onto the island where gods bleed."

The dream began to fade then, the edges blurring and darkening. I tried to hold on to them, but they slipped through my fingers like smoke.

"Do not come after me," Kyler's voice echoed as darkness filled the space. "Stay away, stay safe."

His final warning haunted the darkness, desperate and commanding.

CHAPTER 18

I jerked upright, my chest heaving and my skin slick with sweat. The dream clung to me like morning dew in a field, too real to be mere imagination. I could still feel Kyler's cool touch against my skin, still taste the sweetness of his lips on mine.

"Alora?" Oryn's voice came from beside me, thick with sleep. "What's wrong?"

My mind raced, latching onto the final words that had echoed in my head as the dream faded. "The island where gods bleed," I whispered. An ache bloomed in my chest, and I rubbed at it to try to ease the sensation.

"What?" Oryn sat up, running a hand through his tousled hair.

"I had the strangest dream. I saw Kyler. He said, 'Stay away from the island where gods bleed.'" I turned to Oryn, my heart pounding. "What if it's one of the islands we sailed past?"

"It was just a dream, Love. Sometimes they feel real, trust me. I had the most delicious dream where my sexy wife was riding her other mate while I—"

"No," I cut him off as I shook my head firmly. "Wait, what?"

He hummed in amusement as he began trailing light kisses along the column of my neck. "So, you are interested in hearing how you were such a good girl for me and Kyler in a fun little rendezvous in the woods."

Oryn had clearly enjoyed where his mind had wandered while asleep, but I couldn't shake the urgency burning through my veins.

"No, Oryn," I pushed him away in frustration. "You were in the woods with me and Kyler? That was my dream. We had..." Despite our familiarity, embarrassment began flushing my cheeks as I thought about the part of my dream where we made love.

"Sex," Oryn deadpanned. "You don't need to be embarrassed about it. Did you have a sex dream, too? Or was Kyler just whispering cryptic messages the entire time?"

"That's the thing," I explained. "Oryn, we were in the woods. The three of us." I searched his eyes looking for the shine of realization, disappointment sank like a stone in my gut when his sleepy gaze failed to mirror the recognition I sought. "It sounds like we had the same dream."

"I don't remember Kyler saying anything about islands in mine," he said.

"What are the chances that we both had dreams of the three of us fucking in the woods?" I asked. "In a clearing, I was wearing this same nightdress. I went to Kyler first, and then you appeared behind us and said—"

"'What about me, Love?'" Oryn finished for me, eyes now wide. "How?"

The ache in my chest grew as a new one formed in my head. How? Was this an attempt on Kyler's part to reach out? If it were, then why did he warn me to stay away and wait for him to flee on his own? If he were able to, he would've done it already.

Right?

I continued trying to come up with a logical explanation for the phenomenon, but fell short. Nothing made sense. Nothing but...

"The bond," I said, jumping from the bed to rush to the wardrobe. I pulled open the thick doors and began pulling clothes for

Oryn and me. I tossed his at him and started pulling mine on, discarding my dress.

"The bond?" Oryn caught his items before they smacked him in the face as he stood and put them on.

"Kyler showed me something—a memory—through the bond one time." I explained. Turning to walk over to the desk where my weapons lay in a neat pile, I placed each blade in a secure spot on my person. "We can speak to each other in our minds because of the bond. He was able to show me something because of it. What if... what if the three of us shared that dream?"

"Don't you think that's a little crazy?" Oryn asked. "I'm not saying *you're* crazy," he quickly added. "It's just hard to consider."

"Harder than your father looking for a 'powerful match' and not only finding your mate in that match, but also someone whose powers are tied to a god?" I quirked a brow at him.

He shrugged in agreement. It was truly hard to believe everything we had experienced so far, but fate seemed to have a penchant for throwing us into the fire without a second thought.

Then a thought hit me, if we shared that dream, it meant the connection to Kyler had somehow been opened. Ever since he disappeared into that portal, I hadn't been able to reach him. I closed my eyes, envisioned the golden thread that bound me to him just as it did to Oryn and followed it to the door in my mind that stood between us. Closed, so nothing had changed there. I pushed on it, surprised to find it give until a flood of pain seized me. I dropped to my knees. I could hear Oryn shout my name in the distance as I continued to push the door that led to my lost love. The pain didn't matter when this was the closest I had been to him in weeks.

Until something snapped and I was thrown back, the door once again sealed shut.

"No!" I screamed as the pain subsided back to a dull ache. Tears streamed down my face at the loss of connection. I had been so close to reaching him. To hearing his voice again, to finding out where he was, to saving him.

"Alora, what happened?" Oryn was at my side, holding me in his arms as I sobbed on the floor. My shaking hands gripped onto him, my anchor in this sea of despair.

"We've got to find him, Oryn." My words fractured between ragged sobs, barely escaping my throat. "He can't wait anymore."

AFTER COLLECTING MYSELF, Oryn led me out the door, his typical morning languor replaced by tense alertness. With a firm grip, he directed me through the maze of corridors, unwilling to risk my hand slipping from his grip.

We stopped at Rasher's door first. After several attempts and practically breaking down the door, we finally accepted the lack of response meant he wasn't there. We moved on to the next room, Lucas's.

I pounded my fist against the wood, hearing a startled curse from within followed by hurried shuffling.

When Lucas finally cracked open the door, he peered through a sliver barely wide enough to show his face. His hair was a disaster, eyes bleary, and—was that a bruise forming on his neck?

"Gods, Lor, do you know what time it is?"

"Get dressed," I ordered. "I need to talk to everyone. I think I know where Kyler is."

His eyes widened. "How?"

"I'll explain when everyone's together. Have you seen Rasher? He didn't answer when we knocked."

Lucas's cheeks flushed slightly. "I'll fetch him. Just... give me a minute to get dressed." He tried to close the door, but I stuck my foot in the gap.

"Lucas, what are you—"

"I'll meet you in the dining hall," he blurted. "Fifteen minutes. I'll grab Rasher. I'm sure he's out playing with swords or something." With surprising strength, he pushed my foot back and shut the door firmly.

I stared at the closed door, baffled. "What was that about?"

Oryn shrugged, though a knowing smile played at his lips. "Let's get Luella and Magnus."

Those two were considerably easier to rouse. Luella answered her door promptly, already dressed as if she'd been awake for hours, and Magnus emerged from his room at the first knock, looking battle-ready as always.

"What's happened?" Magnus asked instantly alert.

"Dining hall," I said. "I'll explain everything there."

We made our way down to breakfast, my mind racing through possibilities. The islands we'd visited mere months ago wouldn't be far from the Esmeray coast based on how long the trek had taken from Saints Landing. There had been at least four of them: the one stacked high with cliffs and waterfalls, one filled with a thick jungle, the misty island where we met Death, and the barren one that appeared to be nothing but stone.

The dining hall was nearly empty at this early hour, with just a few servants preparing for the day. We claimed a table near the window, and I paced while waiting for Lucas and Rasher.

"Sit down," Magnus said. "You're making me anxious."

"They're taking too long," I muttered, but complied, drumming my fingers against the tabletop.

Luella tilted her head. "What's going on, Lor?"

I opened my mouth to explain but stopped when the dining hall doors swung open. Lucas strode in with Rasher close behind. Both looked slightly disheveled despite obvious attempts to appear otherwise. Lucas's shirt was misbuttoned, and Rasher had missed a spot near his ear while shaving.

"Finally," I said as they joined us at the table. "What took you so long?"

Lucas avoided my eyes. "Had to find the big guy."

Rasher cleared his throat. "What's this about Kyler?"

A servant approached with a tray of food. I waited impatiently as they gently placed it in the center before they scurried off.

"I had a dream last night. Well it wasn't just a dream—he was really there, somehow."

"A dream," Rasher repeated flatly.

"Yes, but not an ordinary one." I leaned forward. "Before it ended, he warned me to stay away from 'the island where gods bleed.' It has to be a clue to where he's being held."

"Or it could be your subconscious guilt manifesting," Lucas suggested gently.

I shook my head. "No. It was him. I know it."

Oryn had remained oddly quiet, staring down at his hands folded on the table. When I glanced at him, he wouldn't meet my eyes.

"Oryn?" I prompted.

He sighed heavily. "I had the same dream, though without the talk of islands. And if it's what Lor heard, then that's where we should look."

"Wait, you two had the same dream?" Lucas asked.

Magnus frowned. "And you know of an island with bleeding gods?"

"We saw several islands in our travels, could it be one of those? We landed on one where Alora spoke to a god, what's to say the other isles aren't home to the other gods?" Rasher pointed out.

"But which one?" Lucas frowned.

My frustration bubbled up, unable to be contained. "I don't know, but we will search them all!"

"I'm not sure I'll survive another voyage," Lucas grimaced, his face already showing a hint of green.

Luella placed a calming hand on my arm. "What if you spoke with the gods again? They would know which island that is, and surely they could help point us in the right direction."

Rasher nodded. Magnus looked unsure while Lucas sank further in his chair, no doubt thinking about returning to those cursed shores.

Before anyone could voice another opinion, the dining hall doors burst open with a bang. A soldier in Esmeray colors staggered in, breathing hard. His armor was dented and streaked with dirt, his face haggard with exhaustion.

"Captain Rasher," he gasped, stumbling toward our table. "Urgent news from the front."

Rasher shot to his feet. "Report, soldier."

"Oakston is under attack." The man swayed slightly. "Sunnevean forces have burned their way through the woods and have ravaged the farmlands around the town. They launched a massive assault at dawn. They're led by their new queen."

My blood turned to ice. So, Trinity had made her move.

"How many casualties?" Rasher demanded.

"Unknown, sir. I was dispatched when the first wave hit. The city's defenses were holding when I left, but barely." The soldier straightened his spine with visible effort. "The commander requests immediate reinforcements."

Rasher's expression hardened. "Alert the queen. Mobilize the eastern garrison. I want riders ready to move within the hour."

The soldier saluted and hurried out.

"What about Kyler?" I asked as Rasher began barking orders at the soldiers who had filed into the hall as we were speaking.

He turned his gaze onto me, regret shining in his eyes. "Kyler would want his people to be saved before anyone went for him. I'm sorry, Lor. But I have my duties."

My eyes brimmed with tears at the realization that Kyler's rescue would be pushed back once again. Guilt was wrapped around me like a suffocating shroud as Rasher's words settled in. He was right. We both knew which choice Kyler would make in this situation.

"Then I'm going, too," I declared, rising to my feet.

Oryn, Magnus, and Lucas stood with a resounding 'aye'. Luella went to stand, but Magnus shook his head at the young girl.

"I can fight with the rest of you," she said, crossing her arms across her chest.

"Magnus is right. I know you'd stand by us, but I won't be able to live with myself if you got hurt following us into battle, Luella," I said. "Please stay here, for me."

She chewed her bottom lip before nodding. "Fine, I'll continue our research. But I'm sailing with you all."

"We wouldn't leave without you." I promised.

"One hour," Rasher ordered. "Meet at the eastern gate, ready for battle."

As we scattered to prepare, the echo of Kyler's plea to stay away rang in my mind. If he was there, nothing in this world or the next would keep me away—not even his wishes.

First, we had to save his people. Trinity had taken action. Now it was our turn.

CHAPTER 19

I watched Oryn strap on a sword that was lying around Kyler's room, meticulously checking the length of leather before moving on to slide a dagger into his boot. We were both dressed in battle leathers, mine new, though a little stiff. Kyler had ensured my ensemble was as dark as night, allowing me to blend into the shadows if needed. Filling each hidden pocket with daggers felt comforting. It was something I had done hundreds of times, but it still gave me a sense of security even when heading straight into a fight.

Despite the stiffness of the new leather, they felt comfortable. The thought of how much care my mate had put into selecting them eased the pain in my chest. Oryn's came from the Esmeray armory, but they fit as if they'd been crafted for him. It was odd to see him in the dark colors, highlighted in glistening silver. I had only ever seen him in rich browns, bright golds, and the occasional ruby red of Sunneva.

"You don't have to come," I said, breaking the silence between us. "Those are your men we're about to fight, people you know. It would be understandable."

His blue eyes flicked up to meet mine. "Yes, I do. Those are my *father's* men. I won't let innocents suffer under his hand."

No further explanation was needed. Oryn would follow me into battle just as I would follow him. That's what we'd both do for Kyler.

I wondered if Magnus would have difficulty raising his own blade against those he knew, but I shook the thought away. He vowed to protect me even before he learned I was his daughter. If I could trust anything, it was having him on our side.

We headed to the eastern gate, where a small contingent had already gathered. Rasher stood tall among them, shouting orders and organizing the soldiers into formation. Magnus waited with two saddled horses, my father's face wore grim determination as his eyes found mine.

But I was too distracted by the horse that stood out against the rest.

My steed. My beautiful, strong, stubborn steed.

Magnus handed me Raven's reins. "He was a bastard trying to get him saddled, and Lucas refused to go anywhere near him."

I smiled at my beloved steed, patting the soft fur on his snout.

Raven snorted and nuzzled into my neck affectionately.

"I missed you," I murmured into his fur before turning back to my father. "He puts up a fight for everyone, but he likes you. Thank you for getting him ready for me."

"Oh, don't thank me, you owe the stable hands an ale or two for the fight he gave them." The older man chuckled.

"Well, thank you for waiting here with him at least. And thank you for joining us. I feel better with your sword at our side."

Magnus's eyes softened briefly before hardening again. "Always."

Lucas arrived moments later, looking unusually serious as he mounted a chestnut mare. His light hair was pushed back, and the focused intensity of an assassin hunting his prey had replaced his usual joking demeanor.

"Why do you insist on riding that demon?" he said.

"Why are you still afraid of him when he hasn't done anything to you?" I chuckled.

Disbelief colored his face as his hand went to his chest as if he were offended. "I have been brutally assaulted by him too many times to count. I demand payment for my suffering."

"How about I knock you out before we head to the islands?" I offered.

A ghost of his usual smile painted his face. "Oh Lor, you always know how to take care of me."

A voice cut through the air. "Maybe the Sunneveans will take care of you, and you'll no longer be our problem." Candra strode toward us, her twin axes gleaming at her hips. Her partially shaved head and fierce expression made her look every inch the warrior she was. "Don't expect me to save your asses," she said bluntly, mounting her own horse.

"Wouldn't dream of it," I replied dryly.

Rasher called for silence, his voice cutting through the noise. "We ride hard and fast. Oakston is less than half a day's ride if we push our mounts. Be ready for battle the moment we arrive. No hesitation, no mercy."

With that, he swung onto his own horse, a massive dappled stallion that matched his imposing presence. I caught myself staring, amazed that he had found a steed large enough to carry him.

"For Esmeray!" he shouted.

"For Esmeray!" The soldiers shouted.

WE THUNDERED THROUGH THE GATES, hooves pounding against the earth as we raced toward Oakston. The wind whipped through my hair, carrying the scent of smoke long before we could see it. My stomach twisted into knots as we crested a hill and I caught my first glimpse of what awaited us.

Black smoke billowed into the sky, obscuring the sun and casting an eerie twilight over the countryside. The forest that bordered the town—once lush and vibrant—was now a charred wasteland of broken, smoldering trees. Fields that should have been golden with harvest were blackened and trampled.

"By the gods," Magnus breathed beside me. I looked to Oryn on my other side and could see the guilt hiding behind his calculating eyes as he assessed the destruction.

We will rebuild, I assured him through the bond. *You and Kyler can mend all that has been done. I know you both can.*

I worry there may be nothing left to mend by the time my father's finished.

Have hope, my love. I gave him a gentle smile.

As we drew closer, the sounds of battle reached us—screams, clashing metal, the dull thud of arrows finding their marks. Oakston's outer walls had been breached in several places, flames licking at wooden structures within.

Rasher raised his hand, signaling us to slow. "We'll enter through the west gate. It appears to be holding. Form up, shields forward!"

The soldiers shifted into formation around us. I found myself at the center with Oryn, Lucas, and Magnus, while Candra moved to Rasher's side near the front.

"Stay close," Oryn murmured, his eyes scanning the battlefield ahead. "Something doesn't feel right."

I knew what he meant. There was a strange energy in the air, beyond the chaos of ordinary battle. It reminded me of the night when Trinity appeared—a prickling sensation against my skin that had made my hair stand on end. I pulled shadows to Raven and me. The intimidating look was sometimes enough to make someone hesitate, giving us an opening to cut them down, but tonight, I aimed to blend in. We needed every advantage we had.

We approached the west gate at a gallop. The guards, recognizing Rasher, rushed to let us through. The moment we entered the town, the full horror of the situation became clear.

Bodies littered the streets—civilians and soldiers alike. Buildings burned unchecked, and smoke stung my eyes and filled my lungs. Amid the human defenders and attackers were figures that moved with unnatural precision and strength—Trinity's golems, their granite faces expressionless as they cut down anyone in their path.

"Split up!" Rasher ordered. "First and second units, secure the northern quarter! Third unit, with me to the town square!"

We followed Rasher toward the heart of Oakston, cutting down enemies as we went. I dispatched a Sunnevean soldier with a clean strike across his throat, then whirled to face one of the stone creatures. My blade struck its chest with a jarring clang, barely leaving a scratch.

"Aim for the joints in their armor!" Oryn called out, demonstrating by driving his sword into the gap between the creature's neck and shoulder. It shuddered and fell, crumbling to dust. "If your power is strong enough, it may help." He instructed the rest of the men.

I hopped off Raven, who stamped at the soldiers around us, and followed Oryn's example with the next golem I encountered, finding the weak point where its arm connected to its torso. Its arm crumbled but gave me an opening to jam my blade underneath its armor, in the vulnerable spot where its neck met the rest of its body.

Fighting beside Oryn felt natural, our movements complementing each other as if we'd trained together for years. When a Sunnevean archer took aim at his back, my throwing knife found the man's eye before he could loose his arrow. When I was cornered by two stone soldiers, Oryn appeared at my side, burning one down while I handled the other.

Magnus fought nearby, his experience evident in every calculated strike. Lucas danced through the battle with lethal grace, his daggers finding gaps in the armor with unerring precision. Even Candra, for all her hostility, proved herself to be an extraordinary fighter. Her axes cut wide arcs that left destruction in their wake.

But for every enemy that fell, more seemed to take their place. We were being pushed back, driven toward the town square despite our best efforts.

"Rasher!" Candra shouted, pointing ahead. "The square is surrounded!"

I followed her gaze and saw that she was right. The central plaza had become a battle field, surrounded by golems that herded Esmeray soldiers into an ever shrinking circle. And at the center of all the melee stood a figure I recognized immediately—Trinity.

She wore a crown of gold, her dark hair streaming behind her in the waves of heat from the fires. Her hands glowed with a sickly green light, directing her stone army with casual gestures. She looked every inch a queen of death and chaos.

"Fall back!" Rasher ordered, but it was too late.

Stone soldiers closed in behind us, cutting off our retreat. We found ourselves being herded into the square with the remaining defenders, our backs literally against the wall as Trinity's forces tightened the noose.

"Well, well," Trinity's voice carried across the square as she spotted us. "My lovely daughter has returned to me."

I gripped the obsidian dagger tighter in my hand, fury and fear battling within me. "Where's Kyler?"

She laughed, the sound sending chills down my spine. "So obsessed with a subpar fae. I'll take you to him if you join me. Willingly. I'll even spare your little friends."

My gaze swept the square, assessing our chances. We were outnumbered at least five to one, and our lack of knowledge of Trinity's powers gave her an overwhelming advantage.

"You'd let everyone go and leave Esmeray alone?" I demanded, stalling as I tried to form a plan.

"Sure, sure." Trinity waved a hand as a cruel grin spread across her face. "Esmeray and I are new allies anyway, so I'll leave it be for now."

"Esmeray would never ally itself with you," Rasher growled.

Trinity's smile widened. "Are you sure about that? Your queen and I had quite a productive little chat."

A murmur ran through the Esmeray soldiers. Rasher's face darkened. "You lie."

"Do I?" Trinity raised an eyebrow. "Ask her yourself."

She waved her hand as her forces parted.

"Give me my son!" Wynaria stepped out from the wreckage of her city. The queen's head held high with confidence as she moved among Trinity's forces, who didn't bat an eye.

We'd been played.

"Sorry, dear," my mother said to Wyneria, "the deal was that *you* hand over my daughter. It seems she's done it herself before you could lift a finger." Trinity shrugged.

Her soldiers sprang into action. One wrapped Wynaria's burgundy locks around a thick hand while another buried their blade into her abdomen. Tears sprang from the queen's eyes as she fell to her knees, realizing the bounty she had tried to win was never going to be given.

"You won't get away with this," Oryn snarled, stepping forward to shield me.

Trinity's gaze shifted to him, her expression changing to one of interest. "Prince Oryn. Your father sends his regards. He was quite upset when you disappeared after the death of your mother."

Oryn's face paled with fury. "My father is a fool and a traitor to his own family."

"Perhaps. But he's a useful fool." Trinity's hands began to glow brighter. She thrust her palm forward, sending a blast of green energy straight towards Oryn. I screamed his name, but before I could move, Magnus shoved Oryn aside, taking the full force of the blast himself.

"NO!" I watched in horror as Magnus was thrown backward, his body slamming against the ground. Green energy coursed over him like lightning, his back arching in agony as he writhed in the dirt.

I rushed to him, dropping to my knees beside his crumpled form. "Magnus!"

Magnus's eyes fluttered open, blood trickling from the corner of his mouth. "Alora," he whispered, his voice barely audible.

His hand reached up, trembling, to touch my face. I caught it in my hand, holding it against my cheek as tears blurred my vision.

"Stay with me," I begged. "Please, we only just found each other. Father, please."

"My daughter, I'm so...proud," he gasped, his breath rattling in his chest. "I...love you..."

His eyes fixed on something beyond me, growing distant before I could utter the sentiment back. The hand against my cheek went limp.

"No," I whispered, then louder, "No!"

Something broke inside me—a dam holding back more than just grief. It threatened to pull me back to the throws of my depression, when almost every living soul I knew departed this realm. Tears prickled my eyes as I lost yet another one, another person I'd come to love. The grief pulsed within me as the fear of going through this once again tried to take over. Power surged through my veins, white-hot and all-consuming. Fire erupted in waves that pushed everyone back. I heard Trinity shout something, but the roaring in my ears drowned her voice out.

Through tear-filled eyes, I saw my hands glowing with a brilliant white light that sparked with embers of flame. I felt lightheaded, disconnected from my body as power continued to pour out of me.

"Alora!" Oryn's voice penetrated the haze of my rage and grief. He was trying to reach me, fighting against the force of my power.

I turned to him, and from the shock on his face, I knew my eyes had changed, too.

"Get back," I warned, my voice sounding strange even to my own ears.

Trinity shouted orders to her stone soldiers, directing them toward me. But as they approached, my power lashed out, reducing them to dust with a mere thought. The Sunnevean soldiers backed away in terror, some turning to flee.

Trinity's expression shifted from interest to excitement. She raised her hands, green energy gathered between them. "You are so much more than I had expected," glee laced through her words.

A swirling portal began to form behind her, dark and ominous. She thrust her hands forward, sending a net of green energy toward me. I tried to deflect it with my power, but my control was still erratic. The net ensnared me, yanking me toward the portal.

"Alora!" Oryn shouted, lunging for me. His fingers closed around my wrist just as Trinity's magic pulled me into the portal's opening.

"No! Release her!" Trinity snarled, trying to separate us.

"Never," Oryn growled, his grip tightening as we were both dragged into the void.

"I've got you!" Lucas appeared, grabbing for my other hand. For a moment, I thought he might pull us both free.

Then Trinity lashed out with another burst of power, striking Lucas squarely in the chest. Blood bloomed across his shirt as he staggered backward, his face a mask of shock and pain.

"Lucas!" I screamed as he collapsed to the ground, unmoving.

It was the last thing I saw before the portal swallowed Oryn and me whole, the darkness closing around us like a fist. The sensation of falling overwhelmed me, Oryn's hand still clasped tightly around mine as we plummeted through nothingness.

Trinity's gleeful cackling echoed in the void, following us down, down, down into the unknown. My last conscious thought was of Magnus's lifeless body and the shock in Lucas's eyes as his knees hit the ground. I had been powerless to save them.

The momentum of the drop began to make my thoughts blur as Oryn and I barreled through until we hit a hard floor. My mind spun as we reached our destination.

"Quickly, give it to them before they recover." Trinity's barked command was the only noise that stood out from the buzzing in my ears.

We were in the monster's den, and I could only pray to the gods who played cruelly with our lives that we would find our missing piece and make it out of this.

Alive.

Preferably alive.

CHAPTER 20

Darkness, thick and suffocating, pressed against my eyelids. My head throbbed with each heartbeat, a steady rhythm of pain that pulled me from unconsciousness. I tried to lift my hand to my temple, but something cold and unyielding bit into my wrists.

Iron.

The bitter scent flooded my nostrils as awareness returned.

I pried my eyes open, blinking the world back into focus. A dim room materialized around me—stone walls slick with moisture, a single torch casting ghoulish shadows across the floor. The air was stale and carried the stench of mildew and something else... something coppery.

Blood.

Memories crashed over me violently. Wynaria's betrayal. Magnus dead in my arms. Lucas crumpled to the ground. The portal whisked Oryn and me away.

"Oryn?" My voice came out as a rasp, my throat dry as parchment.

A groan answered from somewhere to my right. I turned my

head, ignoring the way it made the room spin, and found him slumped against the wall. His hands were bound like mine, heavy iron manacles connected to chains that hung on the stone wall behind us.

"Alora." His voice was thick and slurred. "Are you hurt?"

"Just sore. I think they drugged us when we came out of the portal." I tugged at my restraints, testing their strength. They didn't budge. "Where are we?"

"Sunneva," a familiar voice answered from the shadows across the cell.

My heart stopped.

A figure shifted in the darkness of the cell beside us, chains rattling as he moved into the meager light. Dirty, bruised, with dark circles beneath his eyes—but unmistakably him.

"Kyler," I whispered. This moment I had begged the gods for had finally arrived. My mate, the love of my life, before me in the flesh.

Alive.

He looked thinner than when I'd last seen him, his sharp cheekbones more pronounced. His hair had grown longer, hanging in his eyes. A patchwork of bruises decorated his jaw and disappeared beneath the torn collar of his shirt. But his eyes—those dark, fierce eyes—were the same. They locked onto mine with an intensity that stole my breath.

"You shouldn't be here," his voice was rough from disuse.

"You know us better than that," Oryn said, struggling to sit up straighter.

Kyler's gaze shifted to Oryn, and something passed between them—an understanding, a shared pain. "You look like shit," Kyler told him with a ghost of his old smirk.

"Speak for yourself," Oryn shot back, but the relief in his voice was palpable.

I strained against my chains, desperate to touch him, to make sure he was real and not some cruel hallucination. "We didn't stop searching for you..."

"I know." His eyes softened as they returned to me. "Sometimes, I felt you through our bond, but only when they... when whatever they kept giving me wore off."

"Drugs?" Oryn asked, frowning.

Kyler nodded, holding up his own chained wrists. I noticed now the bruising marks along his forearms, some fresh, others healing. "Something that mutes the bond and our powers. Makes it impossible to reach out." His voice dropped lower. "But the other night, it was different. I saw you, heard you, Alora."

The dream. My breath caught in my throat. "You were really there."

"For the first time in weeks." A muscle in his jaw twitched. "It gave me hope. Though, you didn't listen to me at all."

"You cut me off when I could finally get through to you." I narrowed my eyes accusingly.

He winced. "I couldn't risk you feeling my beatings, the burn of the iron. I only did it to protect you, Princess."

"Well, don't protect me," I snapped. "I don't need your protection."

An exasperated sigh left him as he leaned his head against the wall.

"Noted."

I wanted to tell him everything—about meeting with the witch once again, about Magnus and Candra, and about his mother. But the words caught in my throat as I looked at him, alive but suffering. Instead, I asked, "What happened?"

Kyler's expression darkened. "Trinity had her golems on me the moment I came through the portal. It wasn't hard to overpower me, most come out of there disoriented. The last thing I remembered was feeling a prick in my neck." He looked down at his hands. "Next thing I knew, I woke up chained here, the door to our connection sealed shut."

"She's been busy," Oryn muttered. "Her soldiers razed Oakston. Your mother—"

"Oryn." I cut him off, giving him a scathing look.

"What about my mother?" Kyler pressed on.

I looked down at my shackled hands, picking at my nail beds as I tried to come up with the right words.

"She handed Lor over in exchange for you." Oryn told him.

Kyler cursed, the heat from his rage warming the air around us. It didn't take a mate bond to understand what he felt. "That went bloody well for her. When I see her next, I'm separating her head from her neck. What she did was unforgivable."

Oryn and I shared a solemn glance, but as we looked to Kyler once again, a violent scoff echoed in the room.

"It's about time my mother's shady plans caught up with her." Kyler muttered.

"I'm so sorry, Kyler." After all, she was still his mother, and Esmeray's queen. With her demise and Kyler's imprisonment, where did that leave the northern kingdom?

"I'm not. I mean it, Princess. Her days were numbered the moment she decided your life was worth less than my own. I'd spend hundreds of years here if it meant you lived a happy, full life." His eyes shone with regret. "I really wish you hadn't followed me here."

"Funny," I said, "I'm really glad that I did. Have you learned anything about Trinity's plans?" I asked.

Kyler shook his head. "They've kept me isolated. The only people I see are guards who bring me food and water. Sometimes Trinity comes to... check on me." His expression told me that those visits were far from pleasant. "I've gathered fragments of information, only whispers. Something about a ritual deep in the island made of iron, but nothing beyond that."

"An island that can make gods bleed," I said quietly, I looked to Oryn whose brows pinched in concentration. "But why would she want to bring Chaos to an island that could kill him?"

Oryn's face paled. "What if that's his island? Like you met with Death on his. Maybe a god can only be brought from their realm through the place most connected to them."

"You didn't tell me to stay away from you," I said suddenly, turning to Kyler. "You wanted me to stay away from the island."

"I didn't want you to end up there when looking for me." He corrected. "Knowing you lot, you and Rasher would've figured it out eventually and commandeered a ship, no doubt dragging poor Lucas with you."

The sound of Lucas's name brought tears to my eyes. I had no idea what happened to him, to any of them. For all I knew, Rasher could be dead. Candra too. No, Candra surely got away; she seemed like she'd find a way to slither out of death's grasp.

"Rasher?" Kyler asked.

Oryn shook his head.

"We don't know," I admitted. "Magnus is dead." The words felt like broken glass in my mouth. "He tried to protect me, and she... Trinity killed him."

Kyler's expression softened with pain and regret. "Alora, I'm so sorry."

"Lucas, too," Oryn added, his voice hollow. "Trinity struck him down just as we were pulled through the portal."

"Fuck," Kyler breathed, closing his eyes briefly. When he opened them again, they burned with a bitter fury. "We need to get out of here. Stop her before she—"

The creak of hinges cut him off. We all tensed as a door I hadn't noticed before swung open, casting a wider rectangle of light across the stone floor.

Trinity stepped through, resplendent in a gown of deep crimson that matched the gems of the crown that sat upon her head. Two stone soldiers flanked her, their expressionless faces inhuman and haunting in their stillness.

"Well, isn't this touching," she purred, her lips curving into a smile that never reached her eyes. "Reunited at last with your little mate."

I lunged against my chains, teeth bared. "You murdered Magnus and Lucas."

"They were in my way," she replied simply before turning to Oryn. "As were you until I realized it would be better this way."

"And what way is that?" Oryn growled.

Trinity's gaze slid to Kyler, cold calculation in her eyes. "She is the vessel." Her eyes returned to me, hungry and appraising. "You felt it in Oakston, didn't you? When your grief overtook you? The power in your veins is older than you can imagine. An ancient power."

The memory of white flames pouring from my hands flashed through my mind.

"I don't know what you're talking about," I lied.

Trinity laughed. "Of course you do. Humility will get you nowhere, girl." She stepped closer, her skirts brushing the filthy floor without her seeming to care. "The gods chose you, Alora. Handpicked and made in their image. You were meant for greater things, far greater things than being an ordinary girl."

"For what?" Kyler demanded.

"To bring back what was lost," Trinity answered, her voice taking on an almost reverent quality. "To restore the balance that was broken. The glory of our gods will return once again!"

"You mean, bring Chaos back," I spat. "There's no balance where he goes."

"What an ignorant way to think," she chided. "I knew I shouldn't have left you in that godforsaken village. You would have benefited from a more worldly education. But alas, that was not the path Fate had set for us." She shrugged. "Chaos is not just destruction—it can be rebirth. Chaos is whatever the wielder demands it to be. It is the ultimate source of power. It's time for the kingdoms to be torn down for the new ways to rise." She crouched before me, bringing her face level with mine. "And you, my daughter, are the key that unlocks the door."

I recoiled from her, pressing back against the wall. "I won't be unlocking shit for you."

"No?" Trinity raised an eyebrow. She stood, moving to enter into the cell beside us. Her gliding steps halted where Kyler sat, his eyes tracking her every move like a predator. Without warning, she plunged her hand into his hair, yanking his head back to expose his throat. A dagger materialized in her other hand, its edge kissing his skin. "Not even to save your precious mate?"

"Don't touch him," I snarled, white-hot rage flooding my veins.

A thin line of blood appeared where Trinity's blade pressed. "Here's how this will work, Alora. You will cooperate. You will lend your power to me. In fact, you will do everything I ask without question." She scraped the knife against his throat, more blood trickled from the wound. "Or I will kill them both while you watch, starting with this one."

Kyler didn't flinch, didn't beg. His eyes found mine, steady and certain. "Don't you dare give her what she wants," he said softly.

Trinity slammed his head back against the wall. "Quiet."

Oryn strained against his chains, the metal cutting into his wrists as he fought to reach Trinity. "You touch him again, and I'll tear your heart out with my bare hands."

"Such devotion," Trinity mocked, releasing Kyler with a shove. "It's too bad I don't have one. You'll have to be a bit more creative with your threats." She turned back to me. "Well, Alora? What will it be?"

My mind raced, searching for a way out. If I refused, she'd kill them both. If I agreed, she might still kill them once she got what she wanted. Either way, Chaos would rise, and the world as we knew it would end and be reshaped into whatever she willed.

Unless...

"If I agree," I said slowly, "what happens to them?"

Trinity's smile widened. "They'll live, of course. You'll all be free to roam the palace, under supervision. The king will welcome you back with open arms, and you'll be treated as you should with your stations." Her eyes glittered. "I'm not unreasonable, Alora. I don't desire their deaths for their own sake. They're merely... leverage."

"And if I refuse?"

"Then they die." She shrugged. "You'll be my prisoner and you'll still have to help me. Your cooperation merely makes things more pleasant, less messy."

Kyler's eyes burned into mine. *Don't,* they seemed to say. *Whatever happens, don't give her what she wants.*

But what choice did I have?

"I need time to think," I said, stalling.

Trinity laughed. "No, you don't. You've already made your decision—I can see it in your eyes." She approached me again, crouching to meet my gaze. "You'd do anything to protect them. It's pathetic, but has its use."

I wanted to spit in her face, to tell her to go to hell. But the image of Kyler's throat under her blade kept me silent.

"Fine," I whispered finally. "I'll help you. But if you harm either of them—"

"You'll what?" Trinity interrupted. "Kill me? With those pretty chains binding your power?" She reached out to stroke my cheek, her touch like ice. I jerked away, and she laughed. "You have no power here, Alora, you're in no position to bargain. Take the kindness I so rarely offer. You'll do as I say because the alternative is watching your princes die slowly and painfully while their blood seeps into your clothing, your skin."

She straightened, smoothing her hands down her gown. "Guards," she called to the stone soldiers. "Prepare the prisoners for transfer to the west wing. Clean them up—they reek of the dungeons." She wrinkled her nose. "And bring the witch. She needs to examine the vessel."

"Alora," Kyler said, his voice tight with desperation. "Don't do this. Whatever she wants, it's not worth it."

Trinity turned to him with a razor-thin smile. "How noble. Sacrificing yourself for the greater good." She stroked his cheek mockingly. "There are forces at work beyond your comprehension, prince. Chaos must rise... but what comes after is what truly matters."

"Seems like death and ruin only follow Chaos," Oryn growled.

Trinity chuckled. "We shall see." She turned to leave, pausing at the door. "I expect the three of you to behave, my kindness only stretches so far."

The door slammed shut behind her, plunging us back into the semi-darkness.

"I'm sorry, I can't watch you both die," I whispered. Too many loved ones have been ripped from me already. My heart was a wasteland until my princes came into my life. It would kill me to watch the life leech from their eyes.

"We know," Oryn said softly, "but we need to get out of here." He pulled against his chains again. "Find a way to escape before the ritual."

I nodded, but despair threatened to overwhelm me. The iron manacles blocked my power completely—I couldn't even sense the now familiar warmth of my fire. Without it, or my shadows, how could we possibly escape?

"Together," Kyler said suddenly, his eyes intense as they moved between Oryn and me. "Whatever happens, we face it together. I won't lose either of you again."

Despite everything—the dread, the fear, the looming shadow of Chaos and the unknown—warmth bloomed in my chest at his words. We'd found him. Against all odds, we were together again.

Whether that was a blessing or a curse remained to be seen.

CHAPTER 21

The doors to our cells opened with a groan, and three stone guards entered, their movements mechanical and unsettling. I'd barely had time to exchange whispered reassurances with my mates when they yanked us to our feet. They unlocked our chains from the wall, leaving the heavy iron manacles still clasped around our wrists.

The guards remained silent, their stone faces expressionless as they pushed us forward. Their grip was unyielding, fingers digging into my arms hard enough to bruise. I glanced at Kyler, noting the tightness around his eyes that betrayed his pain as they handled him roughly. Oryn looked ready to kill, his jaw clenched so hard I feared he might crack his teeth.

We were marched through dim, torch-lit corridors that twisted and turned. Despite having lived in this castle for many months, the newly established dungeons were unfamiliar territory, and I quickly lost my bearings.

Eventually, we emerged into more familiar hallways. The polished marble floors and ornate tapestries were a stark contrast to the dank stone of the dungeons. Guards—fae ones—lined the corridors, their eyes averted as we passed. Whether from fear or indifference, I couldn't tell.

"They're taking us to the royal wing," Oryn murmured, his voice barely audible.

My heart clenched as we approached a familiar doorway Our chambers—mine and Oryn's—from before everything fell apart. The guards pushed us inside, and I stumbled, catching myself against the back of a chair.

The room looked exactly as we'd left it. The massive four-poster bed still had its rich burgundy coverings. The bookshelves lined one wall, filled with volumes I had yet to read. The sitting area near the fireplace where the three of us had bared our souls to each other, still looked the same.

It felt like stepping into a memory, or perhaps a nightmare.

"Well, this is a sorry state of affairs," a familiar voice announced.

Miss Gregoria stood near the bathroom door, her hands clasped tightly before her. Her face was a mask of carefully controlled emotion, but I caught the slight widening of her eyes as she took in our battered appearances.

"Miss Gregoria," I whispered, unsure whether to feel relief or dread at seeing the old crone. She had never been warm to me, choosing to let Luella deal with me on most days. The times I had spent with her, she was nothing short of totalitarian and rigid.

"Lady Alora," she replied with a small nod. "Prince Oryn, Captain." Her gaze lingered on the two men. "I've been instructed to oversee your... preparations."

As if on cue, several maids entered from the bathroom, carrying towels, soaps, and fresh clothing. Steam billowed from the open door, suggesting a bath had been drawn.

"You're to be made presentable for dinner with His Majesty and Lady Trinity," Miss Gregoria explained, her tone formal but her eyes revealed nothing but cool detachment.

As the maids approached us, I lifted my wrists, jingling my new accessory. "How are we supposed to bathe with these on?"

"They remain," one of the stone guards rumbled, speaking for the first time. His voice sounded like gravel grinding together. "Lady Trinity's orders."

Miss Gregoria's lips thinned, but she nodded to the maids. "Proceed."

One of the younger maids approached me with scissors in hand, reaching for the tattered remains of my clothing. I instinctively stepped back, bumping into Kyler.

"Don't touch her," he growled, his voice low and dangerous despite his weakened state.

The maid froze, her eyes wide with fear.

Oryn moved to stand beside me, his posture protective despite the chains binding his power. "I will not have my wife exposed to these," his shackles ground together as he attempted to wave his hand toward the guards, "things."

Tension flooded the room like static. The stone guards stood motionless, menacingly still as Oryn gave the old woman a hard stare.

Miss Gregoria assessed the situation with shrewd eyes before letting out a sigh that could have been irritation or resignation. My coin would be on the first. "Leave us," she ordered the maids. "I will see to their needs myself."

"But—" one of the older maids protested.

"I said, leave." Miss Gregoria's tone left no room for argument. "I've been managing this household for longer than you've been alive, girl. I can handle the three of them."

The maids exchanged uncertain glances but ultimately filed out of the room, leaving only Miss Gregoria and the two stone guards.

"You," she pointed at the guards, "wait outside. I doubt they'll attempt anything foolish. The windows have been sealed shut, and the only exit is that door. You'll be called if needed."

The guards hesitated before one nodded stiffly. "Ten minutes."

After they left, Miss Gregoria's shoulders sagged slightly, her formal demeanor cracking. "Quickly now," she urged, ushering us toward the bathroom. "We don't have much time."

The bathroom was filled with steam, the large tub in the center filled with hot water that smelled faintly of citrus and jasmine. Under different circumstances, it would have been inviting. Now, it seemed another form of torture—comfort dangled before us like bait.

"I cannot remove those," Miss Gregoria said, gesturing to our shackles. "But I can give you privacy. Help each other as best you can." She handed us soap and cloths. "I wouldn't do anything to gain ill favor with the new lady. She is…" The old crone hesitated, considering her next words. "She is ruthless."

Before I could respond, she turned and left, closing the door behind her.

"Those may have been the kindest words she's ever graced me with," I said.

We stood awkwardly for a moment, the reality of our situation setting in. With our wrists confined, undressing would be difficult, if not impossible, without tearing our clothes further.

"Turn around," Kyler said suddenly. "I'll help you first, Princess."

I did as he asked, feeling his fingers gently work at the laces of my tattered shirt. Despite our circumstances, my skin tingled where he touched me. When he loosened it as much as he could, he pulled the fabric taut between his teeth and his hands and ripped at it, tearing it at the shoulders and down the sides. The tattered bits of cloth dropped into a pile on the floor. He helped me pull my pants off until I was finally bare. We worked together to repeat the process until the three of us were left covered only in dirt and grime. By the time I lowered myself into the water, frustration had built a knot in my throat.

The hot water stung cuts I hadn't realized I had, but the heat was heavenly on my aching muscles. I scrubbed the parts I could reach as quickly as I could, turning to help my mates with their backs.

Washing away the evidence of the battle we had fought gave me little peace. The memories of my long-lost father and my best friend continued to haunt me. Lucas had brought me back from the dead, every idiotic joke and flirty smile cracked away at the walls I had built around myself after losing Maël. He had my back more times than I could count, and when it mattered, it felt like I had failed to have his. I should have protected him, somehow, even if it meant dragging him through the portal with us. At least I would've known he was alive. And Magnus was the man I never truly got to know, but deep down I had wanted to open up, to know what it would've been like to have a father. Two more deaths to add to the many I had witnessed. Two more loved ones were gone. I shoved the grief down, trying to draw every ounce of strength I had to survive the coming days.

By the time we'd all bathed, steam had fogged the mirrors and our skin was flushed from the heat. We emerged from the bathroom wrapped in towels secured as best we could manage with our shackled hands, to find Miss Gregoria waiting with clean clothes laid out on the bed.

But she wasn't alone.

An older woman with sharp features and calculating eyes stood near the window, her hands clasped before her. I recognized her immediately—Elvirana, the Royal Mage. Beside her stood one of the stone guards.

"Finally," Elvirana said, clicking her tongue impatiently. "How am I supposed to make a proper assessment of the vessel with those ridiculous things on?" She gestured dismissively at our shackles.

"I do not know." The guard's response reminded me of a reflex, a mindless action.

Elvirana rolled her eyes. She reached into a pouch at her waist and withdrew three gleaming bands of metal, tossing them to the guard. "Put these on them instead."

The guard caught the bands but continued to stand there.

"They're iron bracelets, you simpleton. Enchanted, of course.

Lady Trinity has approved them. They'll block their powers just as effectively while allowing me to conduct my examination without interference."

My heart quickened. Could we use this to our advantage? If the bracelets were less restrictive than the shackles...

But as if reading my thoughts, Elvirana fixed her gaze on me. "Don't get any ideas, girl. These are just as powerful, merely more subtle. Appropriate for court. Unless you'd rather show up to dinner stark naked with your hands bound in front of you?"

The guard approached Kyler first, who tensed but allowed the exchange. The dainty band of metal was placed onto his wrist before the guard removed his shackles, eliminating the risk of using our powers within a moment. The same process was repeated with Oryn, and finally, me.

The bracelets were slim and deceptively elegant, almost like jewelry rather than restraints. But the moment mine closed around my wrist, I felt the same suffocating absence of my power that the iron had caused. My connection to the shadows, to my fire, even to my mates—all remained frustratingly out of reach.

"There," Elvirana said, satisfied. "Now you can dress properly without being the laughingstock at dinner."

Miss Gregoria stepped forward. "I'll assist them—"

"Later," Elvirana cut her off. "I need to examine the girl first. Leave us."

Miss Gregoria hesitated, glancing at us with concern before nodding stiffly and departing. The stone guard remained, standing like a statue before the door.

Elvirana approached me, her eyes narrowed in concentration. "Hold still," she commanded, lifting her hands to hover on either side of my head.

A sensation that I could only describe as walking through a hall of cobwebs brushed against my mind. It wasn't painful, but deeply unsettling—as if someone were rifling through my thoughts, my very essence.

"Interesting," she murmured. "Very interesting indeed."

Her hands moved lower, hovering over my heart. The sensation intensified, and I gasped as something cold seemed to reach inside me, probing at my core.

"Stop," Kyler growled, stepping forward. The guard immediately moved to intercept him, stone hand gripping his arm with bruising force.

"I'm not hurting her," Elvirana said without looking away from me. "Merely... studying."

Her examination continued for what felt like an eternity. Finally, she stepped back, her expression troubled.

"Your well of power has grown," she said, mostly to herself. "There's something different within you, something I didn't sense when we first met." She stepped back, addressing the guard. "Tell Lady Trinity the vessel is viable and that we can move forward with preparations."

The guard nodded curtly.

She turned to leave, then paused, looking back at us with an expression I couldn't decipher. "Treasure these moments," she said cryptically. "When Chaos rises, nothing will be as it was. Not even you, Alora."

With those harrowing words hanging in the air, she departed, leaving us shaken and confused.

We dressed in silence, not risking speaking in front of the guard now that we knew they could communicate. How many poor souls have spoken cross words only to have Trinity punish them for it?

The clothes laid out for us were decadent—silks and velvets in rich warm colors—as if we were honored guests rather than prisoners. The absurdity of it wasn't lost on me.

Once dressed, we huddled closely on the sofa, hoping for a moment of reprieve from the guard's watchful gaze. Not once did he blink, nor did he leave us.

If this was what we had to look forward to every day, then escape was hopeless. Any step out of line was sure to end in torture for my mates. I needed to play the part, complete whatever it was Trinity wanted from me, at least until I could get Oryn and Kyler out safely.

A sharp knock at the door interrupted the silence of the chamber. Worried glances were exchanged between my mates and me as the guard moved to answer it.

What fresh hell awaited us now?

CHAPTER 22

The stone guard pulled open the door, revealing Shefferd's stout frame. The Hand to the King looked noticeably thinner than when I'd last seen him, his jowls were less pronounced, and his eyes more sunken. But he still surveyed us with a critical gaze, his lips pressed into a thin line.

"You're presentable. Good." He cleared his throat, the nasal quality of his voice remained as grating as ever. "I've been sent to escort you to the throne room. The king wishes to make a formal reintroduction of you three to society now that you've returned home."

Home. The word felt like poison when the place of reference was nothing but a gilded prison.

"I think you mean that he intends to parade us around," Oryn sneered.

Shefferd's eyes darted to the stone guard and back to us. "I'd advise against such... candor... when in His Majesty's presence."

He gestured with trembling hands for us to follow him. Six fae guards fell into formation around us—two in front, two behind, and one flanking each side. Their expressions were blank, but the way they gripped their swords in fear in our presence was amusing. Frightened of the people who want to help, yet blindly follow their leader into the dark.

As we walked through the corridors, the changes in the castle became increasingly apparent. The normally bustling hallways were eerily quiet. Where nobles once gathered in clusters, whispering court gossip and plotting alliances to gain their riches, there was now only the occasional servant hurrying past with downcast eyes.

"Where is everyone?" I whispered to Shefferd.

He kept his gaze forward. "Much of the court has retired to their country estates. For... health reasons. The ones who've stayed are likely already in attendance."

In other words, they'd fled. For once, they've shown a sliver of intelligence, or at least, self preservation.

We passed a corridor that was often used by the maids who carried fresh linens to guest rooms, a place that had buzzed with chatter. Now it was empty save for a stone golem standing sentinel at the intersection. Its blank eyes seemed to follow our movement.

"They're everywhere," Kyler murmured, nodding toward the golem.

"Yes, they've been quite the eyesore," Shefferd said, tight lipped.

An eyesore that would be a big problem if we find the opportunity to escape.

We turned a corner, and I nearly stumbled. Where a beautiful tapestry depicting the founding of Sunneva once hung, there was now a massive banner in blood red. A symbol I didn't recognize was embroidered in black thread—a twisting, chaotic pattern that made my vision blur when I stared at it.

Oryn placed a steadying hand on my lower back. "You okay?"

I nodded, though *okay* wasn't remotely accurate. We were in dangerous waters where there were sure to be unknown monsters lurking about.

As we approached the throne room, the large double doors stood open. The usual herald was absent, but we could hear voices inside

—not the usual cacophony of court chatter, but a subdued murmur that cut off abruptly as we entered.

The throne room was filled with Sunneva's nobility, but the atmosphere was tense. Without the lively revelry, the nobles stood in small clusters having hushed conversations. Their eyes tracked us as we walked down the center aisle, a mixture of fear and contempt followed our every step. There were very few ladies who still looked upon Oryn with adoration, none more so than Ingrid, whose face lit up as if her long lost love had returned to her. She went to take a step towards us until her eyes locked onto my murderous glare. With a huff, she twisted away, but not before one last longing look at the object of her desires.

At the far end, the king sat upon his throne, looking older than I remembered. Beside him, on the queen's throne, sat Trinity. She wore a gown of gold, her obsidian hair elaborately styled with a delicate crown nestled within it. Her lips curved into a satisfied smile as she watched our approach.

We were brought to stand before the golden thrones, our guards spreading out around us. The newfound space left us exposed, vulnerable—a sensation made worse by the iron bracelets that diluted our natural defenses. With eyes constantly on us, I hadn't yet pilfered a weapon.

But I had agreed to behave and to do whatever Trinity asked of me willingly. I could live with it, reconcile it as I had with every assassination I'd completed. What I couldn't survive was knowing my mates were hurt, or killed, and it would be my fault.

I refused to watch another loved one fall.

The king rose, arms outstretched in a gesture of welcome that was as warm as his smile—frigid.

"My son," he boomed, his voice carrying throughout the hall. "And his lovely wife. How pleased we are to welcome you home to Sunneva."

Oryn's jaw tightened beside me, but he remained silent.

"And of course," the king continued, his gaze sliding to Kyler, "the guard's captain. Our soldiers will surely flourish under your command once again."

A murmur rippled through the crowd. I caught snippets of whispered conspiracies.

The king raised a hand, silencing the whispers. "I know there have been distressing rumors circulating about recent events at court. Rumors that my son and his mate were somehow involved in the tragic passing of our beloved queen."

My heart pounded against my ribs. Was he actually going to admit to killing her? Or did he plan to serve his own son on a spit in the most public way possible?

"I wish to put these rumors to rest once and for all. They are false. Nothing more than childish gossip." The king's voice grew stern. "A sudden illness—a condition that was mistakenly attributed to poisoning, is what took our queen from us. The true cause of her death was lost within the confusion and grief that followed."

Beside me, Oryn choked in disbelief. I slipped my hand into his and squeezed. It was the only thing I could do to show him that I knew the truth, and would never let his mother's death be in vain.

"The physicians have since confirmed her illness, and I will not have my son slandered by baseless accusations." The king's gaze swept the room. "He and his wife departed the capital to grieve in private, as was their right. Now they have returned."

The murmuring began once more. Some nobles nodded in apparent acceptance; others exchanged skeptical glances. I searched the crowd and found Davian, Oryn's little brother, seated off to the side. Hollow eyes stared off, focused on demons only he could see. Where there was once a confident young man, now sat a ghost of the smiling kid I once knew.

"Therefore," the king continued, "I am pleased to formally welcome

Prince Oryn and Princess Alora back to court. May our empire blossom with your return."

More murmurs, louder this time. I caught a noblewoman openly glaring at us, her hand clutching her husband's arm with white-knuckled intensity.

"As for our captain," the king added, "it brings me great pleasure to announce his true identity. Due to the ongoing war, it was too dangerous, you see, to reveal himself to be working against his homeland. But now that we are in a place to offer him sanctuary while we rebuild the empire, I'd like to introduce to you Prince Kyler of Esmeray. Over the years, we have worked together to merge the kingdoms to stop the war, and soon that day will come. He will be our esteemed ally for as long as he wishes to remain."

Kyler's expression didn't change despite the lively applause. I wished I knew how he was handling his identity being revealed so callously and to be painted as a traitor to his own people in the process. The king's story of a secret alliance could be devastating to Esmeray. I hoped his people would see past the poisonous fabrications of the boastful king. I wondered if this was his way of saving face or if it were simply a story Trinity whispered in his eager ear like sweet venom.

"And now," the king said, his voice softening as he turned to Trinity, "I have the great pleasure of introducing you all to our new queen."

Trinity rose gracefully, extending her hand to the king. He took it, pressing a kiss to her knuckles with a tenderness that made my stomach turn.

"We were married in a private ceremony only a few days ago," the king announced. "A union that will strengthen our kingdom in these uncertain times."

Murmurs of surprise and sharp hushes fell over the crowd of nobility, many faces appeared unsure, while others forced smiles. One by one, the nobles dropped to a deep bow, until we were the only ones left standing except for the guards.

The air surrounding us felt lethal. Oryn's rage was palpable as he gripped my hand to keep himself under control.

Trinity's smile was pure triumph as she gazed out at the crowd.

"I look forward to serving Sunneva as its queen," she said, "and to healing the rifts that have divided us for too long. You may rise, your loyalty has been shown in earnest."

The nobles straightened up and applauded her pretty words. Several hands remained conspicuously still.

I glanced at Kyler, whose stoic face covered his true thoughts like a well practiced mask. He met my eyes briefly, a silent message passing between us: Trinity had engineered herself into the position.

She killed a queen in cold blood and then took the place of another. Yet she still sought to mess with the affairs of gods.

The king commanded the room's attention once again. "Let us adjourn to the dining hall. A feast has been prepared to celebrate this joyous occasion."

I nearly sagged with relief. Maybe we'd have a moment to breathe, to strategize among the relative chaos of a formal dinner.

But as the king moved to step down from the dais, Trinity placed a hand on his arm. "One moment, darling," she said. "There is one more matter to address."

The king paused, looking momentarily confused before nodding. "Of course, my queen."

Trinity stepped forward, her gilded dress caught the light like a thousand tiny suns. "Before we celebrate the return of our prince and princess, there is one small matter of business to conclude." Her gaze swept over the assembled nobles. "Our enemies still lurk within the shadows, threatening the greatness of Sunneva. But the sun's light will reveal the threats that lurk among us." She turned toward one of the side entrances. "Guard," she called out. "Bring forth the traitor."

The creak of a door was accompanied by the stomp of the stone soldiers. Two of them carried a lanky figure between them, a muddied rucksack covered the prisoner's head. They tossed the unfortunate soul at our feet.

"Our own capital harbored this man who fed information across our borders, helping our enemy. Rest assured, there will be one less obstacle on our path to greatness before the night is over." She gestured toward the crumbled man. The nearest guard lumbered toward him, yanking the sack off his head.

My blood turned to ice.

If I had eaten, the contents of my stomach would be coating the floor.

Battered and bruised, Augustus showed no sign of reaction as the crowd gasped. Despite the beating he took, his face was still recognizable.

The guard forced him up. He was only an arm's length from where we stood. My brain still couldn't comprehend the reality before me. Augustus here in the flesh, and painted as a traitor. I had hoped Vanya would have whisked him away somewhere safe. Just where had the old bookshop owner gone that brought him back here to be another decoration on the king's grand wall of death?

"You may leave as we deliver justice to this wretched man." She ordered the room. The room had gone quiet, with nothing but the sound of shuffled steps as the nobles filed out.

I waited to be escorted out, to be forced to leave my ally, the grumpy man who had pretended to be my beloved uncle. But no one came.

Once the room had emptied except for the royal family and its guards, Trinity glided down from the dais towards me.

"Daughter," she regarded me, her cold hands captured my own, one digit playfully tapped my new jewelry. "I have decided to bestow the honor of protecting our kingdom onto you." She raised one hand and, with a snap of her fingers, the guard beside me held out their sword.

They offered the sword to me. They meant for me to use it.

"Now, I don't think I need to remind you what's at stake," she smirked. Our personal guard detail closed in on Kyler and Oryn.

No, I could never forget what was at stake.

With shaky fingers, I took the weapon and slowly brought myself closer to Augustus. For the first time, he didn't regard me with his usual snark. No, the will to fight had left this man who looked at me with nothing but regret.

His lips parted with a whispering wheeze.

"It's alright, lass," his words were barely audible. "It's... alr..." His chest shook as a fit of coughs overtook him. It didn't matter whether I followed through with Trinity's plan or not; he was already dying.

But would he forgive me for what I was about to do?

I looked to Kyler and Oryn once more, hoping they could forgive me, too. Turning back to Augustus, I raised my blade.

"I'm so sorry," I whispered to him. A lump caught in my throat and I fought back angry tears.

I held his gaze for one more moment, that seemed to stretch on forever. Then, I plunged the sword into his chest. A swift death was the only comfort I could provide him. The hilt slipped from my fingertips as he crumbled to the floor, his blood pooled at my feet.

Despite feeling betrayed by them, I sent a silent prayer to Death, demanding there be sunflowers greeting the old man when he reunited with the woman he loved.

CHAPTER 23

The blade hit the floor with a clatter that echoed through the silent throne room. Blood soaked the hem of my gown and spread like a crimson river across the marble floor. Augustus's eyes—once full of gruff wisdom and kindness—stared unseeing at the vaulted ceiling.

I turned to Trinity, my jaw clenched so tight my teeth might shatter.

"How does this benefit you?" I asked, my voice deceptively calm. "The blood of old men who sell books?" I gestured at the growing pool at my feet. "I hope your new kingdom rebels once they see how much blood you're eager to spill."

Trinity's smile faltered for a fraction of a second before returning, wider and more venomous.

"Careful, daughter. I can always find more of your little friends for you to kill." She trailed a finger down my cheek. "Though I must say, you do it so efficiently. Like you were made to deliver death."

I recoiled from her touch and stepped back toward Kyler and Oryn. In an instant, Oryn's arms wrapped around me, drawing me against his chest. His hands trembled against my back.

"It's not your fault," he whispered into my hair, too low for anyone else to hear.

The king descended from the dais, his nose wrinkling in disgust as he skirted the pooling blood. "Have this cleaned up immediately," he ordered one of the guards. "We can't have the blood seeping into the hall."

"Of course, we wouldn't want anything to spoil your appetite," I muttered.

The king's eyes flashed with rage, but Trinity placed a calming hand on his arm.

"Pay her no mind, my darling. She's merely having a tantrum." She beamed at me. "But she did wonderfully, didn't she? Such devotion to Sunneva. So willing to cut down any traitor in her path."

The king's anger faded under her attention, and he nodded offering her his arm. "Indeed. Let us celebrate our union and the return of my son and his... companions."

Guards moved in to escort us from the throne room. I couldn't look back at Augustus's body as we left. I'd seen enough death to last lifetimes, but this one will leave a scar.

Could Vanya ever forgive me? Or should I expect to see her while she delivers my last rites?

The corridors passed in a blur. I was vaguely aware of Kyler and Oryn flanking me, their bodies creating a protective barrier between me and the rest of the world. But I wasn't truly there. My mind had retreated somewhere far away, somewhere safe where I didn't have to feel the weight of what I'd done.

Another name added to my ledger. A death that would weigh on my conscience.

"Lor," Kyler's voice came from somewhere far away. "Stay with us."

I nodded on instinct, but my thoughts remained fragmented. The dining hall doors loomed ahead, the sound of forced merriment filtering through.

We entered the grand hall, where tables had been arranged in a horseshoe shape. The king and Trinity sat at the center of the main table, with places clearly marked for us nearby. The nobles who remained at court filled the other seats, their conversations hushed and strained.

"Your Highnesses," a servant bowed, gesturing to our seats.

I moved without conscious thought, taking my place between Kyler and Oryn. The plate before me gleamed with golden trim, the goblet filled with deep red wine that reminded me too much of the blood still drying on my dress.

"Eat something," Oryn murmured, placing a small portion of roasted meat on my plate. "You need your strength."

I stared at the food, unable to imagine putting anything in my mouth. My hands remained folded in my lap, one thumb absentmindedly tracing the cold iron of the bracelet circling my wrist.

Trinity's laughter rang out from the head of the table, artificially bright as she charmed the nobles seated near her. The king watched her with fascination, hanging on her every word.

"Are you there, Princess?" Kyler asked quietly, his shoulder pressing against mine.

I blinked, trying to focus on his face. "I'm here."

But I wasn't. Not really. I was back in that throne room, watching the life drain from Augustus's face. Even if he wasn't my real uncle, he may as well been. Then I was in Oakston with Magnus, holding him as he died in my arms. And in Briarwood facing Maël as he turned to ash.

Death clung to me like a plague.

Kyler's hand found mine under the table. "We're going to get out of here," he promised.

Across the table, Davian sat in silence, pushing food around his plate. Our eyes met briefly, and I saw my own haunted expression mirrored in his. Was this what he'd been surviving since his mother's demise?

Servants brought course after course. Platters of delicacies that once would have made my mouth water but now turned my stomach. The nobles ate and drank, their initial tension gradually dissolving as the wine flowed freely.

"A toast!" The king rose suddenly, lifting his goblet. "To my beautiful new queen, who has brought such joy to Sunneva in these troubled times."

The court raised their glasses in unison. "To Queen Trinity."

I lifted my untouched goblet, not quite bringing it to my lips.

"And to the return of my son and his princess," the king added, almost as an afterthought. "May they serve Sunneva proudly." His eyes gleamed with malice as they met mine.

More toasts followed. Cheers to the prosperity of the kingdom. Cries of victory against their enemies. They ended the toasts with declarations of the sun-blessed future that awaited them all.

Each proclamation rang hollow in my ears. The voices around me muddled into meaningless noise. I caught fragments of conversation —nervous speculation about absent nobles, hushed concerns about the stone soldiers patrolling the castle, or of flattery directed at the new queen to earn her favor.

"You need to eat," Oryn whispered, his breath warm against my ear.

"I can't," I whispered.

Kyler shifted beside me, his body tensing. "As much as I hate this, we need to appear normal," he said, his voice so low I barely caught it. "All eyes are on us."

He was right. Even as conversations swirled around the hall, I could feel the weight of wary gazes. Nobles watching us from the corners of their eyes, servants lingering longer than necessary when refilling our goblets.

I forced myself to pick up a piece of bread, tearing off a small corner and placing it on my tongue.

It tasted like ash.

"A bit more," Oryn encouraged, his hand finding my knee under the table.

I managed a few more bites, washing them down with water instead of wine. The food sat like stones in my stomach.

Trinity held court from her seat, gesturing animatedly as she regaled those nearby with a tale that had them hanging on her every word. The king showered her with affection, more than the former queen ever received.

"Do you think Augustus would forgive me?" I asked suddenly, my voice barely audible.

Oryn's hand tightened on my knee. "Don't do this to yourself, Lor."

"He was already on his deathbed when they brought him in," Kyler added grimly. "You ended his suffering, and I'm sure he was grateful it came swiftly."

But the words brought no comfort. I had killed a friend to save my mates. The justification felt hollow, even if the alternative was unthinkable.

As the main courses were cleared and desserts brought out, movement at the edge of the hall caught my attention. A woman in a green gown detached herself from the group of nobles and made her way toward our table. Her brown hair elaborately styled, gems woven through the braids crowning her head.

Ingrid.

Despite the last time she crossed our path, I recognized the calculating gleam in her eyes. She paused behind Oryn's chair, her hand coming to rest on his shoulder with familiar ease.

"My prince," she purred, leaning down so her lips nearly brushed his ear. "How my heart soared when I heard of your return! The court has been worried about you."

Oryn stiffened under her touch but maintained his composure. "Lady Ingrid. I see you've forgotten my warning the last time you thought to lay your hands on me."

She laughed, a practiced, musical sound. "There is nothing you can do to me here. You see, I've gained favor with our new queen. I believe she sees me as a daughter of sorts." Her fingers traced small circles on his shoulder as she spoke.

I watched with detached interest, as if observing a scene from far away. Some distant part of me recognized I should feel jealousy or anger, but those emotions seemed locked behind a wall of ice.

"You look tired, my prince," Ingrid continued, her voice dripping with false concern. "Perhaps you need more... attentive care than you've been receiving." Her eyes flicked dismissively toward me. "I'm sure the queen wouldn't mind moving me to the room beside yours so I can attend to your needs."

Oryn removed her hand from his shoulder. "I assure you I'm well cared for, by my *wife*. Maybe you should ask your queen for a room beside hers, since you seem so close."

Undeterred, Ingrid shifted her attention to Kyler. "And Prince Kyler, what an unexpected turn of events!" She dipped into a curtsy that displayed more of her cleavage than was proper. "I'd be honored to show you our kingdom's newest... delights."

Kyler regarded her with cool indifference. "I'm familiar enough with Sunneva, thank you."

"But surely you never had the time to really enjoy it," she persisted, her hand now trailing down his arm. "Being the captain was a busy job, I'm sure it left you with no time to spare. I could help you enjoy what we have to offer in a much more... intimate way."

Something cracked inside me. The numbness that had encased me since Augustus's death shattered like thin ice under too much weight. Heat rushed through my veins, chasing away the cold detachment.

"Remove your hand," I said, my voice low but carrying enough that nearby conversations faltered.

Ingrid turned to me with feigned innocence. "Princess Alora, I was merely—"

"Remove. Your. Hand." Each word fell like a stone. "Unless you'd like me to remove it for you. Permanently."

Ingrid's fingers jerked away from Kyler's arm. "I was simply being hospitable to our distinguished guest."

"No, you were pawing at my mates like a cat in heat." I rose from my seat, the chair scraping loudly against the floor. The dining hall quieted as heads turned our way. "Let me make something perfectly clear, Lady Ingrid. Touch either of them again, and you'll find yourself with more than just fewer fingers."

Her face flushed an ugly red. "How dare you threaten me? I am the daughter of—"

"I don't care if you're the daughter of a king." I leaned closer, dropping my voice so only those nearest could hear. "I've already killed one person today. Shall we make it two?"

Fear flashed in her eyes as she took a step back. "You're unhinged," she hissed. "Claiming another man as your mate when your husband is right there. You're unworthy of your title."

"Perhaps," I agreed, a cold smile spreading across my face. "But at least I'm not pathetic enough to continually throw myself at men who have never wanted me. Maybe if you weren't such a whore, you would've found a proper husband by now."

Ingrid retreated, nearly tripping over her gown in her haste to put distance between us. Conversations resumed around the hall, though now with a new undercurrent of tension.

I sank back into my chair, the burst of anger leaving me as quickly as it had come. But the numbness didn't return. Instead, I felt every emotion I'd been suppressing—grief, rage, guilt—crashing over me like a tidal wave.

Kyler's hand found mine under the table, his fingers interlacing with mine. "Thank the gods, I thought you were truly gone for a moment there," he murmured.

On my other side, Oryn's lips twitched in a barely suppressed smile. "I'm not sure what I enjoyed more. You tormenting the girl or publicly claiming both of us while putting the fear of death in her eyes."

"It was stupid," I whispered, though I couldn't bring myself to regret it. "I shouldn't have drawn attention. And now we'll surely be all everyone talks about."

"Our names would pass their lips regardless," Kyler said, "it was inevitable."

From across the hall, Trinity watched me with narrowed eyes, her perfect composure momentarily disrupted. I met her gaze steadily, letting her see that her puppet strings had frayed.

I might have killed for her today, but I wouldn't be her weapon forever. And when the time came to turn the blade—I'd be ready.

CHAPTER 24

No one spoke to us for the rest of the evening. The nobility went back to their frivolous conversations while becoming drunker with each passing moment. No one blinked when the stony guards came to escort us to our room. They continued their revelry, and at some point, a few were dancing on the tables.

It was a blessing to be able to leave the rowdy crowd, but our journey through the halls felt endless. The deep thud of the golem's feet was a steady rhythm almost in time with my heart.

Still, Augustus haunted me. Was there not something more I could've done for him? I was Death's Wraith, surely I could have liberated all of us from this golden prison. So why did I feel so helpless, so utterly lost?

A sudden shove broke my thoughts.

"The queen demands you stay inside," one of the guards ordered as he pushed me, Kyler, and Oryn inside Oryn's room. "Do not leave."

The heavy oak door closed behind us with a final thud. We stood in tense silence, listening to the retreating footsteps of our escorts. Only when they had faded completely did the tension ease.

Kyler prowled the perimeter of the room, checking the windows despite knowing they'd been sealed. His shoulders were tight, the muscles in his back bunching beneath the fine silk shirt they'd provided. "They've thought of everything," he muttered, running his fingers along the windowsill. "These are sealed with both magic and iron."

"How can something be of magic and iron?" I asked. "I thought one cancels out the other."

"It seems like they've found a way," Kyler sighed.

Oryn had gone straight to the hearth, stoking the fire to chase away the chill that had settled in my bones. "At least they've left us alone for now."

I stood frozen in the center of the room, blood still crusted my feet. Augustus's blood. I couldn't take my eyes away from the parts of my gown that had turned dark, a reminder of what I'd done.

"Lor." Kyler's voice cut through my spiraling thoughts. He crossed the room in three long strides, taking my hand in his. "Look at me."

I raised my eyes to his, finding no condemnation there, only concern.

"You did what you had to do," he murmured. "Augustus knew that, and I would've made the same choice."

"I killed him," I whispered. "He was my friend, and I killed him."

Oryn appeared at my side, his hand warm against the small of my back. "You gave him mercy. You saved him from a slow, painful death."

The truth of his words did nothing to ease the hollow ache in my chest. I pulled away from them both, wrapping my arms around myself. "How many more will die because of me? Magnus, Lucas, Augustus... who's next?"

The feelings I've shoved down bubbled to the surface, taking hold of all of my senses and causing me to crouch, holding my knees as I sobbed. The ache in my chest only grew as I cried for them, for my friends.

"They would still be here if it weren't for me," each word tumbled out broken between sobs. "It should have been me instead."

"None of this is your fault," Kyler insisted.

"Isn't it?" My face lifted towards them, my voice breaking. "Trinity wants me. And I agreed to help her. I might as well have signed everyone's death warrant."

"You agreed because she backed you into a corner," Oryn countered. He crouched beside me, gently unwinding one of my hands from my leg to draw me back up. "That doesn't mean we've given up."

The blood on my hands seemed to burn. "I need to wash," I said abruptly, turning toward the bathroom. Washing away the evidence of what I'd done was the only thing I cared about in this moment, the only thing I could do right now. I needed to be clean, even if I could never truly cleanse my conscience.

I'd barely made it three steps when Kyler caught my wrist, his touch gentle despite its firmness. "Let us help you," he said, his dark eyes holding mine.

Something in his gaze broke through the fog of guilt and grief that threatened to consume me. I nodded silently, allowing him to lead me toward the bathroom where water steamed in the large copper tub. Miss Gregoria must have had the servants filling baths before everyone returned from the meal.

Oryn followed, closing the door behind us. Without a word, he began to work at the fastenings of my blood-stained dress while Kyler removed my shoes. Their movements were synchronized, practiced from our earlier bath, but this was filled with tenderness rather than necessity.

"Arms up," Oryn murmured, and I complied, letting him pull the silk over my head. The fabric made a soft sound as it hit the floor, quickly followed by my undergarments.

I stood naked between them, shaking, vulnerable in every sense of the word. Kyler's fingers traced the iron bracelet on my wrist, his jaw tight with anger.

"We'll find a way to remove these," he promised, pressing a kiss to my pulse point.

Oryn guided me to the tub, his hands steady as I stepped into the warm water. The heat enveloped me as I sank down, my muscles relaxing despite the turmoil in my mind.

Kyler rolled up his sleeves and knelt beside the tub, taking a cloth and soap in hand. He began with my hands, gently scrubbing away the blood that stained them, treating each finger with reverent care.

"Close your eyes," Oryn instructed softly from behind me. I felt his fingers in my hair, working through the tangles before pouring warm water over my head.

They worked in silence, washing away the physical remnants of the day. I surrendered to their ministrations, letting their touch anchor me to the present when my mind threatened to drag me back to that throne room.

"I keep seeing his face," I whispered, my voice barely audible over the gentle lapping of water. "The moment the blade went in... he looked relieved."

Kyler paused, his hands stilling on my arm. "He saw the end of his suffering."

"It doesn't make it right."

"No," Oryn agreed, his fingers massaging my scalp. "Nothing about this situation is right. But you are not the villain here, Love."

I leaned back against the edge of the tub, looking up at them both. "Aren't I though? I'm the one who wielded the blade. I leave nothing but death in my wake."

"You're not," Kyler said. "You're the hero who's saved countless lives, including my own."

"Well, you did kidnap me," Oryn added with a wink. My eyes rolled as Kyler let a deep chuckle slip. Oryn brushed a hand down my cheek, bringing it further down until it rested on my heart. "Nothing Trinity says or demands of you will ever change the good that's inside you."

A tear slipped down my cheek, followed quickly by another. "I'm so tired of losing people," I admitted. "I'm tired of fighting and losing."

"Then let us fight for you," Kyler said, wiping away my tears with his thumb. "Let us keep your demons away."

I looked between them, these two men who had become my entire world, even despite the many times I tried to resist them. Thanks to the iron on my wrist, our bond was dulled, but it couldn't fully erase how connected the three of us were. "Please," I whispered. "Help me forget... just for a little while."

Something shifted in the air between us, the tenderness giving way to a different kind of intensity. Kyler's eyes darkened as he leaned forward to capture my lips in a searing kiss that stole my breath. His hand cradled my jaw, tilting my head back to deepen the connection.

Behind me, Oryn's lips found my neck, trailing fire along my skin. "We've got you," he murmured against my pulse.

Water sloshed over the edge of the tub as they lifted me out, quickly drying me with towels before they carried me to the bed. My skin prickled with goosebumps, not from cold but from the heat in their eyes as they laid me on the silk sheets.

They shed their clothes with swift efficiency, their bodies soon pressing against mine from both sides. Skin against skin, hearts beating in a rhythm that seemed to synchronize with every touch.

"You don't know how much I longed to have you like this," Kyler breathed, his fingers tracing the curve of my hip. "You're so fucking beautiful."

Oryn's mouth found my breast, drawing a gasp from my lips as pleasure sparked through me. "We're going to worship you," he said against my skin. "Let us remind you who you belong to."

And they did. With every kiss, every caress, every whispered word of devotion, they reminded me how they owned every single part of me. Kyler's hands mapped my body like he was memorizing every curve, every dip, every place that made me gasp. Oryn's mouth followed, trailing fire wherever it touched.

I surrendered to them, letting each sensation wash away the things that haunted me. There was no room for guilt, fear or doubt in the space they created—only pleasure and connection and a fierce, burning love that consumed everything else.

They consumed my soul and rebuilt it piece by piece until all that was left was them, their souls tied to mine. All that remained was us.

When Kyler finally moved above me, his body joining with mine in one smooth thrust, I cried out his name. His forehead pressed against mine, our breaths mingling as he held me tightly to him, moving with deliberate slowness, drawing out each sensation.

"I dreamed of this," he confessed, his voice rough with emotion. "Every night in that cell, I dreamed of holding you again."

Oryn's hand found mine, squeezing tight as he watched us with hungry eyes. "Are you going to give your mate what he's been missing?"

As the pressure began to build, the friction of our bodies brought me to that edge, threatening to throw me off. "Y-yes," I stammered. "Just don't stop."

"Never, Love. We'll never stop when it comes to you."

The world narrowed to just the three of us. When Kyler and I found our release together, his name tore from my throat in a sob of pure elation. And when he rolled to my side, Oryn took his place.

"Already so wet, Love. I bet you can't wait to be filled and dripping from both of us." He placed a hand between my legs, collecting what was already seeping out of me and using two fingers to shove it back in. His vulgar words caused a mewl to escape me as my body squeezed around his thick digits.

Kyler's hand stroked my hair. "I think she needs more than your fingers, Ryn."

Oryn tsked. "Such a greedy mate, no wonder the gods blessed her with us."

He removed his fingers only to replace them with his even thicker cock. Slowly, he stretched me, giving my body a moment to adjust to the sudden shift until he was fully seated.

"Fuck, you feel amazing," he sighed, his hips starting a rhythm that had my back arching off the bed.

"Our perfect mate," Kyler mused. He shifted to his knees just beside my head and pulled my chin towards him as I let out a deep moan. "Open your mouth, Alora."

The command shot more heat down to my core as I locked eyes with him while opening for him. The taste of the two of us overwhelmed me as he slid himself against my tongue until he was hitting the back of my throat. My mates alternated. When one thrust in, the other pulled out. Drool dribbled down my chin with every muffled moan around Kyler's length, but I didn't care. I only wanted more. Oryn brought a thumb to my clit, massaging that bundle of nerves while hitting that sweet spot inside me.

"Let go for us, Love." Oryn growled.

And I did. Stars burst from behind my eyes while Oryn moaned my name as he pumped into me. After I rode the aftershocks of pleasure, both slid out of me, praising me while I caught my breath. Kyler disappeared into the bathroom only to emerge a moment later with a cloth. They cleaned me up before cleaning themselves. The bed bounced when they collapsed beside me afterward.

As we lay tangled together, sweat cooling on our skin, reality began to creep back in. The iron bracelets still encircled our wrists, cold against our flushed skin.

"We need to find a way out of here," I said.

Kyler pressed a kiss to my shoulder. "We will."

Oryn sat up, his eyes scanning the room. "We need to find something to get these damn things off." He lifted his wrist, the iron bracelet glinting dully in the firelight.

We separated reluctantly, dressing in simple clothes before beginning our search of the room. We checked every drawer, every hidden corner, and every loose floorboard we could find. Kyler even went so far as to dismantle part of the bed frame, looking for anything sharp enough to pry them open, or something that could shatter them entirely.

"Nothing," he finally said, frustration evident in his voice. "They've been thorough."

Oryn sat heavily on the edge of the bed. "We may have to leave them on, at least for tonight. We'll wait for an opportunity."

I leaned against the windowsill, gazing out at the night sky through the sealed glass. "We may not have that luxury. It feels like any day now Trinity can fetch me for her ritual."

"Soon," Kyler said with certainty. "She's confident, almost too much. It feels like the odds are stacked in her favor."

The weight of what was coming settled over us like a shroud. I crossed the room to sit between them, drawing strength from their presence.

"Whatever happens," I said, taking their hands in mine, "we stay together. We'll find a way to stop her."

They nodded, determination hardening their features. No more words were needed as we curled together on the bed, fully clothed but somehow more intimate than before. My head rested on Kyler's chest, his heartbeat steady beneath my ear. Oryn pressed against my back, his arm thrown protectively over both of us.

Exhaustion claimed me quickly, pulling me into a dreamless sleep. The last thought I had before darkness took me was that at least we were together. Whatever horrors awaited us tomorrow, we would face them as one.

The door crashed open with a bang that jolted me from sleep. Sunlight streamed through the windows, momentarily blinding me as I sat upright, disoriented.

"The queen requires your presence," a stone guard announced, his voice echoing unnaturally in the room.

Kyler and Oryn were already on their feet, positioning themselves between me and the intruder. The guard remained impassive, his rocky features betraying no emotion.

"Give her a moment to dress properly," Oryn demanded.

"Now," the guard insisted, stepping further into the room. "The vessel comes with me now."

My blood ran cold at the word 'vessel.' I rose from the bed, straightening my rumpled clothes. "It's alright," I told my mates, though it was anything but. "I'll go."

"Like hell you will," Kyler growled, his body coiled tight with tension. "Not alone."

The guard took another step forward. "Only the vessel."

"Her name is Alora," Oryn snapped.

I placed a hand on each of their arms. "I'll be fine," I said with more confidence than I felt. "I agreed to cooperate, remember? This is part of the deal."

Kyler's eyes burned into mine. "If she hurts you—"

"She won't," I cut him off, knowing full well that the likelihood of being a part of Trinity's sinister games was almost assured. "Not if she needs me for her ritual."

The logic seemed to reach him, though the muscle in his jaw twitched. Oryn looked no less pleased but nodded reluctantly.

"We'll be waiting," he promised.

I squeezed their hands one last time before turning to the guard. "Lead the way."

As I followed the stone soldier from the room, I felt their eyes on my back. Two men who would tear the world apart to find me while I doomed it to save them.

Whatever Trinity had planned for me, I would endure it. I would play along, bide my time, and find a way to turn her own game against her. Because I was never fighting for myself.

I was fighting for us. For all of us.

And even gods should fear what I would do to keep my mates safe.

CHAPTER 25

The stone golem led me through the gilded corridors. More banners replaced what used to be the ornate furnishings, blood red with that twisted symbol. We passed guard after guard—both stone and fae—their eyes followed our every step.

We descended a staircase I'd never noticed before, hidden behind the sharp curve of one of the lesser traveled halls. The air grew cooler with each step, the thick scent of dampness mingled with something... unnatural. The flickering torch in the golem's hand cast long shadows that danced across the narrow walls. If I had access to my powers, I could've made those shadows swallow me whole and sneak us out of here. After facing Candra, I could've also used them to shove this guard down these steps.

It was a nice thought, imagining him tumbling forward, his stony limbs hitting each step, but with my magic bound, it remained nothing but a fantasy.

At the bottom of the stairs stretched a long corridor lined with iron doors. Most were closed, but from behind one came the faint sound of weeping. I shuddered, wondering what poor soul languished there.

The golem stopped before the last door and pushed it open, revealing a chamber that froze the air in my lungs.

A laboratory stretched before me, larger than seemed possible given its underground location. Tables covered with glass vials, tubes, and strange instruments filled the space. Shelves lined the walls, holding jars of substances I couldn't identify—some glowed faintly in shades of blue and green, others seemed to move of their own accord.

But it was the centerpiece that froze the blood in my veins.

A metal table dominated the room's center. Thick leather straps hung from its sides, and channels carved into its surface led to collection bottles at the bottom.

I'd seen this table before. Not this exact one, perhaps, but the Alchemist had strapped me to one just like it, cut into me, and harvested my blood for their experiments.

My lungs seized and my vision narrowed as the memories of the past haunted the present. I could almost feel the cold of the metal against my back, the restraints digging against my wrists and ankles, and the sharp burn of needles.

"You're late," Trinity's voice cut through my rising panic.

She stood at a workbench across the room, her back to me as she arranged bottles of brightly colored liquids. Her hair was pulled back in a tight bun, and she'd traded her royal finery for a simple black robe with tight sleeves.

"The princes were reluctant to let her go," the golem reported.

Trinity turned, her lips curving into a smile that made her eyes shine with malice. "I'm sure they were." She approached me, circling slowly like a predator assessing its prey. "But you followed my orders beautifully today, just as you had yesterday. Augustus's death was... efficient. I appreciate efficiency, though I do wish there had been more dramatics."

My stomach churned at the memory of the blade sliding into Augustus, the way his blood had pooled at my feet.

"I didn't have a choice," I said flatly.

"No, you didn't." Her smile widened. "And you don't have one now either. On the table, please."

The stone guard's hand closed around my upper arm, but I shook it off. "I can walk."

Each step toward that table felt like wading through quicksand. My heart hammered against my ribs, memories of another time threatening to overwhelm me.

A bottle on a nearby shelf caught my eye—a familiar deep purple liquid that pulsed with its own inner light. I was certain it was the exact same concoction the Alchemist had injected into me before. Next to it sat a jar filled with what looked like liquid darkness, swirling and coiling like living smoke. I'd seen that too, in the moments before they—

"Is there a problem?" Trinity's voice was sharp with impatience.

I forced my legs to move, approaching the table with wooden steps. As she adjusted instruments on a small tray beside the table, bands of jagged ink decorated Trinity's exposed forearm, their harsh lines a barely visible green. The markings looked eerily similar to those that had covered the Alchemist's skin.

"It was you," I whispered, the realization hitting me like a physical blow. "The Alchemist worked for you."

Trinity paused, her head tilting slightly. "He... assisted me. Poor thing, failed his first ever real taste of power." She gestured to the table. "Lie down."

My body refused to obey. The mere thought of being strapped to that table sent tremors through my limbs. Images flashed behind my eyes—needles piercing skin, blood flowing through tubes, pain lancing through my body as I was injected with who knows what. Being in and out of consciousness was the worst part. What had they done to me without my knowledge?

"I said, lie down." Trinity's voice hardened to steel.

The golem moved behind me, its stone hands pressing heavily on my shoulders. With one push from him, I'd be forced onto the table.

"I'll cooperate," I said quickly, twisting away from the guard's touch. "Just... no restraints. Please."

Trinity considered me for a moment, then nodded. "Very well. As long as you remain still."

I forced myself onto the table, the coolness of the metal surface seeping through my clothes. My muscles tensed involuntarily, preparing for pain that hadn't yet come. The flickering light from the candles surrounded the room with an eerie glow.

Trinity stepped towards me, looking down at me with calculating eyes. "This won't hurt," she said, surprising me with her false gentleness. "Not today at least. I simply need a fresh sample."

The false comfort evaporated as a cool, wet cloth wiped across the crook of my elbow. The sharp pinch of a needle followed, and I forced my face not to react, not to flinch. Warm blood flowed from my veins into a glass vial that Trinity held with practiced hands.

"You know, he was once normal," she said. "A scholar obsessed with magic and gods. He's the one who introduced me to alchemy. After one experiment, his mind was never the same, altered just as his body had, but he still had his uses." She watched the flow with keen eyes. "Perfect," she murmured, removing the needle and pressing a cloth to the small puncture. "Hold this."

I pressed my fingers to the cloth while Trinity moved away, taking my blood to her workbench. The golem remained at my side, its blank stone face hovering at the edge of my vision.

"Is that what caused those marks on your arms?" I asked.

Trinity halted for a moment. "Yes," she answered. "There's a risk when working with such ancient magic. I was more fortunate not to be as close when everything turned. Rodrick, or The Alchemist, as you call him, was not so lucky. He was scarred much the same as I, but his entire flesh was consumed by it."

"Rodrick," I tested the name. How could my torturer have such a mundane name? Whenever I thought of *The Alchemist*, it was never without a touch of fear from what I lived through. But *Rodrick* was...

laughable. I was sure I had killed a Rodrick in some fleeting moment of my life, a different one.

"You know," Trinity called over her shoulder as she worked, "you should be honored. Few are capable of being vessels for the gods."

I sat up slowly, keeping the cloth pressed to my arm. "Why me?"

"Because you're special." She uncorked vials of colored liquids, adding drops of blood to each. "Your power signature is... unique. The perfect conduit for Chaos to enter this world."

"And what happens to me when Chaos enters?" I asked, though I feared I already knew the answer.

Trinity's shoulders shook with laughter. "Does it matter?"

I watched as she mixed my blood with various substances, each vial turning a different color when she was done. The final one glowed with an inner emerald light that pulsed like a heartbeat.

"The other gods cared little for us," she continued, her voice taking on a fervent edge. "Turned their backs on us. But Chaos loved his people. Everything we have to this day was a gift from Chaos. His return will be the end of all our struggles."

"And what does Chaos want in return?" I asked, trying to keep her talking while my eyes darted around the lab, cataloging anything that might be useful later. If only I knew what these concoctions were. Some bubbled in their bottles; others had dark bits floating in them. Glasses, bits of iron, and scrolls littered the tabletops.

"To restore balance." Trinity held the glowing vial up to the light, studying it with fascination. "The balance the other gods disrupted to begin with so they could leave this realm. He will give that power back to those who deserve it."

"The fae," I guessed.

"The worthy," she corrected. "Only they can save us from what we've become."

I thought of the nobles upstairs, of how many had already fled the castle. "And what about the kingdoms? I can't imagine what your husband will do with such power."

Trinity turned to me then, a sinister smirk playing on her lips. "Don't worry about him. His... usefulness... has done its part."

The implication hung heavy in the air. The king was a puppet, just as I was. But unlike me, he didn't know the strings were a noose around his neck.

"There," she said, setting down the last vial. "Initial tests confirm what I suspected." She wiped her hands on a cloth. "We'll continue tomorrow. Daily samples will be necessary as we approach the solstice."

"Solstice?" I echoed, my mind racing. That was less than two weeks away.

"The veil between worlds thins at the solstice." She approached me again, her eyes glittering with anticipation. "The perfect time for a god to cross over."

Fear clenched my gut, but I kept my expression neutral. Knowledge was power, and every moment in this laboratory gave me more of it.

"You're dismissed for now," Trinity said, waving a hand. "I'll see you at supper." She turned to the golem. "Take her back to her room. The princes have my permission to leave their chambers with supervision for now. Consider it a reward for your compliance, Alora."

The golem nodded its stone head and gestured for me to follow. I slid off the table on shaky legs, relief flooding through me at the prospect of escape from this chamber of horrors.

"Oh, and Alora?" Trinity called as I reached the door. "I expect the same level of cooperation tomorrow. Remember what's at stake."

The image of Augustus falling at my feet flashed before my eyes. I nodded stiffly and followed the golem out, my mind whirling with everything I'd learned.

The journey back through the winding corridors seemed shorter than before. With each step away from that laboratory, my breathing came easier, though the phantom sensation of cold metal biting into my arms lingered.

When we reached our chambers, the golem pushed open the door without announcement. I barely had a chance to step inside before strong arms engulfed me and the door was slammed shut in the stone soldier's face.

"Lor!" Kyler's voice was rough with relief as he pulled me against his chest. His hands roamed my arms, my back, my face, checking for injuries. "Are you hurt? What did she do to you?"

Before I could answer, Oryn was there too, his arms wrapping around both of us. "We were going out of our minds," he murmured against my hair. "You were gone for too long."

"I'm fine," I assured them, though the words felt hollow. "She just took some blood."

Kyler pulled back slightly, his eyes searching mine. "What else?" he demanded, seeing what was hidden under my carefully placed mask.

"The laboratory," I whispered, unable to keep the tremor from my voice. "It was like being back with the Alchemist. The same table, the same equipment. The same scent of wrongness and death. They were working together."

Understanding dawned in their eyes. Oryn's jaw tightened, and Kyler's arms tightened around me.

"She's planning something at the solstice," I continued, needing to share everything while it was fresh in my mind. "Something about Chaos crossing over. She needs my blood for it."

"The solstice is ten days from now," Oryn said grimly.

"Nine," Kyler corrected. "We don't have much time."

I leaned into their embrace, drawing strength from their warmth, their solidity. "We have a small advantage now. She's given us permission to leave these rooms with supervision."

"A tether is still a tether, no matter how long," Oryn muttered.

"But it's something," I insisted. "We can catalogue what's changed, shift rotations. Find the weak points."

Kyler nodded slowly, his tactical mind already working. "We

need to get these off first," he said, tapping the iron bracelet on my wrist. "Without our powers, we're vulnerable."

"We'll find a way," I promised, though I had no idea how. "We have to."

Oryn guided me to the sofa before the fireplace, pulling me down between them. Outside the windows, the afternoon sun gave the castle grounds a golden glow. I had been down there for hours.

"Tell us everything," he said. "Every detail you can remember about the laboratory, and about what Trinity said."

I closed my eyes, forcing myself to recall every moment of my time in that underground chamber. Each word Trinity had spoken, each vial on the shelves, each instrument on the tables. Knowledge was our only weapon now, and I would sharpen it as best I could.

Because in nine days, Trinity planned to bring a god into our world.

And I was the key that would unlock the door.

CHAPTER 26

The iron bracelet chafed against my wrist as we stepped into the hallway, flanked by our stone guardian. Despite being allowed out of our chambers, the freedom felt like another kind of cage—one with invisible bars and watchful eyes.

I threaded my arm through Oryn's as we began our carefully casual stroll through the palace. Kyler walked on my other side, his posture relaxed but his eyes constantly moving, cataloguing everything.

"The castle seems emptier," I observed, keeping my tone conversational. It wasn't just for show—the corridors echoed with our footsteps instead of the lively bustle they used to. "Do you think more nobles left?"

"If they were smart," Oryn replied, nodding to a passing servant who quickly averted her eyes, "yes. The only ones left no doubt value the king and new queen's favor over everything else."

We turned down the main corridor that led to the grand hall. Two stone soldiers stood motionless at each intersection, their blank faces betraying nothing as we passed. I counted silently. four intersections, eight golems, all positioned to control movement throughout the castle.

"Do you think they'll serve roasted chicken tonight?" Oryn asked loudly, obviously for our escort's benefit. "I'm starved."

I played along, summoning a smile that felt foreign on my face. "I'm sure they will, my love."

"If you're that hungry, we could just visit the kitchens." Kyler joined in. I felt the brush of his thumb stroking small circles on the back of my arm until he dropped his hand.

"I could use a bite to eat," I said.

Our guard remained impassive, seemingly uninterested in our quest for food. I noticed Oryn's eyes darting to the windows as we passed, noting which were sealed and which were merely latched.

The buzz of magic hung heavy in the air. How did the castle change so much in such a short amount of time?

We rounded another corner and collided with someone. A flash of green silk and elaborate braids disappeared behind a column, but not before I caught a glimpse of Ingrid's pinched face. She'd been watching us—probably hoping to catch Oryn alone.

Or perhaps it was me she stalked, determined to finish the job and force poison down my throat.

It was amusing how lofty her dreams were.

"Are you alright?" I asked Oryn, who brushed invisible remnants of the encounter off his shirt.

Oryn's face darkened. "That woman doesn't know when to quit."

I pictured her hands on him at dinner last night, her fingers trailing down Kyler's arm. The memory sent a fresh surge of anger through me. The fact that we were trapped in this castle with *her* didn't sit well.

"Maybe we should give her a reason to stay away," I suggested, a dangerous edge to my voice. "Since the threats we've given haven't sunk in."

Kyler looked towards the column and then turned back to me. His hands came up to cradle my face, forcing me to meet his eyes.

"She is the last thing you need to focus on. Save your energy for the real threats. Don't waste it being the villain in some hopeless girl's story."

He waited for me to nod before releasing me, only to hook a finger under my chin to press his lips against mine. The kiss deepened, his hands weaving into my hair as a small moan escaped me. Growls rumbled from both my mates as Kyler stepped away, a satisfied smirk on his face.

Warmth bloomed from my cheeks as I caught the breath that had been stolen so quickly. "What was that for?" I asked.

"I didn't need to be in your mind to tell you wanted to go after Ingrid. Since I can't strip you bare and kiss the place I know will ease your tension, this was the next best spot." He winked as he gestured toward the path we had been taking.

"Maybe we should do that anyway," Oryn whispered in my ear, eliciting a giggle from me. I grabbed onto his arm and allowed him to steer me from the spot. What my silly mates didn't realize was that I could hold a grudge. For a very, very long time.

We continued down the hall, passing the open doors to the library where empty shelves gaped like missing teeth. Several books had been cleared out, leaving nothing but dust.

Voices drifted from around the next corner. We slowed our pace, exchanging glances as Shefferd's nasal tones became distinguishable.

"—must be perfect, Miss Gregoria. The queen insists on the finest wines from the cellar. Nothing else will do for her first official banquet as queen."

We turned the corner to find Shefferd gesticulating wildly at the castle's head of staff. Miss Gregoria looked harried, her usually immaculate hair escaping its pins.

"Of course," she replied, her voice strained. "But with so many of the kitchen staff gone, I'm not certain—"

"Excuses!" Shefferd snapped. "The banquet is tomorrow night, and it will showcase the kingdom's strength and our monarch's perfect union." His eyes landed on us, widening slightly. "Ah, Your Highnesses. Out for some air?"

I forced a pleasant expression. "Just stretching our legs."

Miss Gregoria bobbed a curtsy, her eyes never quite meeting mine. "Prince Oryn, Princess Alora, Captain... I mean Prince Kyler. I trust you've been enjoying the day?"

"We have," Kyler replied, his jaw tightened. "Though I admit we're curious about this banquet."

Shefferd puffed up importantly. "A celebration of Their Majesties' union and the bright future of Sunneva. All nobility will attend." His eyes narrowed slightly. "As will you three, naturally. The queen specifically requested your presence."

"We wouldn't miss it," Oryn said dryly.

Shefferd nodded briskly. "Now, if you'll excuse me, there are countless details requiring my attention." He scurried off, but not without giving Miss Gregoria a sharp look.

The woman lingered, her hands fidgeting with her apron. "Is there... anything you require?" she asked, with a strange hesitation in her voice.

"Nothing at this moment," I answered, studying her. There was something in her eyes—fear, certainly, but something else too. Guilt? Regret? "Actually, have you seen Luella? I would prefer she be assigned to me once again. She knew my preferences."

Her face went white, but she controlled it quickly. "I'm afraid we had to let her go. She had an urgent family matter that needed her attention," she said.

An interesting lie for a girl who I knew fled this place.

"Alright, well that was all," I said, making a mental note to try to keep better tabs on the woman. She was hiding something, but what?

She nodded and hurried after Shefferd, leaving us alone with our silent guardian.

"Did you notice how many guards were posted in this section?" Kyler murmured as we continued walking.

"Four stone, two fae," Oryn replied. "Less than the other halls."

"They're concentrated near the exits," I observed. "And that staircase that leads to Trinity's laboratory."

We completed our circuit of the main floor, carefully noting guard positions and potential weaknesses. The golem followed without comment, its heavy footsteps a constant reminder of our captivity.

Back in our chambers, the door closed behind us with a heavy thud. Our stone escort remained outside, its presence felt even through the thick oak.

"What did you see?" Kyler asked the moment we were alone.

"Eight stone soldiers guarding major intersections," I said, slipping off my shoes. "Four more near the main entrance. The windows near the kitchens didn't appear to be sealed with magic, just iron latches."

"The fae guard rotations seem to be the same," Oryn added, pacing the room. "But I didn't see a single area that was solely guarded by fae."

Kyler nodded, his tactical mind processing the information. "They've eliminated anyone slipping by during meal times or when the soldiers are exhausted. The golems never tire, never feel hunger. They're able to keep watch while the normal guard changes out. Still, the banquet tomorrow night might be our best chance. With the nobles present, attention will be divided."

"And the wine flowing freely," I added, remembering Shefferd's insistence on the finest vintages. "Sunneva's guard will be focused on the hall, not the corridors."

"Which leaves us with the golems and these damn bracelets," Oryn growled, twisting the iron band on his wrist. "If we can find weapons long enough, we might stand a chance against one or two golems. But without our powers, we're at a disadvantage against eight."

I sank onto the edge of the bed, turning my own bracelet. The metal was smooth, without visible seams or locks. "These shouldn't be possible unless," I said slowly, "I saw jars with rings similar to these. Maybe that's how they're being made? Trinity calls it alchemy... maybe that's how they're able to imbue iron with magic."

Kyler's eyes met mine, understanding dawning. "They'll be taking you to the laboratory tomorrow morning."

"And I'll try to grab some notes or something," I finished. "There has to be a trick to it, something we're missing."

"It's too dangerous," Oryn protested. "If she catches you—"

"She won't," I said, confidence firm in my voice. "She's very focused on her work. Besides, I've trained with one of the best thieves around, Lucas." The ache that plagued me returned as his name left my lips, causing me to catch my breath.

Kyler sat beside me, taking my hands in his. "If you can figure out how to remove them, we make our move during the banquet." His eyes were intense, determined. "We'll slip out when everyone's distracted, find weapons in the guard room—"

"And then we run like our assess are on fire," Oryn finished. "Back to Esmeray, where we can regroup and figure out how to stop this ritual before the solstice."

I nodded, hope flickering to life for the first time since our capture. "Nine days until the solstice. We can make it."

We spent the rest of the evening going over the plan, refining the details, and accounting for contingencies. The servants brought our evening meal, which we picked at, more focused on escape than sustenance.

As night fell, we prepared for bed with a new sense of purpose. Tomorrow could mean freedom—or disaster.

"I still don't like you going to her alone," Oryn said as we lay in darkness, his arm draped protectively across my waist.

"Neither do I," Kyler agreed from my other side. "But we have to play by her rules, for now."

I nestled between them, drawing strength from their warmth. "I'll be careful," I promised. "Just be ready tomorrow night. We leave together unless..." I swallowed, knowing my next words would cause strife. "You two have to get out at all costs. Even if you have to leave me."

Deadly silence filled the space as the bed suddenly became stiffer.

"No," Kyler said.

"Like fucking hell, Love," Oryn added.

I sighed. "I need you two to get out of here. I'm still going to fight like hell to join you, but you're the only leverage she has over me. If one of us is forced to stay behind, it has to be me. Otherwise..." I couldn't voice my next thought, afraid of the universe taking it and making it reality. If either or both of them were caught, they would die.

"It's not going to happen, Princess," Kyler stroked my hair as he spoke. The action calmed me, but I still worried about the worst outcomes of our plan. "It's all three of us."

"All or nothing," Oryn said, scooting closer to me.

Sleep came fitfully, my dreams haunted by Augustus's dying face, Magnus's lifeless one, Lucas collapsed on the ground, and Trinity's cold smile. I woke before dawn, my body tense with anticipation.

I slipped from between my sleeping mates, padding to the window to watch the sky lighten.

Today would determine everything.

I had to be ready, to be sharp. I needed to be Death's Wraith, waiting in the dark for the opportunity to strike.

The first rays of sun had barely crested the horizon when heavy footsteps approached our door. I was dressed and waiting when it swung open, revealing our stone escort.

"The queen requires the vessel," it intoned.

This time, I didn't wait for my mates to wake fully. I pressed quick kisses on their foreheads and murmured, "I'll see you soon."

Kyler caught my wrist, his eyes still heavy with sleep but sharp with concern. "Be careful."

"Always am," I replied with a grin.

Oryn snorted beside him at the sentiment.

Yeah, I wouldn't believe that lie either.

I followed the golem through the quiet halls, my mind racing through what I needed to look for—notes on the bracelets, if there was some sort of tool or key, anything I could exploit later.

The descent into the underground corridor felt less intimidating this time. I was prepared for the dank air, the eerie silence broken only by the golem's heavy footfalls. Knowledge was power, and what better place to gain it than a laboratory?

We reached the aged door, and the stone soldier pushed it open without a word. I stepped inside, bracing myself for the sight of the table that still haunted my nightmares.

Trinity stood before it in a simple black robe, her marked arms exposed. From afar, the marks were difficult to make out, looking more like slivers of scars than remnants of magic.

"Ah, Alora," she said, looking up from the vial she was examining. "Right on time. Get on the table and we'll get started."

<h1 style="text-align:center">CHAPTER 27</h1>

I climbed onto the table, suppressing the shudder that threatened to race through me. The surface bit through my thin clothing, and I forced myself to lie still as Trinity moved around me with practiced efficiency.

"Roll up your sleeve," she instructed, reviewing her arranged instruments on the small tray that lay on the table.

I complied, watching her movements while trying to appear disinterested. My eyes tracked the shelves behind her, searching for anything that might hint at the bracelets' weakness. Papers littered a desk in the corner—could one of them hold the answer?

Trinity tied a tourniquet around my upper arm, her fingers surprisingly gentle. "You know, I never dreamed of having kids, or a family. But for my daughter to be the vessel, it's an honor to be your mother."

The needle slid into my vein with barely a pinch, the pain kept me from rolling my eyes at the motherly sentiment. I kept my gaze fixed on a point past her shoulder where more vials glimmered in the candlelight.

"Lucky you," I said flatly.

225

She laughed like brittle ice cracking beneath a heavy boot. "Oh, Alora. You have no idea how long I've waited for this moment. How many years I've planned and plotted to return Chaos to our world."

Blood flowed dark and rich into the collection vial. Trinity's eyes gleamed with unholy delight as she watched it fill.

"Growing up in that suffocating village with my mother was torture," she continued, switching to a second vial. "Eleni was content with her herbs and helping people, happy to live in obscurity. But I knew I was meant for more."

A paper on the desk caught my eye—something about iron and enchantments. If I could just make out the rest...

"Bridgedale saved me," Trinity said, her voice taking on a dreamy quality. "Mother would send me there for supplies, and suddenly I could breathe. The energy, the possibilities... I felt alive for the first time."

She capped the second vial and reached for a third. "That's where I met your father, you know. Magnus was so handsome then, all brooding and strong. At twenty-two, I was foolish enough to think he'd be my ticket out of that hell. That we would fall in love and it would last forever."

I forced myself to respond, needing her distracted. "But it didn't?"

"He left to join the guard, and I was forced to return to my prison," she said with a bitter smile. "I lingered as long as I could, loitering at a bookshop, before finally going home, but not without two gifts from the gods: a book and a growing womb."

She removed the needle, pressing cotton to the puncture. "That one book changed everything. Do you enjoy reading, Alora?"

I gave her a slow nod.

The corner of her mouth lifted in amusement. "You must have gotten that from me. That book spoke of Chaos, of his love for our people, of the power he granted freely before the other gods grew jealous and kept him from returning to us." Her movements became more animated as she moved my blood to her workstation. "That night, I heard his voice for the first time."

She began adding drops of various substances to my blood, each vial changing color as she worked. A green liquid made one vial of blood bubble. A silver one made the blood glow.

"For weeks, I thought I was losing my mind," she admitted. "The whispers in the dark, the dreams of a world remade. It wasn't until I turned twenty-three that I realized a god had chosen me as his prophet."

Movement near the desk drew my attention. The golem had shifted slightly, and I could see more of the papers now. One clearly showed a diagram of iron circles with annotations about "harmonic disruption" and "frequency nullification."

"Chaos speaks to you?" I asked, trying to keep her talking while memorizing what I could see.

"Every day." She held up a vial that now throbbed with an otherworldly light. "He tells me about the paradise we'll create together. The freedom he'll give me to help shape this land into something greater. No more weak kings. No more diluted bloodlines. The fae will reclaim their birthright, and those worthy will rule as we were meant to."

"And those who aren't worthy?"

Her smile turned predatory. "They'll serve or they'll perish. Chaos is not a merciful god, but he is just."

She continued working, mixing and measuring with manic precision. "Do you know what the beautiful irony is? Your grandmother never understood what she had. She wanted a quiet life serving others, not an ambitious bone in her body. Who would've thought she would birth the one that would bring this kingdom to a new age?"

"She wouldn't want this new age if it meant harm to others." I muttered, knowing the old woman would throw me a scathing look if she heard this. I could even imagine the hum of pans flying past our heads... ones she would surely be throwing at her daughter.

Trinity's hands stilled. "And she would perish for such views. There's no room for weakness in our new world."

"Your husband already ensured she wouldn't meddle," I scoffed. "He and his goons destroyed everything."

Trinity waved a hand at me as if dismissing what had happened as a trivial complaint. "He's merely an errand boy, Alora, a means to an end. Besides, that destruction forged you, did it not? It wasn't intentional, my orders were to leave no one alive, but you emerged from the wreckage worthy of this honor you'll fulfill. It has worked out the way Fate has always intended."

She... of course she gave the orders. Why else would the king focus on such a tiny village or even know of its existence? My mother's corruption ran deeper than I had thought. Not a single piece of her cared for anything but herself and her god, so callous and quick to kill, to destroy. If I weren't his chosen, I would think she had been speaking to Death himself.

She gave no value to life, not even her own mother's.

"But you," she turned back to me, her eyes blazing with fanatical fervor, "you're everything I would have hoped for in a daughter. Strong enough to carry a god across realms. Ruthless enough to do what needs to be done. Even if you don't see it yet."

She began cleaning up her instruments. "The solstice approaches quickly. Nine days to prepare for what must be done. Nine days until Chaos walks among us again."

"What happens to me?" I asked once again. "You use me to bring Chaos over, and then what?"

"If all goes well, you will help me turn his vision for this world into reality," she said. "Otherwise, you'll be disposed of once your usefulness has run out."

I sat up slowly, rubbing my arm where the needle had been. The papers on the desk were still partially visible. Something about "soaking" jumped out at me.

Trinity noticed my wandering gaze and moved to block my view. "Curious about my work?"

"Just wondering how you managed to make iron work with magic," I said carefully. "I thought they opposed each other in all forms."

Her eyes narrowed slightly, then she smiled. "Clever girl. Yes, iron naturally repels all magic. But with the right alchemical processes, the right frequencies and materials, you can create pockets within the iron where magic can exist. Like creating tiny cages within the cage itself."

"Sounds complicated."

"Devastatingly so. It took years to perfect. One wrong calculation and..." she trailed off, gesturing vaguely. "Well, let's just say I've had to replace several assistants over the years."

She moved to a cabinet and withdrew a leather journal, flipping through it absently. "But the results speak for themselves. Those pretty bracelets you wear? They contain several magical suppressors, all nested within the iron matrix. Even if you found a way to break one suppression, the others would hold."

My heart sank. We had only nine days to pick several complicated, tiny locks in our bracelets.

"Of course," she continued, snapping the journal shut, "the physical destruction of the bracelet would release them all at once. But the explosive magical backlash would kill the wearer, so I wouldn't recommend it. They're nearly indestructible though, not even my soldiers have been able to crush them. And they can crush *anything*."

She returned the journal to its cabinet—I noted which one—and turned back to me with that unsettling smile.

"You're dismissed for today." She approached me slowly, reaching out to cup my chin. Her touch was like the caress of death itself. "Go straight to your room. No detours, no exploring, no 'getting lost' in the castle halls. Rarely do I extend trust, and the price you'll pay for disobeying me will be higher than you're willing to pay."

I nodded, keeping my expression neutral despite my racing

thoughts. This was an opportunity—as long as I didn't get caught wandering about.

"Understood."

"Good girl." She released me and stepped back. "Run along now. I expect you to be on your best behavior at the banquet. Your men, too."

I turned and left the laboratory, forcing myself to walk at a measured pace despite every instinct screaming at me to run. The corridors seemed wider without the golem's bulk leading me. My footsteps echoed too loudly in the silence.

Three turns, up the stairs, then past the portrait gallery—I committed each landmark to memory. The castle had always been a maze to me, and with few servants running around, it was unlikely I could get help if I were to get turned around.

I'd just rounded the corner toward the royal wing when a door flew open. Before I could react, a pair of hands yanked me inside, the wood slamming shut behind me.

The room was dim, heavy curtains drawn against the afternoon light. My eyes adjusted quickly, taking in the sparse furnishings—a bed, a washstand, and a mirror. Ingrid stood between me and the door with something sharp glinting in her hand.

"Finally," she breathed, and there was something wild in her eyes that hadn't been there before. Her usually perfect hair hung in disarray, her dress wrinkled as if she'd been wearing it for days.

"Ingrid." I kept my voice calm, though my muscles tensed for a fight. "Is there something I can help you with?"

She laughed, high and brittle. "Yes, yes, you can, Alora. The princess who steals everything."

"I didn't steal—"

"Shut up!" The knife trembled in her grip. "You don't get to talk. You should never have landed a prince, let alone two. You're nothing but a thief. Living the life you've stolen from me. He should have been mine!"

I barked out a laugh at that. "My life? You think you want my life?"

"I was supposed to marry Oryn!" Her voice cracked. "I spent years preparing, learning every stupid court dance, memorizing trade agreements, suffering through endless etiquette lessons. I made myself perfect for him. Then you show up—some nobody from nowhere—and suddenly none of it matters!"

"You're right," I said, watching the way she held the knife—too tight, knuckles white. She'd never used one as a weapon before. "It's not fair."

That seemed to throw her. "What?"

"It's not fair. You did everything right, followed all the rules, and still didn't get what you wanted." I thought of Rasher, how he'd talked about accepting fate's cruel hand. "But that's not my fault, Ingrid. That's just... fate being a bitch."

"Fate?" Her laugh turned manic. "You're blaming fate? Not the fact that you've schemed your way into royalty?"

"I didn't scheme—"

"I am nothing because of you!" Tears streamed down her face now, but her grip on the knife never wavered. "I was *born* to be a princess, raised to rule alongside him. And you've fucked that all to hell!"

There was no reasoning with her sense of entitlement.

"You think I wanted any of this?" My own voice rose despite my efforts to stay calm. "You think I asked to be forced to marry someone? To be tortured? To watch my friends die? You want my life so badly, Ingrid? You want the nightmares, the blood, the constant fear that everyone you love will be ripped away?"

"Oh, don't try to play the 'poor princess' act," she sneered. "You've gotten your happily ever after."

"That's not—"

"I'm done watching you laugh in my face." Her tears stopped as suddenly as they'd started, replaced by an eerie calm. "I'm done waiting for Oryn to see you for who you really are. If I can't have the life I deserve, then you don't get to have yours either."

"Ingrid, think about this—"

"I have thought about it. Every day since you arrived. Every night while you were in his bed and I was alone." Her smile was too wide, she looked crazed. "I already wrote your last words. The poor princess lost her mind and took her own life. And I'll be there to comfort her widow."

"You're not a killer," I said, recognizing the desperation in her eyes. I'd seen it in my own mirror too many times. I just needed to disarm her. For a moment, I tried to call my shadows, but the bracelets kept my power at bay.

"You don't know what I am!"

Then, she lunged.

CHAPTER 28

I ducked, the knife missing my face by inches. She crashed into the wall behind me, already spinning back with surprising agility for someone who'd spent her life in court dresses.

"Hold still, you little wretch!" she screeched, slashing wildly.

I backed away, calculating. The room was small, leaving little space to maneuver. The door was behind her, and I had nothing to defend myself with.

"Ingrid, you don't want to do this," I said, though I knew reasoning with her was pointless now. Her eyes had that feverish glaze of someone who'd passed the threshold of sanity.

She laughed high and unhinged. "Oh, but I do. I've dreamed of nothing else for months."

She charged again. This time I sidestepped and grabbed her wrist, twisting as Lucas had taught me. But she wasn't an experienced fighter—she was a desperate woman with nothing to lose. Instead of dropping the knife as expected, she drove her other fist into my stomach.

The blow knocked the wind out of me. I stumbled back, gasping.

"Not so deadly now, are you?" Ingrid taunted, circling me like a predator. "Your threats are nothing more than petty words. You thought you could get rid of me, scare me away, but you're the one who should be afraid."

Fury rose within me as my back hit the edge of the washstand. I felt behind me, my fingers closing around a ceramic pitcher.

"You don't know how wrong you are," I spat.

"I'm never wrong," she sneered. "You're nothing more than a harlot who stole my prince by spreading her legs. You've bewitched the man I was supposed to marry, turned him against everything he wanted."

"Is that what you tell yourself?" I shifted my weight. "That it couldn't possibly be that he just didn't want you? That he'd rather have his *mate?*"

Her face contorted with rage. "You don't deserve him! You don't deserve any of this! The gods were wrong!"

She lunged again. I swung the pitcher, connecting with her forearm. The knife clattered to the floor between us.

We both dove for it.

Her fingers reached it first, but I slammed my elbow into her face. Blood spurted from her nose. She howled, scrambling backward with the knife still clutched in her hand.

"You broke my nose!" she shrieked, blood streaming down her chin, staining her green silk dress. "My face!"

"I'll do worse if you don't drop the knife and let me leave," I warned, rising to my feet. Getting out of here quickly was the highest priority. The opportunity for more observation was too important, and I refused to let Ingrid take any more of my time. The word of one guard saying I strayed from the path would have Trinity pull her generosity without a second thought.

"Never." She wiped blood with the back of her hand, smearing it across her cheek. "I'd rather die than watch you live the life that should have been mine."

Something shifted in my chest—a cold, hard certainty. This would not end without more bloodshed. I saw myself as she did: the thief who stole her dreams, her future, her prince. In her story, I was the villain who needed to be vanquished, just as I had once viewed Lydia when she set her eyes on Maël.

But this wasn't her story.

"This is your last chance," I said quietly.

She answered by leaping towards me.

I dodged sideways, but the blade still caught my arm, slicing through my sleeve. A line of fire blazed across my skin. Blood welled, hot and sticky.

Ingrid laughed, her teeth red with her own blood. "You thought you were untouchable. I wonder if your princes will still yearn for you while I'm warming their beds after you're gone. Or will they only remember the carvings I gave to that pretty face?"

The pain awakened something inside me—a familiar dark cloud that followed me since my arrival in Epherinia. Every sneer Ingrid had ever directed my way, every poisonous word, every calculated touch on Oryn's arm or Kyler's shoulder—they all flooded back.

I remembered the goblet she'd poisoned, meant to kill me. The way she tried to turn every lady against me the moment they met me. Her smug smile while dancing with Oryn.

Rage coiled in my belly like a serpent waking from slumber.

"Your last attempt on my life was a failure at best," I said, my voice dropping lower. "Do you really believe you could kill me with that little knife?"

"You should have died then," she hissed. "It would have been kinder than what I'll do to you now."

The iron bracelet burned against my skin. I couldn't reach my power, not fully—but I could feel it responding to my anger, pushing against its constraints. My fingertips tingled with a familiar coldness.

Ingrid didn't notice the shadows beginning to gather around my hands. She was too focused on her hate, her perceived injustice.

"You took everything from me," she said, slashing the air between us. "I can't wait to attend your funeral. I'll console Oryn, he'll turn to me in his time of grief, of course. And maybe I'll take your Esmeranian prince too, just to prove I can."

The bracelet seared against my flesh, fighting against the power I was pulling through it. But my rage was stronger than whatever Trinity created within the metal band. I felt my shadows responding, weak but present, wisping around my fingers like smoke.

It wasn't much, but it would be enough.

Ingrid charged again, knife aimed at my heart.

This time, I didn't dodge.

I caught her wrist with one hand, my fingers digging into her flesh. With my other hand, I drove my palm into her chest, sending her stumbling backward.

"You've never fought for anything in your life," I said, advancing on her. "Everything you have you've been given. And when you didn't get what you wanted, you blamed everyone but yourself. Even if I didn't exist, Oryn would never willingly marry you."

"Shut up!" She swung the knife wildly. "Just die already!"

The shadows around my hands grew darker, more substantial. The bracelet seared my skin, but I welcomed the pain. It fueled my determination.

"I didn't steal your life, Ingrid." I backed her against the wall. "It was never yours to begin with."

She screamed and lunged forward in desperation. I sidestepped, grabbing her knife arm and twisting until something snapped. The knife fell from her fingers.

Ingrid howled in pain, clutching her broken wrist. "You beast! You monster!"

I picked up the knife, testing its weight in my hand. "I am forged by the gods," I said. "And I am the deliverance of death."

"Guards!" she screamed. "Someone help me!"

I knew no one would come. The stone soldiers didn't care about human squabbles, and the fae guards were nowhere in sight.

"No one's coming to save you, Ingrid," I told her. "It's just you and me now."

Her eyes darted around the room, seeking escape. Finding none, she drew herself up, a sneer twisting her bloodied face.

"You won't kill me," she said, but uncertainty wavered in her voice. "You're all talk, too weak. That's why Oryn will never truly love you—you're not the strong queen he needs by his side."

I laughed harder than I had in weeks. "You still don't understand, do you? I've killed more people than you've ever met. And every one of them was stronger than you."

The shadows coiled more tightly around my hands, flowing down the blade of the knife. The bracelet was a band of fire around my wrist, but I barely felt it now. My power responded to my call like water finding cracks between rocks; it was determined to be let loose.

"You're lying," she whispered, but her eyes showed her fear. "You're just a village nobody."

"I am Death's Wraith," I corrected her. "And you should have left me and my mates alone."

I moved faster than she could track, my body humming with adrenaline. The knife slashed once, twice. Ingrid gasped, her eyes widening as she tried to breathe but could only choke on her own blood. Blood spilled from her throat, the corset of her dress soaking the liquid eagerly and turning dark. Her legs buckled, her body crumbling to the floor.

"It didn't have to be this way," I told her softly. "You could have *lived*."

Her eyes locked with mine, hatred still burning even as the light began to fade from them. A wet, gurgling sound escaped her throat. Her body convulsed before it went still. The hatred in her eyes gave way to the vacant stare of death.

I sat back on my heels, the shadows fading from my hands as my rage subsided. The bracelet cooled against my skin, keeping my powers at bay once again.

They weren't as perfect as Trinity believed, which means we had a chance of breaking free of them. I just had to push through the pain.

Looking down at Ingrid's body, I felt nothing. No triumph, no satisfaction, no remorse. Just the quiet certainty that this had been inevitable from the moment she pulled me into this room.

I stood, wiping blood from my hands onto a cloth from the washstand. My mind worked methodically, assessing the scene.

Ingrid had planned my suicide. Perhaps I could arrange the same for her.

I positioned her body on the bed, arranging her limbs to appear as if she'd lain down deliberately. In one of her hands, I placed the knife, moving her arms in a way that made it seem like she slit her own throat. Her blood soaked into the bedclothes, but there wasn't much I could do about that.

I smoothed her hair and closed her eyes. In death, the pinched tension had left her face. She looked younger, almost peaceful.

"May you find peace beyond the veil," I murmured.

My gaze fell on a piece of parchment on the bedside table. I picked it up, skimming the words.

> *I can no longer bear the shame of my failure. I cannot live knowing I will never bear Prince Oryn's heir. May the next life be kinder than this one.*

I scoffed at the message. Ingrid's handwriting was elegant, flowing—the script of a woman who'd spent years perfecting her penmanship. But the note she'd planned to leave in my name was ridiculous. Sure, it may convince the nobility that I'd taken my life out of despair, but Oryn would've seen right through this.

How fitting that it would now serve as her own suicide note.

I tucked it partially under a corner of the pillow, making it appear as though she'd placed it there before her final act. Anyone finding her would have no reason to doubt the narrative—a heartbroken noble woman, spurned by the prince she had loved, taking her own life in despair. Her public acts only served as evidence of her affection towards him, and his continued dismissal proved the love was one-sided.

I examined the room one last time, ensuring I'd left no obvious traces of my presence. A few spots of blood on the floor might raise questions, but a partially cleaned floor would be more suspicious.

Satisfied, I moved to the door, listening carefully before cracking it open. The corridor remained empty. I slipped out, the door eased shut behind me. I walked steadily toward my chambers, toward my mates. My arm throbbed where Ingrid's knife had cut me, but the wound was shallow. I could hide it easily enough.

As I turned the corner toward our rooms, I felt a strange lightness. One less enemy to worry about, one less thing getting in our way tonight. And I'd discovered something valuable—the bracelets could be overcome, even if just for a moment.

That knowledge alone was worth the blood on my hands.

CHAPTER 29

I pushed open the door to our chambers, the blood on my clothes dry and flaking against my skin. The iron bracelet chafed my wrist.

Kyler paced the length of the room like a caged animal, his jaw tight, hands flexing at his sides. His head snapped up at my entrance, eyes widening as they landed on me.

Oryn sat on the sofa facing the door, leaning forward with his elbows on his knees. The moment I stepped inside, his face transformed, relief washing over his features as he surged to his feet.

"Lor," he breathed, rushing toward me. His arms opened to pull me into an embrace but froze mid-motion when he noticed the bloodstains. "What happened?" His voice dropped to a dangerous whisper.

Kyler was beside us in an instant, his eyes darkening as they scanned me from head to toe. "Who did this to you?" he growled, fingers hovering over the cut on my arm where Ingrid's knife had sliced through.

"I'm fine," I said, wincing as Kyler's finger grazed the wound. "It's shallow."

"That's not what I asked." Kyler's voice had turned to ice. "What the hell was Trinity doing to you? If I had known—"

"It wasn't Trinity."

Kyler waited for me to elaborate, one eyebrow raised.

"Ingrid," I explained. "She pulled me into her room on my way back and attacked me."

Oryn cursed, his hands curling. "I knew I should have killed her. This is the last time she ever hurts our mate. Where is she now? I swear to the gods—"

"Dead," I cut him off, my voice hollow. "I killed her. She won't be a problem anymore."

Silence fell between us, heavy with unspoken questions. Kyler's eyes never left my face, searching for signs of... something while Oryn's gaze dropped to my clothes.

"Good," Kyler finally said, the word a sharp declaration that left no room for debate.

"We need to get you cleaned up," Oryn added, his voice gentler as he took my hand. "Come on."

"Wait," I pulled back slightly. "We don't have much time. The banquet is tonight, and we need to go over our plan."

"The plan can wait a few minutes," Kyler insisted, guiding me toward the bathroom with a firm hand at the small of my back. "You're bleeding."

"It's mostly her blood," I muttered, but allowed them to lead me.

The bathroom was warm and bright, sunlight streaming through the small window high on the wall. Kyler immediately filled the basin with water while Oryn helped me out of the soiled clothes, his movements careful as he peeled the fabric away from the cut on my arm.

"Do we need to go clean up a body after this?" Kyler asked.

I shook my head, though he didn't appear to be surprised by that answer. His mate was the professional killer he chased after for a long time, and he would've caught me long ago had I been too sloppy to clean up after myself.

"Tell us what happened," Oryn said as he examined the wound. "All of it."

I winced as Kyler pressed a damp cloth to the cut, cleaning away the dried blood. "Trinity took some of my blood again today. She said, she needs daily samples as we get closer to the solstice." I hissed as he dabbed at a particularly tender spot. Now that the adrenaline had worn off, aches began to bloom all over my body from the events earlier. "She's been talking to Chaos for a while. She truly believes she's bringing him back for the greater good, even if that means enslaving humans and half-bred fae."

"And Ingrid?" Kyler prompted, his touch gentle despite the tension in his shoulders. "Where was the golem that escorted you? How did she get to you?"

"She was waiting for me when I left the laboratory. Trinity told the golem to stay behind, said I could walk back alone." I closed my eyes, seeing Ingrid's face twisted in hatred. "Ingrid had a knife and was completely unhinged. Said I'd stolen the life that should have been hers."

"She's always been exceptionally entitled," Oryn said. "I don't think she would be so desperate to trade places if she knew what you've been through."

"That's exactly what I told her," I said with a humorless laugh. "She didn't appreciate the irony. No, all she cared about was you and the crown."

Kyler wrung out the cloth, the water in the basin turning pink. "Did anyone see you?"

I shook my head. "No. I made it look like she killed herself. She even had a suicide note ready—meant for me, but it worked just as well for her. Apparently, I was so distraught with my shame for not being able to bear Oryn's children that I would have taken my own life."

Heat flashed in my men's eyes. "Let's prove that thought wrong," Oryn purred. "No one but you would ever bear children for me."

"Or me," Kyler added. "Whenever you're ready, Princess, just say the word."

Heat bloomed across my cheeks as I tried to process their words before giving up. Now wasn't the time, and this certainly wasn't the place.

"Just think about it," Kyler murmured, pressing a clean cloth to my arm. "Hold this."

I pressed the cloth against my arm while Kyler went to fetch a fresh basin of water. Oryn knelt before me, taking my free hand in his.

"I'm sorry I wasn't there to protect you," he said, his thumb tracing circles on my palm.

"Don't be, I can handle myself. And there was a personal score to settle, which now, it has." I gave him a reassuring smile.

He sighed with relief. "Did you learn anything while you were with Trinity?"

I nodded eagerly. "That's the one good thing that came out of today. I saw notes in her laboratory—she's somehow embedded these bracelets with pockets of carefully crafted magic to make them nearly impervious." An earnest grin stretched across my face. "But they're not as perfect as she thinks."

Both men stilled, their attention razor-sharp.

"What do you mean?" Kyler asked, returning with fresh water.

I lowered my voice, though we were alone in our chambers. "When Ingrid attacked me, I was able to use my shadows—just barely, but they were there. The bracelet burned like hell against my skin, but I pushed through it."

Oryn's eyes widened. "You broke through the suppression?"

"Not completely," I admitted. "It was just a trickle of power, but it was enough to help me overpower her. These things have weaknesses, which means we can break them."

Kyler's expression turned thoughtful as he began to wash the blood from my skin with gentle, methodical strokes. "If you can access even a fraction of your power..."

"We might have a fighting chance tonight," Oryn finished.

I nodded, wincing slightly as Kyler's cloth moved over a bruise forming on my shoulder. "Trinity also mentioned something else. She said the physical destruction of the bracelet would release all the suppressions at once, but the magical backlash would kill the wearer."

"Convenient warning," Kyler muttered, his jaw tightening. "Anything else?"

"She said they're nearly indestructible. Even her stone soldiers can't crush them."

Oryn cursed under his breath. "So, removing them is still our primary obstacle."

"Maybe not," I countered. "If I can access my shadows, even just a little, maybe you two can as well. Maybe we don't need to remove them if we can work around them."

Kyler paused, his hands stilling against my skin. "It's worth a try."

Oryn nodded, a spark of hope igniting in his eyes. "We should test it now, while we have time."

The water in the basin had turned a murky pink from the blood Kyler had washed away. He emptied it and refilled it once more, this time helping me into the tub for a proper bath.

"Tell me about the laboratory first," Kyler said as he worked soap into my hair. "What else did you see?"

I closed my eyes, leaning into his touch. "It's underground, through a hidden staircase behind the east wing. At least eight stone guards patrol the corridor. The lab itself is filled with strange equipment, vials of colored liquids, and ancient-looking books."

"Any weapons?" Oryn asked, sitting on the edge of the tub.

"Nothing obvious, but plenty of glass bottles we could break if needed."

Kyler's fingers massaged my scalp, the sensation soothing despite our dire conversation. "And Trinity? What exactly is she planning?"

I sighed, allowing myself a brief moment to enjoy the warmth of the water and their care before diving back into the horror of our situation. "She needs my blood for the ritual. Something about me being the perfect vessel for Chaos to enter this world. She's been preparing for this for years."

"Did she say what happens to you during this ritual?" Oryn's voice was carefully controlled, but I could hear the fear beneath it.

"Not explicitly, but she didn't deny it when I asked if I'd be disposed of afterward." I opened my eyes to see both their faces had hardened with fury. "But that's not important right now. What matters is stopping her before the solstice."

"Days," Kyler murmured, pouring water over my head to rinse away the soap. "We only have a few days to figure out how to escape and stop a god from entering our world. Hardly more than a week."

"Starting with our escape tonight," I said firmly. "During the banquet."

Oryn reached for a towel as I stood, water cascading down my body. He wrapped it around me with gentle hands, his touch lingering. "The banquet will be our best opportunity. With more people present, security will be divided."

"And hopefully everyone is drunk," Kyler added, a grim smile playing at his lips. "Guards get careless when there's celebration. I suspect the added soldiers made of stone have only made the fae more lenient."

I stepped out of the tub, secure in the towel Oryn had wrapped around me. "We need to go over the details one more time, this has to be perfect. There's no room for error."

Kyler nodded, leading us back into the bedroom. "Let's get you dressed first."

They helped me into fresh clothes, simple black pants and a tunic that would allow freedom of movement. As Oryn fastened the laces at my collar, his fingers brushed against my throat.

"I'll kill anyone who tries to hurt you again," he said quietly, the words more promise than threat.

"Not if I get to them first," Kyler added from where he was checking the window latches once more.

I caught Oryn's hand, pressing a kiss to his palm. "We focus on escape first, revenge later."

He nodded reluctantly, releasing me to join Kyler by the window. "So, the plan from the top."

Kyler turned to face us both, his expression serious. "During the banquet, we wait for the nobility to get properly drunk. That should happen within the first hour based on how they behaved last night."

"Trinity will be busy playing queen," I added. "And the king will be too concerned with appearing powerful to notice three people slipping away."

"The stone guards will be an issue," Oryn said, beginning to pace. "But if we can access even a fraction of our powers, we might be able to distract them long enough to make it to the kitchens."

"From there, we slip out of the windows," Kyler continued. "They're not locked, and it leads out to the service exit. It's less guarded than the main gates, and the delivery carts come and go regularly."

I nodded. "Next, we grab weapons."

"From the guard room on the way," Oryn said. "Making a quick stop if it's clear."

"And if it's not—"

Kyler's smile was cold. "Then we make it clear."

"Once we're outside the castle walls, we head straight for the thickest part of the forest," I said. "So Trinity's stone soldiers will have trouble maneuvering between them, and it would provide us cover."

"And from there to Esmeray," Oryn finished.

A dead silence filled the space suddenly as his blue eyes met mine for a moment. We would hopefully find Rasher in Esmeray, likely dealing with cleaning up the mess Trinity left. Luella should still be huddled up in the library in Charmonia, but there were two people who wouldn't be there to greet us: my father and Lucas. The memory of my eccentric friend falling right before my eyes as the portal swallowed me, eyes that always glinted with glee darkened as he disappeared from view and from this world.

He wouldn't come barging into my room at the guild again. Nor would I be subjected to his retellings of his wild nights, and all the little details that came with them.

I was sure my best friend, my brother in the darkness did not leave the battle at Oakston, and I wasn't strong enough to deal with that yet. It made me question why we ever worshipped such cruel gods. If they were just, he would have lived and would be terrorizing a tavern right now.

"What about the bracelets?" I asked, lifting my wrist to examine the seamless band of iron. "We should try to access our powers now, see if we can recreate what I did earlier."

Kyler nodded, coming to stand beside me. "Let's try one at a time. Oryn, you first."

Oryn closed his eyes, his face contorting with concentration. The muscles in his forearms tensed as he focused, and for a moment, nothing happened. Maybe my eyes were playing tricks on me, but I swore for a moment his fingertips had a pale glow, but once I blinked, it was gone, and Oryn was shaking his head in resignation. But suddenly, his bracelet glowed.

A gasp left his lips. "Fuck, that burns," he said. "It's right there, I know it is, but it's just out of reach."

"Kyler?" I prompted.

Kyler's jaw set in determination as he focused on his palm. After a few quiet moments, he too gave up.

"I know it's there," he said through gritted teeth, the bracelet on his wrist glowing just as Oryn's had. "But it's like trying to walk straight through a wall thicker than the ones around the castle."

I took a deep breath and closed my eyes, reaching for the familiar coolness of my shadows. At first, there was nothing—just the emptiness I'd felt since the bracelets were placed on us. But I pushed harder, remembering the moment when Ingrid attacked me. The fear of never seeing my mates again and the rage that she would take them.

The darkness behind my eyelids deepened, a response to my call. The bracelet around my wrist heated, becoming painful against my skin, but I pushed through it. When I opened my eyes, thin wisps of shadow curled around my fingers.

"How are you doing that?" Kyler asked as I focused on maintaining my concentration despite the burning pain. The shadows grew slightly thicker before the bracelet flared hot enough to burn. The shadows dissipated immediately.

"I don't know," I finally answered. "I just called to them and ignored the pain, and thought about the moments during the attack. All I remember is feeling *so* angry and fearful thinking about her succeeding."

Kyler considered my words. "Your power grows when you're enraged, we've seen that with our own eyes."

Oryn nodded. "You must be overpowering the magic in the bands, if we can replicate that," he looked to Kyler, "then we might be able to get through the wall that prevents us from touching ours."

"It won't be enough to sustain a fight," Kyler cautioned, rubbing his wrist where the bracelet had burned him. "But maybe enough for a distraction."

"Or if things get dire," I added. "I might be able to pull enough shadows for you two to get away."

"No," both men said simultaneously.

"We stay together," Kyler insisted. "No splitting up."

"The moment we separate is the moment something goes wrong," Oryn added. "We do this as one or not at all. I will not leave either of you behind."

I wanted to argue, to point out the very real possibility that we might not all be able to escape, but I held my tongue. "Fine. Together."

Kyler's shoulders relaxed slightly. "Good. Now, timing. The

banquet begins at sundown. We wait until the festivities are well underway before making our move."

"We should position ourselves near the east door," Oryn suggested. "It's closest to the kitchens."

"And keep an eye on Trinity," I added. "She can control her golems through her magic, if she thinks we're up to anything, she's going to have them on us immediately."

The three of us continued refining our plan, discussing possible obstacles and contingencies. As the afternoon wore on, our preparation took on an almost desperate edge. This might be our only chance to escape before Trinity's ritual at the solstice.

Kyler's hand found mine, his grip firm and reassuring. Oryn wrapped his arm around my shoulders. I leaned into their embrace, drawing strength from them. "For what it's worth, I'm glad you're both here with me. I couldn't do this alone."

"There's nowhere else we'd rather be than by your side," Kyler said softly. "You never have to be alone again."

Oryn pressed a kiss to my temple. "We're in this together. All the way to the end. Not even the gods can part us."

The light outside our windows had begun to shift, the golden afternoon giving way to the softer hues of early evening. Soon, golems would come to escort us to the banquet. Our plan would be set in motion.

"Whatever happens tonight," I said, looking between the two men who had become my world, "know that I love you both. More than I ever thought possible."

Kyler stiffened. "That sounds a lot like goodbye, Princess, but there are no goodbyes between us." His voice was as stern as the look in his eyes as he looked down at me.

I shook my head, though I knew the truth. "I wasn't saying goodbye, I was just speaking my heart since I can't whisper through our bonds." But it *was* most certainly a goodbye, final words in case we were parted despite our efforts.

"And we love you," Oryn replied, his voice thick with emotion.

Kyler simply nodded, but his eyes said everything his words didn't. He had said everything when we bonded, and when we had come back to this den of snakes. His words always proved true by his actions. The love between the three of us was complicated yet so easy. The bond made it impossible not to fall head over heels instantly, but Kyler had proven so much more with his words, affirmations, and actions. What used to be fights became quiet consolations, conversations uplifting the darkest moments.

And Oryn and I crossed the chasm between us when we had finally laid everything on the line. The part of my heart that I didn't want to admit was his lay before him, while his had been bleeding on his sleeve, patiently waiting for me to see the truth. The three of us had turned a corner, and I would forever be grateful for the moments we had together.

A knock at the door startled us out of our moment.

It was time.

I squared my shoulders, letting my expression shift into the mask I'd perfected during my time as Death's Wraith. Cool, composed, revealing nothing of the turmoil beneath.

Handmaidens swarmed in, arms full of clothing and eager to groom us until we looked like royalty. By the time they finished, Kyler, Oryn, and I glittered in Sunneva's signature gold with red accents. I took in both handsome men one final time before linking my arms in theirs.

"Let's go," I said, moving toward the door. "We have a banquet to attend."

And a kingdom to escape. Tonight, we would either win our freedom or lose everything trying.

CHAPTER 30

A golem stood waiting as we stepped into the hall, its massive stone form blocking half the corridor. Its blank face revealed nothing as it gestured for us to follow. Kyler's hand pressed against the small of my back, a gentle but reassuring presence.

The golem turned and began its thunderous march down the corridor. Each footfall echoed against the marble floors, announcing our approach long before we'd reach the banquet hall. I kept my head high, my expression carefully neutral as my eyes cataloged everything we passed.

Two fae guards stood at the intersection—their eyes skimming over us before returning to their post. They looked bored, perhaps even resentful of their new stone comrades. I counted four more golems positioned at interconnected points along our route, each standing unnaturally still.

"They've doubled the guard since yesterday," Kyler murmured, his voice so low only Oryn and I could hear it.

I gave a slight nod, noting how the golems had been placed to cover every possible exit route. Were they expecting trouble tonight, or was this merely Trinity's paranoia manifesting?

The ritual was too close for her to risk a flaw in her plan. Unfortunately for her, we were determined to exploit that very weakness.

"Smile, Love," Oryn whispered, squeezing my arm gently. "You look like you're heading to an execution rather than a celebration."

I forced my lips to curve upward, though the comparison wasn't far off. "Better?"

"Much." He winked, though the worry in his eyes negated his casual tone.

As we descended the grand staircase, the sounds of the gathering nobility grew louder—voices raised in laughter, the clink of glasses, music from string instruments floating through the air. The facade of normalcy was almost convincing.

Almost.

Two massive oak doors stood open at the entrance to the great hall, flanked by more stone guards. Our escort stopped just short of the threshold.

"Proceed," it commanded, its voice monotone.

The scene before us was dazzling, deliberately so. Chandeliers glowed with hundreds of candles, casting golden light over the room. Long tables groaned under the weight of elaborate food and endless wine. Nobles adorned in their finest silks and jewels milled about, their faces flushed with drink and false merriment.

At the far end of the hall, two thrones stood on a raised dais. The king of Sunneva sat in one, resplendent in crimson and gold, his crown gleaming in the candlelight. Trinity occupied the other, her gown a deep burgundy. Her eyes found mine immediately, a predatory smile spreading across her face.

"Deep breaths," Kyler murmured as we stepped into the hall. "Remember the plan. We stick together."

My fingers dug into his arm, releasing only when I realized how tightly I was gripping him. "East exit," I whispered, tilting my head subtly toward the door I could just make out behind a cluster of courtiers.

"Four guards," Oryn noted. "Two stone, two fae."

"Manageable," Kyler replied, nodding slightly as we moved deeper into the crowd.

Noble faces turned toward us, a mix of curiosity, fear, and disdain in their eyes. I recognized most from the past few days, but there were a few unaccounted for.

"Prince Oryn! Princess Alora!" Shefferd appeared before us, bowing so low I thought he might topple over. "And Prince Kyler. How delightful that you could join us."

His tone suggested it was anything but delightful, though his smile remained fixed in place. The stench of fear wafted from him like cheap perfume.

"Shefferd," Oryn acknowledged with a curt nod. "The hall looks... festive."

"Indeed, indeed! Her Majesty insisted on only the finest decorations for this special occasion." He leaned closer, lowering his voice. "Between us, the queen has been most specific about every detail. Most specific indeed."

His eyes darted nervously toward the dais where Trinity sat watching the proceedings like a spider in the center of its web.

"How fortunate for Sunneva to have such an attentive queen," I said, my voice dripping with false sweetness.

Shefferd's smile faltered for a moment before he recovered. "Yes, quite. If you'll excuse me, I must see to the other guests."

He scurried away, disappearing into the crowd like a mouse fleeing a hawk.

"Let's find a place near the exit," Kyler suggested, guiding us toward the eastern side of the hall.

We navigated through clusters of nobles, nodding politely at those who acknowledged us but avoiding any lengthy conversations. I kept track of every guard position, every potential obstacle between us and freedom.

The king's voice suddenly boomed across the hall, cutting through the chatter. "Lords and ladies of Sunneva, my esteemed guests, my beloved queen—" he gestured to Trinity, who inclined her head with practiced grace. "—I thank you all for coming tonight."

The crowd fell silent, all eyes turning toward the dais, except mine and Davian's.

The ghostly young man sat near the dais, head hanging down in his hands, elbows braced on the table. Whether he was truly listening to the king, I didn't know, but my bet would be he was impatiently waiting for the night to conclude so he could escape this hellscape.

"Tonight, we celebrate not just the union between myself and my queen, but the dawn of a new era for our kingdom." The king's voice carried easily through the hall, each word precise and calculated. "Sunneva stands on the precipice of greatness, of power unlike any the realm has ever seen."

Murmurs rippled through the crowd—some excited, others uneasy.

"In the coming days, you will witness Sunneva ascend to its rightful place as the supreme power of this world. Our enemies will kneel or perish. Our allies will prosper under our protection."

Trinity rose from her throne, her movements fluid as water. "My king speaks true," she said, her voice somehow both gentle and commanding. "The gods have blessed this kingdom above all others. The sun itself favors Sunneva, always has, always will."

Her eyes found mine across the crowd, a secret smile playing at her lips. "Some of you may have heard whispers, rumors of ancient magic being awakened. I stand before you today to confirm those rumors are true—and to assure you there is nothing to fear."

Elvirana stepped forward from the shadows behind the throne, her aged face solemn. "As Royal Mage of the Crown, I have witnessed the power that flows through our queen, through our very land." She raised her hands, her voice rising with them. "Sunneva is truly sun-blessed! The magic that once belonged to all fae will return to us, stronger than ever before!"

Cheers erupted from the more enthusiastic nobles, though I noticed several exchanging worried glances. Not all were convinced by this performance, but they clapped nonetheless, fear keeping them in line.

"Eat, drink, celebrate!" the king commanded. "For you are the chosen few who will witness the rebirth of true fae power!"

The orchestra struck up a lively tune as servants began pouring wine with renewed vigor. The king descended from the dais, Trinity on his arm, to mingle with the crowd.

"They're putting on quite a show," Oryn muttered.

"Keeps the nobles distracted," Kyler replied. "Makes them feel special rather than trapped."

I watched as Trinity laughed at something a courtier said, her hand resting lightly on the king's arm. To anyone else, she might have appeared the perfect queen—beautiful, charming, attentive to her husband. But I could see the cold calculation behind her eyes, the way she surveyed the room like a general assessing a battlefield.

"We need to be patient," I murmured as a servant offered us goblets of wine. I took one but had no intention of drinking it. "Let them get deeper into their cups."

Hours crawled by as we maintained our positions near the east exit, occasionally moving to avoid drawing suspicion but always keeping our escape route in sight. The nobility grew progressively more intoxicated, their laughter louder, their movements less coordinated. Even the fae guards had partaken in some wine, their postures slightly more relaxed than before.

The king sat heavily on his throne, his face flushed with drink, his crown slightly askew. Trinity remained beside him, though I noticed she'd barely touched her wine all evening.

"I think it's time," Kyler whispered as the orchestra began a particularly boisterous piece that had several nobles attempting to dance. "The guards are distracted, and most of these fools couldn't see straight if their lives depended on it."

Oryn nodded, casually setting down his untouched goblet. "Trinity's still too alert for my liking, but we may not get a better chance."

I glanced toward the exit, mentally mapping out the path. Twenty steps to the door. Another thirty through the corridor to the kitchens. Then the window, the gardens, the forest beyond the wall.

"Ready?" I breathed, my heart hammering against my ribs.

Both men nodded, their faces set with determination.

We began to move, slow and causal, as if simply relocating to a less crowded area. I kept my expression neutral, laughing softly at something Oryn said as we edged closer to the door.

Fifteen steps away.

Ten.

Five.

But suddenly, the doors of the great hall burst open with a thunderous crash.

A man staggered in, his wide eyes in shock. "She's dead!" he cried, his voice breaking through the music and laughter like a stone through glass. "Lady Ingrid is dead!" His wild eyes caught beside me as he lifted a shaky finger towards Oryn. "And it's all *his* fault!"

The hall fell silent, all eyes flickering between the distraught messenger and my golden prince.

"What madness is this?" the king demanded, rising unsteadily from his throne.

The man stumbled forward, clutching a piece of parchment in his trembling hand. "I found her in her chambers, Your Majesty. Her throat…" he choked on the words. "She took her own life."

Gasps and whispers erupted throughout the hall. I felt Kyler's hand tighten around mine, a silent warning to maintain our composure.

"Suicide?" The king frowned, glancing toward Trinity, who watched the proceedings with narrowed eyes.

"She left this, Your Majesty." The man held up the parchment. "Her final words."

"Read it," Trinity commanded, her voice cutting through the commotion.

The messenger unfolded the parchment with shaking hands. "I can no longer bear the shame of my failure," he read, his voice wavering. "'I cannot live knowing I will never bear Prince Oryn's heir. May the next life be kinder than this one.'"

All eyes turned toward Oryn, who stiffened beside me. I squeezed his arm in silent support.

"How dreadfully tragic," Trinity said, though her tone suggested she found it anything but. "Lady Ingrid was always so... passionate in her affections. Though I don't see how you can blame the prince. Her final words admitted she acted alone."

Murmurs rippled through the crowd, sympathetic glances directed our way. Our planned escape route was now blocked by a cluster of nobles gathering around the messenger, eager for more details of the grisly discovery.

"Fuck," Kyler breathed, the word barely audible even to me. "We need another way out."

"The west exit," Oryn suggested, his voice equally low. "It's further from the kitchens, but—"

"Too many guards," I cut in, spotting the four stone soldiers positioned there. "We'd never make it."

The king raised his hands, calling for silence. His face had grown somber, though his eyes remained glazed. "Let us remember Lady Ingrid for this moment, whose devotion to the crown was unmatched."

The assembly bowed their heads, though I noted several barely concealing their excitement at such juicy court gossip. Death, especially romantic suicide, was the pinnacle of entertainment for these vultures, regardless that it was one of their own.

"This changes nothing," Kyler murmured as we pretended to pay our respects. "We wait for the commotion to die down, then we slip out."

I nodded slightly, keeping my expression appropriately somber while my mind raced. Had we lost our chance?

"Now," the king declared after what could hardly be called a respectful pause, "let us continue our celebration. Lady Ingrid would not wish for her passing to dampen our spirits on this momentous occasion."

Servants circulated with goblets of wine, as if alcohol could wash away the melancholy that had fallen over the gathering.

"They've blocked the east exit," Oryn observed, nodding subtly toward the two additional stone guards that had appeared near our original escape route.

My heart sank. "She knows. She must have been watching us look for another way out and suspects us."

"Then we need a new plan," Kyler said, his voice hard with determination. "The north exit, through the servant's corridor."

"It's our only option," I agreed, mentally adjusting our route. "We'll have to—"

A deafening explosion rocked the hall, sending nobles staggering and screams echoing off the vaulted ceiling. The western wall erupted in flames and debris, massive chunks of stone crashing down onto the assembly.

"We're under attack!" Someone screamed as chaos erupted.

CHAPTER 31

Boom!

The following blast hurled me backward, heat searing my face as shards of stone and glass exploded. I hit the floor, ears ringing from the deafening roar. Around me, nobles screamed and scattered like terrified mice, their fine clothes suddenly coated in dust and debris.

"Lor!" Kyler's voice cut through the chaos as his body covered mine, shielding me from the rain of broken chandeliers and ceiling fragments.

"I'm alright," I gasped, pushing up against his weight. "What's happening?"

Oryn appeared through the smoke, blood trickling from a cut above his eyebrow. "The outer wall's been breached. Can't tell who's attacking."

The grand hall had transformed from an opulent celebration to battlefield in seconds. Stone golems marched toward the breach, their massive forms creating a barricade. Trinity was commanding her creations, green magic swirling in the air as her attention focused on the threat, but the king was being hustled away by his personal guard, his face twisted with rage.

"This is our chance," Kyler hissed, pulling me to my feet.

We ducked behind an overturned table as another explosion rocked the foundation of the castle. Through the dust and debris, I spotted a familiar flash of dark hair across the hall.

"Davian," I breathed, watching the youngest prince stumble as a guard roughly yanked him toward the exit.

His face was ashen, eyes wide with terror. Not the terror of someone fearing for their life, but the blank horror of someone watching their nightmares materialize.

"We need to move," Oryn urged, tugging at my arm.

I jerked my chin toward Davian. "We can't leave him again. Look what they've already done to him."

Kyler followed my gaze, the muscle in his jaw tightening. "Lor, we don't have time for—"

"He's your brother," I cut in, meeting Oryn's eyes. "And he's been suffering. I know you've carried guilt for leaving him, and I refuse to repeat past mistakes."

Something shifted in Oryn's expression—pain, guilt, resolve. He gave a tight nod.

A third explosion sent more of the ceiling crashing down, creating a diversion that couldn't have been more perfect if we'd planned it. We darted through the panicked crowd, keeping low and moving fast.

"Get down!" Kyler shoved me sideways as a chunk of marble smashed where I'd been standing moments before.

We pressed against a column, watching as stone soldiers marched in perfect formation toward the doors. Outside, the sound of battle rang clear—metal on metal, shouts, and screams.

"Esmeray forces?" I wondered aloud.

"Can't be," Oryn replied, peering through the haze. "The attack's too chaotic, not coordinated enough."

"Rebels, then," Kyler suggested. "Either way, it's a distraction we need."

We weaved through the wreckage, dodging fleeing nobles and guards too occupied with the threat to pay us much attention. Davian and his escort had disappeared down the eastern corridor—toward the royal quarters.

"This way," Oryn directed, leading us through a servant's passage that ran parallel to the main hall. The narrow corridor was mercifully empty, allowing us to move quickly without detection.

We emerged near the intersection of the royal wing, just in time to see Davian being shoved into a chamber by two guards who then stationed themselves outside.

"We need a distraction," I whispered, scanning our surroundings.

As if answering my call, another explosion shook the castle, this one closer. The guards looked at each other uncertainly, clearly torn between their orders and self-preservation.

"Stay with the prince," one finally commanded the other before sprinting toward the commotion.

One guard.

We could handle one guard.

Oryn caught my eye, a silent understanding passing between us. He nodded once, then strode out into the open, affecting the imperious demeanor of the crown prince.

"You there!" he called sharply. "Report! What's happening? Where is your partner?"

The guard straightened instinctively at the voice of command. "Your Highness! The castle is under attack from the east. The king has been moved to safety, and—"

His words cut off abruptly as Kyler materialized behind him, delivering a precise blow to the back of his head. The guard crumpled without a sound.

"Nicely done," I murmured, rushing forward as Oryn dragged the unconscious body into an alcove.

The door was locked, but Kyler made short work of it with a thin blade he'd somehow acquired during the chaos. Inside, Davian stood by the window, watching the smoke rise from the eastern courtyard, his shoulders hunched in defeat.

He winced at the sound of our entrance. Surprise colored his face as he realized who had entered. "Oryn? What are you—?"

"No time," Oryn cut him off, crossing the room in quick strides. "We're leaving. Now. You're coming with us."

Davian backed away, shaking his head. "I can't. She'll kill everyone if I—"

"She's going to kill everyone anyway," I interrupted, my patience wearing thin. "Starting with you once she realizes we've gone."

Indecision warred on his face, tears building in his eyes. "You don't understand. She has contingencies, ways to—"

Another blast rocked the castle, making the decision for him. Kyler grabbed Davian's arm in a grip that brooked no argument.

"We're not asking," he said flatly.

Oryn met my eyes across the room, gratitude shining through the tension. He mouthed a silent "thank you" that warmed something deep in my chest.

We had so few loved ones left that we needed to save every one that we could.

I gave him a quick nod, then checked the corridor. "Clear for now. We need to move fast—who knows what we'll find near the kitchens."

We slipped into the hallway, Kyler keeping a firm grip on Davian while Oryn took the lead. I brought up the rear, hyper-aware of every sound, every shadow. The bracelet felt heavier on my wrist, mocking me with its presence even through the chaos surrounding us.

We descended the servants' staircase, encountering no one. The usual bustle of the castle had vanished, replaced by an eerie silence punctuated by distant shouts and the occasional crash. The fighting seemed concentrated on the western side now, drawing attention away from our escape route.

"Left here," Oryn whispered as we reached the lower level. "Through the laundry and past the wine cellar."

The corridors grew narrower, the air thicker with the scents of soap and starch. Davian stumbled along with us, his initial resistance fading with each step. Whatever Trinity had done to break the joyful, boyish prince I'd first met had been thorough.

"Almost there," I murmured as the familiar smells of the kitchen —yeast, spices, wood smoke—reached us.

We rounded the final corner and froze.

Elvirana stood in the middle of the kitchen, arms outstretched, fingers splayed. The air around her crackled with energy, her white hair floating as if underwater. Behind her, the large window we'd planned to escape through gleamed like a beacon.

"Going somewhere?" She asked, her voice eerily calm amid the chaos.

Kyler pushed Davian behind him while Oryn and I fanned out, instinctively creating a triangle of defense.

"Step aside, Elvirana," Oryn commanded.

The old woman laughed. "You still don't understand, do you? This isn't your kingdom anymore. Nor is it your father's. It belongs to powers far greater than you could comprehend."

"Chaos," I said flatly. "Trinity's pet god."

"Not a pet," Elvirana corrected, her eyes gleaming with fanatical light. "The true creator of all fae magic, returning to claim what is rightfully his. And Sunneva will be the seat of his power."

"You're mad," Kyler spat. "You've allowed yourself to be deceived by a woman who doesn't care how many die in her quest for power."

"Sacrifices must be made for greatness," she replied, raising her hands higher. "The weak will perish. The strong will thrive. That is the natural order Chaos will restore."

I felt a flicker of heat against my wrist as my anger built. The bracelet was warming, fighting against the shadows that responded to my rage. I pushed harder, feeling the cold tendrils of power straining against their prison. We were leaving Sunneva tonight. I didn't care if I had to burn off my hand to do it.

"Natural order?" I challenged, taking a step forward. "There's nothing natural about what Trinity plans. She'll destroy everything, including Sunneva."

Elvirana's smile stretched wider, showing too many teeth. "She will remake it! Stronger! Purer! The greatest kingdom in the world, above all others!"

"She's completely lost it," Davian whispered behind us. "She used to be the voice of reason before Trinity came."

"She was never really reasonable," Oryn said through gritted teeth. "Just hid behind the facade Father gave her."

"You cannot step on others to gain power, at some point, that foundation will crumble, and you along with it," I said, watching Elvirana's movements carefully, noting how her fingers twitched and jerked unnaturally. She was channeling more power than her aging body could safely contain.

"You children cannot stop what's coming," she cackled, light beginning to coalesce around her fingertips. "The solstice is upon us! The vessel is prepared! Chaos will walk among us once more, and we shall bathe in the blood of the unworthy. You, dear, are his to wield. The perfect instrument."

"No one wields me, especially not a god who's worshipped by a cult of insanity," I responded, buying time as I felt my shadows growing stronger. Just a little more...

Her face contorted with rage. "You dare mock the prophecy? You, the very key to his return? Your blood will open the gate, willing or not!"

"I'm afraid her blood is staying right where it belongs," Kyler drawled, his tone deceptively casual despite the tension radiating from him.

Elvirana's hands began to glow brighter, the air around her shimmering with heat. "Then you will die upon the altar of iron once my god has deemed you useless."

She raised her arms, the light concentrating into a ball of pure energy between her palms. I braced myself, calling on every fragment of power I could reach through the burning bracelet. Shadows began to weave around us; a shield of darkness slowly began to materialize.

"For Chaos!" she screamed, the spell building to its crescendo.

The sound of metal slicing through flesh cut off her incantation. Elvirana's eyes widened in shock as she looked down at the bloodied sword tip protruding from her stomach.

The energy dissipated as Elvirana slumped forward, revealing a figure standing behind her. Blood-splattered and grinning, with his light hair disheveled from battle and beads of sweat making his handsome face glisten, Lucas stood with a satisfied smirk on his lips.

"She's as crazy as the witch from the mountain," Lucas said, yanking the sword free and letting Elvirana's body crumple to the floor. "Miss me?"

CHAPTER 32

"Lucas!" I gasped, the shadows I'd been gathering instantly dissolving. The iron bracelet around my wrist cooled as I lost focus on my power. Relief crashed through me like a tidal wave, and I launched myself at him, nearly knocking us both over.

He was here, but more importantly, he was alive.

"Easy there, Lor," he laughed, catching me in his arms. "I know I'm irresistible, but we don't have time for that right now."

Two growls rumbled behind us, my mates unhappy with the implication, though their faces couldn't mask the undeniable relief they felt seeing him in the flesh.

"You're alive," I breathed, pulling back to examine his face. A fresh scar ran along his jawline, and his usually bright eyes were shadowed with exhaustion. "I saw you fall in Oakston. I thought—"

"It takes more than that to kill me," he winked, though I could see the pain behind his bravado. "Though I won't lie, I thought I was as good as dead."

"Behind you!" Kyler shouted.

Lucas spun us both around as two figures burst through the

"

kitchen door. My hand instinctively reached for a weapon that wasn't there before I recognized Rasher's hulking form and Candra's distinctive silhouette behind him.

"We need to move," Rasher growled, blood streaking his face and armor. "Now!"

Candra pushed past him, her twin axes dripping crimson. "The stone soldiers are turning the tide. We're losing ground in the main hall."

"I've ordered a full retreat," Rasher added, his eyes quickly assessing our group. "Who's this?" He nodded toward Davian, who had shrunk back against the wall.

"Prince Davian of Sunneva, my brother," Oryn answered, placing a protective hand on his brother's shoulder. "He's coming with us."

"How do we get out? Our exit has been blocked by those things," Candra asked, ignoring Oryn's words.

Kyler gestured toward the window. "Kitchen courtyard. There's a service gate just beyond it."

Rasher nodded. "Let's go. We've got horses waiting outside the northern side of the grounds."

Lucas moved to the window, yanking it open with a grunt. Cool night air rushed in, carrying the distant sounds of battle. "Ladies first," he grinned, offering me his hand.

I took it, climbing onto the sill before dropping the short distance to the cobblestones below. The others quickly followed, Kyler helping Davian while Candra took up the rear position, constantly checking behind us.

"Where did you all come from?" I asked as we hurried across the small courtyard toward a narrow alley that led to the outer walls. "How did you know we were here?"

"We still have spies everywhere," Rasher explained, leading us through the shadows. "By the time we returned to Charmonia and Lucas had healed, Candra had already made a plan to infiltrate. The announcement of the banquet was a convenient opportunity."

"How did he survive that?" I asked. "That was a fatal wound, I'm sure of it."

"It was," Rasher said. "We returned to the castle, and your little friend came down with one of her books. Next thing I knew, her eyes and her hands were glowing and his skin was weaving itself back into place." He shook his head in disbelief. "I don't understand what she did, but whatever it was, she saved his life."

"And the troops?" Kyler cut in. "Ours?"

"The forces are mixed," Candra said. "Lucas was able to get help through their... guild. Not enough to win, but enough to create a distraction."

We sprinted across the open space toward the servants' gate. I could see freedom beyond it—the dark outline of trees against the night sky, the promise of escape just within reach.

"Alora," Lucas caught my arm as we ran, his voice low and urgent. "Vanya sent a message: 'The shadows know. Bring them to the light.'"

The cryptic words settled into my mind, resonating with something deep inside me. "What does that mean?"

"Hell if I know," he shrugged. "But she said you'd understand when the time came."

We reached the gate, Rasher working quickly to break the lock. The sounds of battle having grown fainter behind us, the retreat was in full swing. Anxiety clawed at my chest—we were so close to freedom.

"Almost got it," Rasher muttered.

The lock clicked open in Rasher's hands, and the gate swung free with a creak of rusty hinges. We slipped through the gate one by one, emerging onto a narrow path that led away from the castle. Freedom beckoned me, the sweet scent of wildflowers and night air replacing the stench of blood and smoke.

"This way," Rasher pointed toward a cluster of trees. "The horses are just beyond—"

A crackling sound split the air, like lightning striking too close.

The hairs on my arms stood on end as a sickly green light illuminated the space before us. The air itself seemed to tear open, revealing a swirling vortex of energy.

Trinity stepped through, her elegant gown now replaced with a battle outfit of black leather. Her hair whipped around her face, which was twisted into a smile of cold triumph.

"Leaving so soon?" she purred. "But the celebration is just beginning."

We froze, the sorceress the last obstacle to freedom. Kyler and Oryn immediately moved in front of me, while Rasher and Candra raised their weapons. Lucas positioned Davian towards the side, as far away as they could get from the wicked woman.

"Trinity," I stepped forward, pushing my mates despite their protests. "This ends now."

Her laughter rang through the cool air. "Oh, my darling daughter. You're right about that." She raised her hands, green magic crackling between her fingers. "This does end now."

Before any of us could react, the portal behind her expanded rapidly, engulfing us all in its sickening light. I felt Kyler's hand grip mine, Oryn reaching for my other arm, but it was too late.

The world dissolved around us, my stomach lurching as we were pulled through space itself. Wind howled in my ears, drowning out the shouts of the others. My skin burned with the magic tearing at us.

Then, just as suddenly, we crashed onto solid ground. My knees hit stone; the impact jarred through my body. Gasping for breath, I looked up.

We were in a vast cavern, its walls glowing with an eerie light that reflected off countless iron surfaces. Iron columns rose to a ceiling lost in jagged shadows. Iron chains hung from the walls. And at the center of it all stood a massive throne, forged entirely of the metal that burned around my wrist. Candles burned in iron holders, casting long shadows across the floor. The air here felt heavy, oppressive, suffused with ancient power and malice.

Trinity stood before the throne, her arms spread wide in welcome.

"Welcome," she said, her voice echoing in the cavernous space, "to Chaos' kingdom. The only place where a god could fall and rise." She smiled, revealing teeth that seemed too sharp. "The solstice may be days away, but I think we'll start the ritual early. After all, we have everything we need right here."

I struggled to my feet, feeling the weight of the iron in the air pressing against my chest. Beside me, Kyler and Oryn were also rising, their faces contorted with pain as the ambient iron burned their fae skin. Rasher seemed less affected, his partly human origins offering some protection. Lucas, fully human, appeared uncomfortable but not in agony.

Candra and Davian were pulled with us, both looking disoriented but intact. We had all been swept up in Trinity's portal.

"The island where gods bleed," I whispered, recalling the words that had spun in my mind for days on end while searching for Kyler.

Trinity's smile widened as she watched comprehension dawn on my face. "Very good, Alora. You see, some rituals require specific locations. And this island has been soaking in divine blood for millennia. Untouched, waiting for the right moment to be of use." Trinity gestured around us. "This is where Chaos was imprisoned by the other gods. They bound him in chains of iron and left him to suffer until they banished him to the other realm." Her eyes gleamed with a fervent light. "And this is where he will rise again, now that the vessel is ready."

Horror washed over me as I realized what she meant. It wasn't just my blood she needed, it was me. Chaos would use my body as his gateway into this world.

"I won't let you," I said, my hand reaching for Kyler's. "I'll die first."

"That can be arranged," Trinity said pleasantly. "Though I'd prefer you alive for the ritual. It makes the transition so much cleaner."

She raised her hands, magic gathering around her fingertips. "Now, shall we begin? I've waited long enough for this moment."

The rough stone hands of her golems clamped down around us, holding us in place.

There was no escape.

CHAPTER 33

Trinity stood before the iron throne, her hands raised in triumph. Green lightning crackled between her fingers, casting eerie shadows across the cavern walls. The sight, and the sheer might of the magic in this place could have been breathtaking if it weren't so terrifying.

"At last," she breathed, her voice carrying an almost reverent quality. "This is the moment I've waited my entire life for."

I struggled against the stone hands that pushed me to my knees, pinning me to the ground. Beside me, Kyler and Oryn were similarly restrained, both fighting with all their strength against Trinity's golems. Lucas and Rasher were thrown against the far wall. Candra now lay unconscious beside them. Davian huddled behind a column, eyes wide with terror.

"Let her go!" Kyler roared, the veins in his neck standing out as he strained against his captors.

Trinity laughed, the sound bouncing off the iron surfaces surrounding us. "Such devotion. It's almost touching." She approached me, crouching to stroke my cheek with cold fingers. "My daughter. My vessel. The perfect conduit for a god."

I jerked my face away. "I'm not your daughter."

"Blood is blood," she said simply, rising to her feet. "And yours is particularly special. The perfect blend of ancient lineages, containing just the right magical signature." She gestured to the golems. "Bring her to the altar."

The stone soldiers lifted me, my feet dangling uselessly as they carried me toward a flat slab of iron positioned before the throne. No matter how hard I kicked or thrashed, their grip remained unbreakable.

"Alora!" Oryn's desperate voice cut through my panic. His face contorted with rage and fear as he fought harder against his restraints. "Trinity, stop this madness!"

"Madness?" Trinity whirled on him, her eyes flashing. "Is it madness to restore what was lost? To bring back the true power of the fae? The gods abandoned us, Prince of Sunneva, but one remained faithful. One whispered secrets, shared visions of glory."

Her golems threw me down on the altar, the cold iron burning against my skin. Before I could roll away, iron shackles snapped around my wrists and ankles, securing me to the slab. I pulled against them, feeling them bite into my flesh.

"This won't work," I spat. "Whatever Chaos has promised you is a lie. The other gods won't allow you to do this."

Trinity smiled, a terrible, serene expression. "Oh, but it will work. Your blood has proven most responsive to my tests." She turned to the stone table beside the altar, where various instruments were laid out in neat rows. "The solstice may be days away, but this place... this sacred place strengthens the connection."

She selected a familiar knife. Its dark hilt and blade of starlight had kept me company for many nights. The last gift my grandmother had ever given me.

"Thank you for returning this to me," she mused as she went to work, cutting thin slits across my arms and legs. I gritted against the sting as dark crimson blood trickled down onto the table and dripped to the floor. Once satisfied with the flow, she walked out of my eyesight, only to return with a glowing orb.

The orb from the book of the gods, the one that I held in Sunneva for Elvirana.

Trinity placed the orb on a pillar beside the throne, focusing entirely on me. She began arranging candles around the altar, placing strange objects at specific points—a black feather, a piece of bone, a vial of swirling silver liquid. With each item, she muttered words in a language I didn't understand, the air growing heavier with magic. My mates begged for this to stop, for my life, even to take my place. Their words fell on deaf ears.

"Trinity," I tried once more, desperate now. "This won't bring back what you think. It won't make you happy."

Her movements stilled momentarily. "Happiness?" She looked genuinely perplexed. "This was never about happiness, Alora. It's about power. About restoring what was rightfully ours." She resumed her preparations. "The humans took over our world, diluted our bloodlines, made us weaker. Chaos will purify us all."

"By killing innocent people? By destroying everything?"

"By rebuilding," she corrected. "Sometimes creation requires destruction first."

I turned my head, seeking Kyler's eyes across the cavern. His face was a mask of determination as he worked at his restraints. Beside him, Oryn was doing the same, blood trickling from his wrists where the stone had scraped his skin raw.

She raised the knife above me. "Your blood will open the gate. Your body will house him. If he deems it."

"And then what happens to me?" I demanded, though I already knew the answer.

Trinity's smile was almost pitying. "Does it really matter? Now," her voice raised an octave. "We begin."

She placed a hand on my forehead, the other holding the knife above my chest. "Blood of my blood, flesh of my flesh, I offer this vessel to you, Great Chaos, last of the true gods!"

The knife descended toward my heart.

"NO!" Kyler's anguished cry rang out as he somehow broke free from his restraints, reaching desperately toward me.

Trinity faltered at his outburst, the knife stopping inches from my chest. She turned, fury transforming her face into something inhuman.

"Hold them!" she commanded her golems.

That final moment, my eyes locked with both my mates. Every word I wished I could say reflected in the tears that started to stream down my face.

"May Fate entwine our paths again," I whispered as the tip of the knife breached my flesh.

I STOOD in a vast emptiness dotted with distant stars—a place between worlds. The air here felt strange, neither hot nor cold, and sound seemed to travel differently, as if through water.

"Alora Satori."

The voice came from everywhere and nowhere, deep and ancient and terrible. I turned slowly, facing the source.

A figure stood before me, tall and imposing. At first glance, it appeared to be a man, but as I looked closer, its features shifted constantly, never settling on one form. Sometimes it appeared as a great beast with molten eyes, then shifted to a swirling vortex of darkness, then transformed into something my mind couldn't grasp. Far different from Death, who hid beneath his hooded cloak.

"Chaos," I said, surprised my voice didn't waver.

The being inclined what might have been its head. "You know me."

"I know you've been banished to this realm by the other gods. That is enough."

A sound like laughter rumbled through the strange space, booming like thunder. "Is that what they say about me, little fae? That my brothers and sisters locked me away?"

"It is."

The being moved closer, circling me with fluid grace. "And you believe that to be true?"

I stood my ground, refusing to show fear. "I do."

"Interesting." The figure stopped before me. "My brother's chosen champions have always intrigued me. His heralds of death had cowered before me. But not you. Even if you know nothing."

"Then enlighten me," I challenged.

"I believe my chosen sent you to me, yes?" He waited for my nod before continuing. "Her devotion is... admirable. But she misunderstands my intentions just as your world has misunderstood its gods' departure."

"So Trinity is your champion?" I asked. "You are the one that's put all of this," I gestured with my arms, "into motion."

"We don't get to choose our champions, little fae," Chaos said simply. "And that is part of the reason we've distanced ourselves. You heathens disrupted the balance that your world once had. Gods and mortals, life and death, order and... well, chaos." The being gestured to itself. "But the mortals who were blessed with a direct connection to us turned. Their souls rotted with an ambition beyond their means."

I frowned, trying to understand. "Your champions destroyed the balance?"

"Indeed. Destruction may be part of my nature," Chaos admitted. "But so is creation. One cannot exist without the other. You see, I gave the people of your world the power to thrive. To help their harvest be bountiful, to bring water to towns in drought, to always be able to light a fire to stay warm. My chosen had begged me on behalf of mortals when blight and famine threatened their very existence. But my gift went astray, and soon the people began harnessing gifts of their own."

"The fae," I said. "That turned into the powers the fae develop on their twenty-first birthday."

"Yes," he continued. "That taste of power only grew. Soon, they requested access to us to help us, they said. Life and Death's were mostly diligent, though sometimes a person would come back to life or too many souls were lost. Fate's grew... troubled with the knowledge of what would come to pass. Power's temple only grew." Chaos continued to pace around me, the vast nothingness stretching endlessly in all directions. "When they gained everything they asked for, they wanted more."

The god's form shifted constantly, skin crackling like obsidian glass with cracks of molten fire beneath, then dissolving into swirling smoke with eyes like distant stars.

"So the gods abandoned us?" I asked, struggling to understand. "Because we asked for too much?"

Chaos made a sound that might have been a laugh. "Not abandoned, little fae. *Limited*. We had to establish boundaries. Our chosen ones had become corrupted by the very power they wielded in our names."

"Your champion," I said, connecting the pieces. "Trinity."

"Not just her," Chaos replied, the form solidifying momentarily into something resembling a tall man with shifting features. "All our champions began to use our gifts for their own gain. Power's chosen became tyrants. Life's chosen became zealots who decided who was worthy of healing. Death's grew to fear their own shadows."

He moved closer, and I forced myself not to retreat. "But yes, my champions were always the most... susceptible. The nature of chaos is freedom, potential, possibility. In the wrong hands, that becomes destruction for destruction's sake."

"You're saying Trinity is corrupted?" I asked, my mind still trying to put the pieces together.

"I whispered to her, yes," Chaos admitted, his voice taking on a distant quality. "But not what she claims. When she found that ancient text, I felt her seeking me. I warned her to stop her search, to close the book, to walk away from the power she sought."

"But she didn't listen."

"She heard what she wanted to hear," Chaos said, darkness rippling through his form. "The corruption had already taken root. She claimed I promised her power, dominion, rebirth. What I offered was balance, harmony, peace."

I stared at him, disbelief coursing through me. "Peace? Your champion has murdered innocents, created stone armies, kidnapped my mates, tried to kill me more than once—all in your name!"

"Not in my name," Chaos said sharply, the space around us trembling. "Only what she believes I am, what humans and fae have reduced me to in their stories—a force of pure destruction."

"But even Death warned me about—"

"Chaos. Pure, uncontrolled chaos. Creation without the right intent. Something dark and insidious," he interrupted. "And he was right to do so."

The being's form shifted again, this time revealing glimpses of what might have been its true nature—something more complex, a beast of a man twice the size of Rasher with glowing eyes. I saw creation and destruction in perfect balance, the birth of stars and their inevitable collapse, forests burning only to be reborn from ash.

"The other gods' champions could handle their gifts," Chaos continued. "They faltered, yes, but they understood the responsibility. Mine never could. The power was too intoxicating, too easily twisted."

"So you cut yourself off," I said, beginning to understand. "All the gods did."

"We limited our interactions, hoping to regain balance." Chaos's voice softened. "But some connections remained—thin threads to those whose souls were naturally attuned to us. We waited until the one Fate foresaw took their first breath of life."

"Me," I whispered.

"Precisely." Chaos nodded. "Only the harbinger of death and flame could survive this."

I swallowed hard, processing everything. The truth reframed everything I thought I knew about Trinity, about the gods, about my own purpose.

"What happens now?" I asked. "Trinity killed me to give you a vessel. But you're not coming to our realm, are you?"

Chaos's form flickered, almost appearing sad. "No. I will not enter your world as she hopes. That would upset the balance further."

"So, she failed." The realization should have been comforting, but something in Chaos's manner made me uneasy. "What will she do next?"

"She will try again," Chaos said simply. "And again. She will sacrifice more innocent lives in her quest to force my manifestation. She is beyond reason now, consumed by her vision of what should be."

Panic rose in my chest. "My mates—Kyler and Oryn—she'll hurt them. And my friends."

"Most likely," Chaos agreed. "Unless someone stops her."

I looked up at the god, sudden clarity washing over me. "That's why I'm here, isn't it? You want me to stop her."

"I cannot intervene directly," Chaos said. "None of us can, not without risking greater imbalance. But you—you walk between worlds already. Death has touched you. And my gift runs in your veins."

"Your gift?" I asked, confused.

"Fire," Chaos replied. "The most primal element of transformation. Destruction that leads to creation."

My heart pounded as the pieces fell into place. "I barely have any control over it."

"The fire is part of you, as are the shadows."

I thought of Oryn's words during training—not containing the fire, but directing it. Working with it instead of against it.

"There is nothing to be done unless you return," Chaos continued. "Only you can restore balance and protect your world now. You are the balance."

"Return?" I echoed. "But Trinity killed me. How can I—"

"Death is not ready to take you, little fae," Chaos interrupted. "You will not cross over yet."

Chaos's form began to blur at the edges, the vast emptiness around us starting to shimmer and warp. "Our time grows short. The veil thins."

"Wait!" I reached out. "You haven't told me—"

"You are the balance, harbinger of flame," Chaos's voice began to fade. "The gods have not yet abandoned you—we have been waiting for you to accept your fate."

The void around me began to dissolve, golden light piercing through the darkness. The world exploded into white light, and I felt myself falling, hurtling back toward my body. My last thought before consciousness claimed me was of Kyler and Oryn, their faces clear in my mind. I would return to them. I would save them.

And I would end Trinity's madness once and for all.

CHAPTER 34

I gasped, air rushing into my lungs like a tidal wave. My body convulsed, back arching off the cold iron altar as if pulled by invisible strings. The wound in my chest burned, then sealed itself in a flash of golden light. Every nerve ending ignited, power surging through my veins like molten metal.

"What's happening?" Trinity's voice pierced through the haze, her tone shifting from triumph to uncertainty.

I couldn't respond, couldn't think. My vision blurred as golden fire erupted from my skin, dancing across my body in intricate patterns. The iron shackles at my wrists and ankles grew hot, then white-hot, then—

Crack.

The restraints shattered, fragments of metal flying in all directions. Trinity stumbled backward, arms raised to shield her face.

"Alora?" Kyler's voice was distant, a mix of alarm and desperate hope.

I sat up slowly, my movements fluid despite the pain that had ravaged my body moments before. The golden fire continued to dance across my skin, curling around my fingers like affectionate serpents. My vision sharpened, colors more vibrant than I'd ever seen them.

"My lord," Trinity whispered, dropping to her knees. "You've come. You've finally come."

She thought *I* was Chaos. That the god had taken over my body.

Let her believe it.

I slid off the altar, my feet touching the stone floor with barely a sound. The iron bracelet that had bound my magic was gone, dissolved into dust. Power flowed through me unrestricted, a heady rush that made my head spin.

"Release them," I commanded, my voice layered with something ancient and terrible.

Trinity prostrated herself, forehead touching the ground. "Of course, my lord. Anything you command." She gestured sharply, and the stone soldiers holding Kyler and Oryn stepped back, releasing their bonds as well as their grip.

My mates staggered forward, their faces reflecting disbelief, hope, and fear in equal measure. The others—Lucas, Rasher, Candra, and Davian—remained quiet, now all conscious, as they watched the scene before them.

"Lor?" Oryn whispered, taking a hesitant step toward me. "Tell me you're still there, Love."

I raised a hand, warning him to stay back. I needed to maintain the illusion for just a little longer.

"My champion," I said, the golden fire intensifying around me. "You've served your purpose well."

She raised her head, eyes shining with fanatical devotion. "Thank you, my lord. I have dedicated my life to your return."

"Indeed." I stepped closer, the flames trailing behind me like a cloak. "Rise. Stand before your god."

She scrambled to her feet, trembling with excitement. "What is your command, Great Chaos? How shall we begin our reign?"

I reached out, placing my hand against her cheek. She leaned into the touch, her eyes fluttering closed in ecstasy.

"With your death."

Trinity's eyes opened. The confusion on her face shifted to horror as understanding dawned. "No—"

"Yes," I snarled, shadows suddenly erupting from my fingertips as my flames turned a brilliant white.

I struck without warning, a whip of shadow and fire lashing out to wrap around her throat. Trinity's scream cut off as I yanked her forward, her feet scraping across the stone floor.

"Did you really think it would be so easy?" I hissed, bringing her face close to mine. "That I would simply surrender my body to a god who doesn't even want it."

"Alora? Impossible," she choked out, clawing at the shadow-fire binding her. "The ritual—"

"Revealed the truth," I finished for her. "Chaos isn't coming to our world, Trinity. He never was. You deluded yourself into believing your own lies."

With a flick of my wrist, I sent her flying across the cavern. She crashed into the iron throne, the impact echoing throughout the chamber. Before she could recover, I was upon her again, shadows and flames weaving around my arms like armor.

Trinity's face contorted with rage. "Then I'll have to bring the fae glory on my own. If Chaos won't take you willingly, I'll tear your soul from your body and leave it empty for him!"

She unleashed a torrent of green energy that cut through the air like a scythe. I raised my hands instinctively, and a wall of white fire materialized before me, absorbing the attack with a deafening sizzle.

"You still don't understand," I said, advancing steadily as she backed away. "He will not join you."

"Lies!" Trinity screamed, hurling another blast of power.

I deflected it with a sweep of my arm, the energy dissipating against the cavern wall. "He spoke to me, Trinity. He doesn't want this, he never did."

"Shut up!" She summoned her stone soldiers with a sharp gesture. "Kill her! Kill them all!"

The golems lurched forward, their massive forms closing in from all sides. I felt rather than saw Kyler and Oryn moving to stand with me, their presence at my back a comfort even in this chaos.

"Stay back," I ordered, gathering my power.

With a roar that tore from the depths of my soul, I released a wave of ivory fire that swept outward in all directions. The stone soldiers closest to us crumbled to dust, their magically bound connection to Trinity severed by the pure force of my will.

But others kept coming, dozens of them filing into the cavern from hidden passages.

"Free the others!" I shouted to Kyler and Oryn as I burned away the bracelets that still wrapped around their wrists. A golem lumbered towards me on my left. With my hand encased in flame, I blocked him from coming any closer to my mates and friends.

Oryn and Kyler sprinted toward our friends, dodging stone fists and stomping feet. I couldn't watch their progress—Trinity was advancing again, her face twisted with hatred as she summoned more power to her hands.

"You could have ruled at my side while Chaos shaped the world for us, stupid girl," she snarled. "With your power, every continent would bow to us."

"I never wanted to rule anything," I snarled, shadows gathering around me like a storm cloud. "I only wanted to live."

We clashed in the center of the cavern, green lightning against white fire, her hatred against my determination. The force of the collision sent shockwaves through the chamber, cracking the stone beneath our feet.

From the corner of my eye, I saw Kyler free Lucas from his restraints, while Oryn worked on Rasher's bonds. Candra tried to tear at Davian's while still restrained herself. Their faces strained as they watched the battle unfold.

Trinity and I circled each other, both panting from exertion. My power was exhilarating but taxing—I could feel it draining my strength with each passing second.

"You're weakening already," Trinity observed, a cruel smile playing on her lips. "This power isn't truly yours. You're borrowing it, like a child playing with a wooden sword."

She struck again, a bolt of energy that caught me in the shoulder before I could fully dodge it. Pain exploded up my arm, but I gritted my teeth and countered with a blast of shadow-fire that sent her staggering back.

"Maybe so," I gasped, fighting to maintain control. "But I'm not finished."

Trinity laughed. "I think you are, daughter. Look around, your friends are fighting for their lives. Your mates are outnumbered. And you—you're barely holding on. All that power wasted on someone so weak. You will all die here."

She was right. Despite my initial surge of power, I was struggling. The fire wanted to consume everything in its path, including me. The shadows threatened to devour the light. Balancing these forces required concentration I couldn't maintain while fighting Trinity.

A crash from behind made me glance back. Kyler had been thrown against a wall by a golem, while Oryn fought desperately to reach him. Lucas and Rasher were back-to-back, surrounded by stone soldiers. Candra had somehow gotten up, defending Davian while her restraints still kept her wrists together.

"See?" Trinity smiled. "Even without a god at my side, you failed."

"I haven't failed yet," I said, straightening my spine despite the pain.

I closed my eyes briefly, remembering Chaos's words. *You are the balance.*

Power wasn't meant to be contained, it needs direction to flow to its destination. It's just like Oryn's words in the training ring.

I took a deep breath and let go, letting my power flow from me.

The fire surged, but instead of fighting it, I embraced it. Instead of trying to hold the shadows back, I welcomed them. The two forces spiraled around me, no longer fighting for dominance but dancing together in perfect harmony.

Trinity's eyes widened as she sensed the change. "What are you doing?"

I didn't answer. Instead, I unleashed a focused beam of shadow-fire that struck her square in the chest, sending her flying backward into the iron throne. The impact bent the metal, fragments breaking off and clattering to the floor.

"Impossible," she gasped, struggling to rise. "You can't possibly control—"

"I am Death's Wraith," I cut her off, advancing steadily. "I am of shadow, harbinger of flame. I am the balance between destruction and creation." Each word carried power, making the very air vibrate. "And I am done letting you hurt the people I love."

Trinity's face contorted with hatred as she summoned every ounce of her remaining power. Green lightning arced from her fingertips, coalescing into a massive sphere of crackling energy.

"You are nothing!" she screamed, hurling the sphere at me with all her might.

I met it with my own blast of shadow-fire, the two forces colliding in midair with a sound like thunder. The shockwave knocked everyone off their feet, stone soldiers tumbling one after another.

We stood locked in a deadly stalemate, neither yielding an inch. Her green energy pushed against my brilliant flames, the point of contact spitting sparks and bolts of wild magic. The cavern trembled around us, dust and small rocks fell from the ceiling.

Sweat trickled down my forehead as I struggled to maintain the connection. My arms shook with the effort, muscles screaming in protest. The fire was burning too hot, too fast—consuming my strength at an alarming rate.

Trinity sensed my weakness, a triumphant smile spreading

across her face as she poured more power into her attack. The green energy began to push back my flames, inch by agonizing inch.

"You see?" she called over the roar of our colliding magic. "You're not strong enough. You never were."

My vision began to blur, darkness creeping in at the edges. The fire was fading, my shadows thinning as exhaustion took its toll.

"Lor!" Kyler's voice cut through the chaos. "Hold it, we're coming!"

"Don't give up, Love!" Oryn shouted, both of their voices giving me strength even as my body failed. They were pushing towards us, but with every golem they took down, two more appeared between us.

Trinity laughed, watching me struggle. "Your mates can't save you, child. No one can."

I gritted my teeth, digging deep for any reserve of power I could find. The fire flickered, threatening to go out entirely. My arms felt like lead; my legs barely supported my weight.

You are the balance, Chaos had said. *The gods have not abandoned you.*

In this moment, it felt like they had.

I thought of everything Trinity had taken from me—my childhood, my grandmother, Maël, my father, my peace. I thought of the innocent lives she'd destroyed, and the pain she'd caused in her mad quest for power.

Didn't I tell you that you are not supposed to die? Maël's warm voice flooded my head. Even my hallucinations knew this was the end. Except, a bright light caught my eye in the space beside me. A specter of Maël stood beside me, looking just as he had on our last night together. A sad smile painted his face.

How can I see you? I asked, fighting back a sob.

I've always been here, Lor. Maël brushed a ghostly finger down my cheek. *Keeping you company when you needed me most, and when you didn't... I waited until you needed me again. And right now, it looks like you need me.*

I don't understand.

That smile grew as the specter leaned closer. *You've saved so many, let the ones you couldn't save save you now. We've been waiting for your call.* He stretched an arm out as more light appeared around us. Surrounding Trinity and me were the ghostly figures of each and every person I knew from Briarwood, and even some I recognized from burning villages and the guild. The dim cavern soon became as bright as a star as it filled with souls.

I looked to my other side as I tracked the faces that had joined us, realizing everyone was seeing what I was. My mates and friends watched as ghosts swarmed, decimating the remaining golems. It wasn't until the last golem fell that I noticed who stood on my other side.

My grandmother's worn face scowled towards her daughter, and beside her, Magnus stood, stoic and strong. His hand rested on my shoulder, and what I would have given to be able to feel it.

I feel like I'm losing each of you all over again. Tears welled in my eyes as I turned my head towards Maël again.

It's not goodbye, we will be together again. When it's your time, of course.

The light increased as the ghosts stepped into the tangle of magic between Trinity and me. One by one, they sacrificed their souls one last time until all that was left was me, Maël, my grandmother, and Magnus.

We're proud of you, girl. My grandmother beamed at me before she and Magnus stepped into the fray, dissolving into the magic.

Maël took a step and stopped before joining them.

Maël, please. I begged, unable to bear losing him again.

I love you, Alora. Live the life you were meant to. With one final smile, he vanished before me, sacrificing his soul.

Their sacrifices broke me, but the surge of magic began to overpower Trinity's, allowing me the much needed moments of reprieve. Within moments, my shadow-fire had almost entirely consumed Trinity's. Even from here, I could see the sweat beading on her brow and the look of sheer panic on her face.

Despite my shattered heart, I found one last spark. I needed to do this for them, for everyone I lost, but also for *me*.

"You're wrong," I gasped, forcing the words past dry lips. "I am enough."

With everything I had left, I pushed back against her power, calling to the fire that burned within my soul. White flames erupted from my skin once more, brighter than before, fueled by something deeper than magic—by love, by rage, by sheer stubborn will.

Trinity's confident expression faltered as my attack gained momentum, pushing her energy back toward her. "No—"

I matched her step for step as she backed away from me. Another step. Then another. Each movement cost me dearly, but I refused to yield. The fire was consuming me from within, my skin blistering with the effort of using so much power, but still I pressed on.

Trinity continued to retreat until her back hit the twisted remains of the iron throne. Fear flashed across her face as she realized she had nowhere left to run.

"It's over, Trinity," I said, my voice barely audible over the roar of our clashing magic.

She bared her teeth in a feral snarl. "Never!"

With a desperate surge, she poured everything she had into one final attack. The green energy swelled, pushing against my flames with renewed force. For a moment, I felt myself sliding backward, my strength failing as darkness crowded my vision.

I can't hold on, I thought, despair threatening to overwhelm me. *I'm not strong enough after all.*

But just as my knees began to buckle, I felt something—a hand on my shoulder, warm and steady. Then another on my back. And another gripping my arm.

Kyler.

Oryn.

Lucas.

Rasher.

Even Candra and Davian.

They stood with me, surrounding me, lending me their strength just as mine was failing. I couldn't see them, couldn't turn my head to look, but I felt them—their presence, their determination, their love.

And in that moment, I understood what Chaos meant.

I am the balance.

I'm not alone. I was never alone.

With a final desperate cry, I channeled everything I had left into the brilliantly white flames. My power surged forward, pushing through Trinity's defense, consuming her green energy as they advanced.

Her eyes widened in terror as my attack breached her final barrier. "This isn't possible—"

The shadow-fire reached her fingertips, climbing up her arms like hungry vines. She screamed, a sound of pure anguish echoed through the cavern. Flames consumed her until nothing but ash was left where she stood.

I let out a breath of relief, releasing my hold on the last threads of my power. Dizziness muddled my brain, my equilibrium unbalanced as I watched the world fall as I fell to the ground.

CHAPTER 35

Light filtered through my eyelids, painting the darkness behind them a soft red. My body felt heavy, weighted down as if I'd been buried beneath a mountain of sand. Every breath required deliberate effort, my lungs expanding painfully against bruised ribs.

I'd been here before—this space between consciousness and oblivion. The familiar sensation of having pushed my body beyond its limits, of having touched death's door only to be pulled back at the last moment.

Voices murmured around me, too distant to decipher. A cool hand pressed against my forehead, followed by a tingling sensation that crawled across my skin like winter frost creeping across a windowpane.

"She's waking up," someone said—Luella's voice, sounding both exhausted and relieved.

I fought to open my eyes, my lids as heavy as ancient stone slabs. When I finally managed it, the world blurred into indistinct shapes and colors before slowly sharpening into focus.

Luella stood over me, her hands glowing with pale blue light as they hovered inches above my chest. Dark circles shadowed her eyes, and her normally pristine appearance had given way to disheveled hair and wrinkled clothing. She looked like she hadn't slept in days.

"Welcome back," she whispered, a tired smile spreading across her face.

"How long?" My voice came out as a rasp, my throat parched and raw.

"Four days," came Kyler's voice from my right. His hand found mine, fingers intertwining with gentle pressure.

I turned my head, wincing at the stiffness in my neck, to find him seated beside the bed. He looked as exhausted as Luella, his dark hair disheveled and stubble shadowing his jaw. But his eyes—those deep chestnut eyes—were bright with unshed tears.

"We thought we'd lost you," he said, his voice breaking on the last word.

"Again," Oryn added from my left, his hand finding my other one. He looked no better than Kyler, his golden hair dull with neglect, dark circles under his eyes.

I tried to sit up, but Luella placed a firm hand on my shoulder. "Not yet. I'm still mending your internal injuries." The blue glow intensified around her hands. "You've suffered greatly, my lady."

"Trinity," I whispered, memories flooding back—the cavern, the altar, the fight. "What happened?"

"*You* happened," Lucas said from the foot of the bed, his trademark grin dimmed but present. "You went full wraith on her ass. Even brought a bunch of spirits into the fight."

My gaze swept the room, taking in the familiar surroundings of Kyler's chambers in Esmeray. Rasher stood near the door, arms crossed but relief evident in his usually stoic expression. Candra leaned against the wall beside him, looking less hostile than I remembered. Davian sat in a chair in the corner, looking young and vulnerable, but far less haunted than before.

"The last thing I remember was..." I closed my eyes, trying to retrieve the fragmented memories. "Trinity turned to ash. And then..."

"And then you collapsed," Oryn finished for me, his thumb tracing circles on my palm. "Your power completely drained. Your heart..." His voice faltered. "Your heart stopped twice on the journey back."

"How did we get back?" I asked, trying to piece together the gaps.

"Lucas and I carried you," Kyler said. "Rasher led us through the caverns to the shore, where we were lucky to find a small boat."

Lucas shivered in the corner.

Luella finished her healing, the blue glow fading as she slumped into a chair that Rasher quickly pushed behind her. "That's all I can do for now," she said, wiping sweat from her brow. "She'll need rest, but the worst of the damage is repaired."

"Thank you," I said, reaching out to squeeze her hand. "For everything."

She gave me a tired smile. "What are friends for if not bringing you back from the brink of death? You freed me from the chains of Sunneva, this was the least I could do."

Carefully, with Kyler and Oryn's help, I managed to sit up against the pillows. The room spun momentarily before settling. "What's happened since the battle?"

My friends exchanged glances, a silent conversation passing between them.

"Where do we even start?" Lucas chuckled, dragging a hand through his hair.

"The beginning would be nice," I replied, my voice growing stronger.

Kyler shifted, sitting on the edge of the bed beside me. "After we got you back to Esmeray, Luella began healing you immediately. She's barely left your side since."

"None of us have," Oryn added. "But while we waited for you to recover, the kingdoms have been... adjusting."

"Adjusting?"

Rasher stepped forward. "The casualties from the banquet were far greater than we anticipated. We've heard the king of Sunneva perished in the battle."

Lucas' eyes turned down towards the floor. "As did Vanya and most of the guild."

"There were very few survivors," Davian added. "The remaining nobles have formed a temporary council until..."

"Until I return," Oryn finished. "They've asked me to take the throne, as is my right."

I looked at him, seeing the conflict in his eyes. "And will you?"

He exhaled slowly. "I don't know yet. There's much to consider."

"Sunneva needs a ruler who understands peace," Kyler said. "After what Trinity and the king did, the kingdom is fractured."

"What about Esmeray?" I asked, turning to Rasher.

A shadow crossed his face. "They have been waiting patiently. The council has named you their queen," Rasher said, a rare smile ghosting across his lips. "In Kyler's absence, they recognized you as his mate and therefore their legitimate ruler."

"But Kyler's here—I can't—" I sputtered, panic rising in my chest.

"Relax," Kyler soothed, squeezing my hand. "It's our tradition to honor our queens first. They're expecting us both once you're better. Rasher has been handling matters in the meantime."

"But eventually..." I trailed off, the implications overwhelming.

"Eventually, we'll figure it out," Oryn said firmly. "Together."

"Then what comes next?" I asked.

Kyler and Oryn exchanged a meaningful look that made me feel like I had missed way more than they had told me.

"We were hoping you could tell us," Kyler said. "You're the one who saved us all, after all."

I shook my head. "I didn't do it alone. I wasn't strong enough."

"You never had to do it alone," Oryn said. "We're stronger together."

I paused, realizing he was right. Fate gave me two mates so I'd never walk this life alone, two very infuriating men who would surely never let me out of their sights for a long, long time. She even gave me friends that I've come to know as family. Despite how much had been taken from me, Fate had guided me to discover gemstones among the ash and ruin.

"I want..." I paused. I wasn't entirely sure what I wanted anymore. Peace, certainly. Safety for those I loved. But beyond that?

"You just want what?" Oryn prompted gently.

"I want to go home one last time before everything changes," I decided.

"You can't travel in this state," Kyler said.

Luella stood, swaying slightly before steadying herself. "No, but you will be travel ready soon. But first, you need to rest. Your body has been through tremendous trauma."

She silently shuffled out of the room, with the help of Davian steadying her. One by one, my friends filed out until all that was left was Kyler, Oryn and me. They slid into bed beside me, careful not to jostle me.

"This is usually where my books end with 'and they lived happily ever after'," I said. "Will we find our 'happily ever after'?"

Oryn brushed a hair from my forehead. "As long as it's the three of us, we'll always have our 'happily ever after.'"

As sleep claimed me, I felt their heartbeats synchronize with mine, three rhythms finding harmony. For the first time in longer than I could remember, I drifted off without fear, without dread, without the weight of a prophecy and destiny crushing my chest.

Just peace, and the warmth of the two men I loved more than life itself.

CHAPTER 36

A few days later, I was well enough to travel by horse to Briarwood. The journey to Briarwood seemed longer than I remembered. Perhaps because this time, I wasn't running for my life or chasing after someone else's. The dirt path leading to my childhood village appeared narrower, the trees taller, the shadows less menacing than they once were in my memories.

Kyler rode beside me, his dark eyes scanning our surroundings with the vigilance that never quite left him, even if our enemies were gone. Oryn stayed close on my other side, occasionally reaching across to squeeze my hand when the silence stretched too long.

"Are you certain you're ready for this?" Kyler asked, his voice low enough that only I could hear.

I nodded, unable to form words around the knot in my throat. The truth was, I didn't know if I'd ever be ready to see the remains of the place where I'd grown up, where I'd lost everything. But I needed to do this—needed to close this chapter before we could truly begin the next.

As we emerged from the thicket, the village of Briarwood came into view. Or the meadow that remained of it.

I pulled my horse to a stop, my breath catching. Where the modest cottages and small shops I'd loved once stood, there was now overgrown land. Nature had reclaimed the space, the ash now carried off in the wind. Wildflowers pushed through the grass, greeting us with a multitude of colors. Saplings sprouted where children once played.

"It's smaller than I imagined," Oryn murmured, sliding from his saddle to stand beside my horse.

I dismounted, my legs still a bit unsteady. "It was big enough. There weren't many of us who called it home."

Kyler joined us, his hand finding the small of my back. "Where was your home?"

I pointed to a clearing just past what had been the village square. Without another word, both men flanked me as I walked toward it, their presence a steady comfort against the ghosts that haunted my memories.

When we reached the spot, I stopped. Nothing remained of the cottage where I'd spent my first twenty-one years. Just wild grass and dandelions dancing in the breeze.

"This was the last place I saw them," I said softly. I closed my eyes and breathed deeply. The air here carried the scent of fresh earth and new growth, nothing like the ash and fear that had filled my lungs the last time I stood on this ground. I opened myself to the feeling of the place, to the memories both painful and precious.

"Thank you," I whispered to the spirits of the land, to my grandmother, to Maël, to all those who had guided my path through darkness into light. "Thank you for helping me bring peace."

The wind picked up, swirling around us in a way that felt deliberate, almost like an embrace.

"You've walked your path," an old voice came from behind us. Oryn grabbed my hand as we turned to face the newcomer. Elisanna stood, her once wild hair smoothed and eyes clear and bright. A serene grin stretched across her face as she looked upon us. "And now, this land may finally come to know peace."

Gone were her manic demeanor and wicked laugh. She almost looked... normal.

"Will there be peace?" I asked.

Elisanna closed her eyes and took a deep breath in, only opening them when she exhaled. "There's still work to be done, but Fate calls for peace for the land united under the throne of stars. That is the first step."

"What throne of stars?" Oryn asked the question I knew was on all of our minds.

A lilting laugh emitted from the old woman. "Why, the one you'll build, of course. Do I have to spell out everything?" With a quirk of a smile, she turned to leave but stopped, looking over her shoulder. "My sister, your grandmother, treasured her garden since we were young, but you girl, you are her most treasured bloom of all." With her mysterious words, she left, vanishing in the wind. The only sign of her presence was the gentle rustle of the trees.

"How the hell are we supposed to build a throne of stars?" Oryn asked once the shock of the witches' sudden appearance and disappearance finally wore off.

"I don't think we're meant to take that so literally," Kyler pointed out. "That witch is rarely so straightforward."

In that moment, standing in the place where my story began, surrounded by the two men who would help me write its continuation, I felt something settle within me. Not an ending, but a new beginning.

"We're going to unite everyone under one throne. The Kingdom of Araceli."

IT'S NOT GOODBYE...

Not ready to say goodbye? Subscribe to my newsletter to get the exclusive Araceli's Blade prequel novella: **The Witch of Fate.**

Acknowledgments

I never thought writing the final book in a series would be so hard. I found myself unwilling to type those two final words that made everything come to a close, I wasn't ready to let these characters go. But Alora, Maël, Kyler, Oryn, Lucas, Rasher, Luella, and the rest of the characters needed the peace they've fought so hard for... at least for now.

So many people played a role in getting Araceli's Blade here, and I couldn't be more grateful for each and every one of you. From artists to editors, thank you for your contributions.

To the readers who jumped head first into the realm and were ready to do it again and again, your support is everything.

To Jess & Ali - the feedback you provided me was tremendously helpful and I am so thankful to have your help.

To Bree, thank you for putting up with my spiraling thoughts and crazy ideas over tea and snacks. You're my favorite book goblin.

My partner in crime, Erin, we do this song & dance with every book, but I truly couldn't do this without you. Our first books brought us together, we've grown so much, & I can't wait to see where we're at in five years.

Janai & Dee - your messages and comments always make my day and I am so thankful for your support.

To Téylie & Isla, my sweet, loving, absolutely wild girls, thanks for bringing the party even when we thought we needed sleep.

To my husband, who is still very much mad at me over Maël and as I'm writing this still hasn't read past chapter 7 of Daughter of Shadows and Ash, thank you for your unconditional love and support. I would not be here, chasing my dreams, if it weren't for you. Thank god the universe tied your soul to mine.

ALSO BY EMBER JOHNSON

About the Author

Ember Johnson was born in California where she spent most of her days reading. Naturally, she developed into a book dragon and is currently working on a book collection to rival her grandfathers. She lives in Alabama with her daughters, husband, and beloved pets.

instagram.com/author.emberjohnson

tiktok.com/@author.emberjohnson

threads.com/@author.emberjohnson

reamstories.com/emberjohnson

goodreads.com/emberjohnson

www.ingramcontent.com/pod-product-compliance
Lightning Source LLC
Chambersburg PA
CBHW070511310726
48976CB00002BA/409